A LESSON *in* LOVE

COYOTE CREEK BOOK ONE

The Gift

Covet the Cowboy Erotic Romance Series:

Corralling the Cowboy (Book 1)

Cornering the Cowgirl (Book 2)

A Lesson *in* Love

COYOTE CREEK BOOK ONE

A NOVEL

KATIE O'CONNOR

SNARKY HEART PRESS

—A Lesson in Love: Coyote Creek Book One—
A Billionaire Cowboy Romantic Suspense
This book is a work of fiction. Names, characters, places, and incidents either are products of the author's imagination or are used fictitiously. Any resemblance to actual events, locales, or persons, living or dead, is entirely coincidental.

Published April 2020
(katieohwrites.com)

ISBN: 978-1-989816-03-5 (Kindle Edition)
ISBN: 978-1-989816-04-2 (Other Digital Editions)
ISBN: 978-1-989816-05-9 (Print Edition)

Design and cover art by P.S. Cover Design
Formatting by Shelley Kassian
Editing by Terri St. Clair

This one's for CR, friend and confidant,
who prefers to remain anonymous.

ACKNOWLEDGMENTS

Countless hands were involved in the creation of this book.

As always, my critique partners and beta readers have been invaluable.

Special thanks go out to The Write Chicks, my newly formed romance writing group.

Thanks to my editor, Terri St. Clair; my formatter, Shelley Kassian; and my amazing cover designer P.S. Cover Designs. You ladies made this book possible.

CHAPTER ONE

Perched on the edge of her high-backed wooden stool, Tricia Paxton leaned one elbow against the raised, rough pine table and watched the dancers whirl around Bar None's crowded dance floor. The popular night spot had a country and western theme. Saddles and horse paraphernalia hung everywhere. Hurricane lamps with flameless candles lit every table and all of the solid, wooden furniture was marked with the brands of local ranches. Time and hard use had worn the finish off the furnishings leaving a welcome, rustic feel. A vague lemony scent failed to completely hide the smell of stale beer. Luckily, the aroma of french fries and burgers hung enticingly in the air. She'd come here tonight with Joanne Mahoney. They'd been best friends since university. Jo had disappeared into the crowd ten minutes ago after vowing she'd only be a jiffy. Tricia had laughed, one thing Jo never got right was timing. She was always punctual for work but in all other aspects of her life, Jo lacked the ability to judge the passing of time.

Tonight, Jo had dragged Tricia out claiming they needed a night on the town because Tuesday marked the start of a new school year. She'd promised conversation and dancing and Tricia loved dancing. She'd be out on the floor if anyone asked her to join them, despite her awkward dance moves. Three women danced alone in the small crowd on the floor, surrounded by couples. She debated joining them, but a night out in a town of two thousand people meant familiar faces rather than city anonymity. Here, where everyone knew each other, she preferred not to show off her uncoordinated side alone. She'd only hit the floor if someone asked her to join them.

She'd only been in Coyote Creek for fifteen months. After losing her previous teaching position in Edmonton, she'd taken a job at the small, north central Alberta town's only school. She'd tried getting a position in a private school, but the blemish on her record made her a risky hire. She'd debated changing careers altogether; but in the end decided she loved interacting with children too much to embark on a new career. Nothing she'd ever done matched the happiness and pride which came from helping a child riddle out a complex problem. When the light of understanding bloomed in their eyes, she knew her reason for walking the earth was to educate children.

She'd lucked out with this position when an accident had taken the previous grade one teacher, Mrs. Chips, out of work. Tricia had filled in as a substitute for the last month of classes.

When the sixty-something teacher had chosen not to return to work, the principal had encouraged the school board to hire Tricia on in her place.

Changing from an enormous, exclusive, city school to a small-town school housing kindergarten to grade twelve was an adjustment. Seeing her coworkers around town daily had taken some getting used to; but she was adapting to the intimacy. There were at least half a dozen teachers from the school in the bar tonight; some dancing, some seated and enjoying their evening with friends and coworkers. She knew them by sight and name, but hadn't had much interaction with them; otherwise, she'd join them.

She wasn't shy, exactly. She just wasn't good at introducing herself to adults; with her students, it was easy. The battle between her urge to socialize and her urge to hide roiled in her stomach like stampeding buffalo.

Across the floor, she saw Riley Flint dancing with a curvaceous blonde. Tricia had met him last spring when he'd picked up his nephews, Gary and Zander, at school. Riley was barely under six feet tall and broad shouldered. He had a lean, almost wiry look. Tonight, his neatly trimmed, dark brown hair was hidden by his usual tan Stetson. Blue jeans and a plaid button-down shirt spoke of his cowboy roots even though he'd left the family ranch for a career as a veterinarian.

Riley's movements were graceful and mesmerizing. His narrow hips swayed and his shoulders dipped as he twirled his partner about. He and the blonde danced in perfect unison. The song ended and she returned to her seat; Riley changed partners and stayed on the floor for several songs; slow, fast and everything in between. It was a pleasure to watch him dance; he was graceful and elegant. Women chose Riley for their partner. If not, he ambled through the crowd until he found a willing companion. He danced and danced and she watched until he left the floor and slipped into a chair beside his brother Carl who sat three tables over with a couple of the mechanics who worked in his repair shop on Sparrow Street. Carl and Riley looked a lot alike except Carl had a second dimple and was shorter and stockier.

Riley sat for a moment and sipped his beer before a redhead grabbed his arm and pulled him to the floor. When the music rolled into a slow waltz, he traded partners, bowed to an elderly woman and led her to the floor. He returned the blue haired lady to her husband. He then turned his green eyes in Tricia's direction. She looked away when he winked and tipped his Stetson. She was glad he noticed her though. Excitement trickled through her; she'd gone two years without a date. It was nice to know she could still catch a man's eye.

She waved at a couple of parents she knew from the school and studied the crowd. She recognized a few welders, some operators from the local sour-gas plant, the town's librarian and a local hunting guide. Unless she was mistaken, the kids in the corner worked at the ski hill and skateboard park north of town.

She searched the dancers for Jo. Unable to find her, Tricia debated the merits of abandoning her and heading home. She discarded the idea, she'd never ditch a friend, even in Coyote Creek.

Though Tricia had been in town teaching just over a year, it felt much longer. Probably because she didn't have much of a social life. There'd been a few staff dinners and lots of girls' nights with Jo but she usually spent her evenings at home. Alone. The solitude was wearing thin. Before she'd been wrongly accused and fired from her previous position, her social life had been active. Coworkers, university friends, neighbors and her fiancé; there'd always been something going on.

Here, not so much. She should socialize, make the first move and join her fellow teachers. Why was it so hard to make the initial overture of friendship? They were nice people, she chatted with them in the staff room everyday, yet something held her back.

The music morphed from quick paced to a slow, sexy love song. The dance floor emptied leaving only a few couples wrapped tight in each other's arms, oblivious to the crowd. Beautiful. What would it be like to feel the love she saw shining in their eyes again? She shrugged the thought off. No sense fretting over something unattainable. She wouldn't risk opening her heart again to the pain love could bring after the disaster with her ex-fiancé. If he'd loved her, he would have stayed by her side when things had gotten rough in Edmonton; instead he'd bolted and taken up with one of her closest friends. She'd lost her two closest confidants that day. Anger and disappointment at their duplicity surged anew making her stomach ache.

A bark of deep masculine laughter rose over the twang of country music and she pivoted to find the source. Riley leaned against the bar looking more like a model than a veterinarian in his Wranglers, Stetson and cowboy boots. She did not want to be interested in a cowboy like him, no matter how good looking he was. She'd look her fill and move on; he had a reputation as a lady's man which put him miles out of her league.

All five of the Flint brothers were utterly dependable and danged good looking. Riley's three sisters were as beautiful as his brothers were handsome. Eight kids. As a teacher, she couldn't fathom having that many children. Who could survive a family with eight kids? It was one thing to have twenty kids for a few hours a day, but all day, every day? No thank you.

Tricia scanned the floor again for Joanne, she'd been dancing with Riley's best friend and business partner, Houston Jackson. She spotted her redheaded friend across the room; headed out the door on Houston's arm. Her cell phone vibrated in her pocket. She pulled it out to find a text from Jo. *Sorry to abandon you. Riley will give you a ride home. He's a great guy. You'll like him. Call you in the morning.*

Tricia groaned, slid off her stool and reached for her light cotton jacket.

"Hey, Tricia." Riley ambled into view. "Jo told me you'd need a ride home. I'm here to oblige."

She rocked back on her heels. "No thanks. I'll take a taxi."

"Not likely. Well, my brother Carl owns the cab and it's in the shop. Blew the tranny this morning." Riley answered, a sexy grin curving his lips.

"Figures. Isn't there more than one?" She asked with a

mental eye roll. Well, the exercise wouldn't hurt her and this was the safest town she'd ever lived in. Crime was almost non-existent.

"No. I guess two more have been ordered from the dealership but haven't come in. Carl's lamenting not buying a couple more cabs earlier on. People will have to walk or catch a ride with a friend. Which is what I'm offering you. It's no trouble."

"No. Thanks anyway." She smiled.

"Come on. Dance with me and then I'll take you home." His eyes looked into hers and pulled her in. Even in the dim light of the bar, those unmistakably Flint-green eyes were mesmerizing. Everyone in town talked about green eyes being a Flint family trait. Riley smiled and tipped his hat like a gentleman. She hesitated; temptation prodded her to accept.

"I don't think so. Thank you. I'll just go home." She inched backward.

"Well, I'll be hanged. You don't know how to dance, do you?" He chuckled and a dimple appeared in his right cheek.

Bananas. She was such a sucker for those green eyes and his dimple. "I do know how to dance but I'm an elementary school teacher. I am concerned about what people would think."

"Tricia, I've only ever seen you in the bar twice. I'll bet you haven't had a single drink since you arrived in town. Frank, the bartender, tells me you're drinking iced tea. Therefore, your reputation will come out unscathed." He said lightly, a teasing grin wreathing his face.

He'd asked the bartender what she was drinking?

"Look over there." He pointed to a table in the corner. "The principal, the vice principal, the secretary and the physics teacher. They're all having a beer. Nobody cares. This is Friday night in Coyote Creek." He dragged the word into three distinct syllables the way everyone in town did; rhyming the first syllable with my. Ky-oh-tee.

She followed his gesture. Once again, she was tempted. Too tempted. Not to drink, but to dance with him. Maybe she would. She'd really like to. A cashier from the grocery store slipped in between her and Riley. With her back to Tricia, she slid her arms around Riley's neck and kissed him on the cheek. "Dance with me, Riley."

"Sure." He gave Tricia one last, disappointed look and followed his new partner onto the floor." The music changed from slow to a fast-paced Jive-type beat. Riley grasped the woman's hand and spun her in an exaggerated circle. They dance and twirled. Together, they could have won a dance competition. Envy rocketed through Tricia. She should have accepted his offer. The man danced like a pro. Her gaze glued to them, she flushed when Riley flashed her a grin as they spun by.

Dang.

Okay, this was it. She marshalled her courage as the song came to an end. A deep breath and she stepped onto the dance floor, heading straight toward Riley. He must have noticed her coming, he turned, a wide smile on his face.

"I'm not much of a dancer, but I think I'd like to dance with you." She smiled nervously.

He sketched a slight bow and offered his hand.

Eagerly, but with a touch of shyness, she placed her icy hand in his warm, strong one. A brief brush of fingers and he whirled her across the floor, his other hand light on her upper arm. He guided her through half a dozen steps and into a spin. Expecting her usual klutziness, she discovered, under his guidance, she barely stumbled at all. In his arms, she felt like she was floating on air.

"Riley Robert Flint. I demand an explanation!"

His eyes went wide, he stumbled to a halt and grimaced. He dropped Tricia's hand and turned with a false smile. "Mom?"

Sue Flint, Riley's stepmother was a force to be reckoned with and not one of her eight children dared disobey her. Nor did any of her four grandchildren. She glared at her son, her blue eyes flashing in anger, her hands on her hips.

"Good evening, Mrs. Flint. Constable Baxter." Tricia greeted the newcomers. Amy Baxter, RCMP constable, her long blonde hair in a neat braid hanging down her back, stood beside Mrs. Flint looking deadly serious. They greeted her and turned their attention to Riley.

"What?" He looked back and forth between the two women and then stared at the shiny toes of his boots, like a boy caught doing something wrong.

"I never thought I'd see the day when the police showed up on my doorstep looking for one of my grown sons. I taught you better. Amy tells me there's a baby at the police station with your name on it." She shook her head disapprovingly and made a tsking sound.

His gaze flew up, eyes wide. His mouth flapped

soundlessly. He swallowed hard, Adam's apple bobbing harshly.

"What?" He croaked out. "I never…"

"Not a baby, exactly. A small child. I don't want to discuss this here. Come with us," Constable Baxter suggested. Her uniform was immaculate. She rested her hand on her holster as if she were expecting trouble. Whatever this was about, it must be serious business.

"If there's a kid. It's not mine. I never, ever, mess around without protection."

Sue pinched his ear. "Don't you sass. You're coming with us and we're going to straighten this out. Now." She frog-marched him toward the door, Constable Baxter followed, grinning, in their wake.

The bar fell silent, even the band stopped playing. Nobody moved or said a word until they were out the door. Pandemonium erupted.

Jeepers, and she'd been worried about dancing. She paid her tab and headed for home. Good thing she'd worn comfortable shoes for walking. First Jo ditched her and now, her other ride option was gone as well.

Riley Flint, bachelor extraordinaire, had a child? He didn't seem to think so. Curiosity gnawed at her. He didn't seem careless. She shook off the thought. He did date a lot; but he was friends with all his exes, though, according to Jo, he never dated anyone more than a few times. There'd never been even a hint of a rumor involving Riley fathering a child.

He wasn't a paragon of virtue by any stretch. He drank a bit, but never drove under the influence and he had a flawless reputation as a veterinarian. He was beyond handsome. Too bad their dance had been cut so short; she'd been enjoying herself. Well maybe it was for the best.

She turned her mind away from him, walked two blocks north and turned right on Main Street. Luckily the evening was warm. A soft pine-scented breeze ruffled her hair as she strolled along the south side of the street and admired the buildings across the wide road. The angle parking stalls were virtually empty. Her favorite shop had to be the bubble-gum pink chocolate shop called Sweet Heaven. It had the most adorable white gingerbread trim and a lovely shaded deck where you could sip coffee and eat treats. The rock shop and bookstore were next.

With two lakes and a small ski hill nearby, Coyote Creek businesses relied on the tourist trade to keep going. As a result, there were numerous specialty shops. It was, in effect, a mini-Banff dropped smack dab in north central Alberta.

The ski hill was man-made, constructed by an entrepreneurial farmer and his engineer son who'd grown tired of the insecurity of farm life. They'd bought some equipment, hired a crew and turned a huge portion of their five thousand acres of hilly land into a small ski hill. It wouldn't challenge an experienced skier, but for beginners and people looking for an escape from the province's larger hills, it was a cozy destination hill just twenty minutes north of town. Recently, they'd added an extensive skateboard park and picnic area.

Skiing brought winter tourists; the lakes brought summer guests. Gunderson's Tours offered hunting, fishing and backpacking to visitors. The surrounding mixed arboreal forests providing plenty of opportunity for all kinds of outdoor activity year-round. Last summer, Tricia had gone on a wonderful four-day backpacking excursion with Jo.

She turned north again for two more blocks, enjoying the waning evening light and late summer breeze. She felt safe walking the few blocks to her apartment building, directly across from the Kinsmen's Play Park, and kitty-corner to the curling rink and attached arena. She smiled as she approached the first of two identical buildings and jogged up the brown painted concrete steps. The building manager who had a green thumb and gift for decorating kept the lobby and front steps decorated for every season. Pumpkins, gourds and witches were sprinkled amongst the marigolds and lobelia overflowing their pots on each stair and on the landing. Tricia stopped to admire the display, sniffed the alyssum blossoms and opened the outside door.

Modeled after a brownstone, the three-story brick building had been her home for the past year. She'd been lucky to find the perfect apartment. The vacancy rate here was low. Her two-bedroom suite overlooked Fifteenth Avenue on the front and Spruce Street on the south side. She stepped into the vestibule of her apartment complex and unlocked the inner door. She padded quietly up the carpeted stairs to her third-floor suite and let herself inside.

Her suite number was four-ten. She laughed at the irony of being on the third floor with a four-hundred number. Numbering started with the basement suites being one-oh-one and one-oh-two.

She eased the door shut behind her and leaned against the wall. Home. Her home. Her comfort zone. The furnishings weren't the top end leather and chrome pieces from the apartment she'd shared with her fiancé. Instead they reflected her tastes. A light and airy floral couch and two burgundy wing chairs flanked a small television. The TV stand, end tables and coffee table were garage sale finds but in good shape. They matched the maple kitchen table and chairs her aunt had given her.

Tricia set her purse on the table beside the door, hung her jacket in the closet, placed her shoes inside and closed the bi-fold doors. She grabbed her slippers because while the modern tile floor was beautiful, it was hard on her feet. She'd buy some throw rugs next time she was in Edmonton. Maybe something in a forest green to accentuate the profusion of greenery growing in her windows.

She padded down the hallway into her bedroom and exchanged her jeans and blouse for shorts and a T-shirt. It was early yet; she'd pull out the cozy mystery she'd bought yesterday and make herself some tea.

She could have, no should have, joined her coworkers. She shook her head at her own cowardice. Instead she'd let Riley rattle her and bolted for home and another night alone.

CHAPTER TWO

"Seriously?" Riley frowned at Amy Baxter as she pushed his head down and herded him into the back seat of her RCMP cruiser. "Am I under arrest?"

She slammed the door and climbed into the front seat beside his mother. "You are not under arrest, but your presence is required at the station. Buckle up."

"Someone want to tell me what this is all about? Why did you haul me out of the bar? The night's young and I've only had one beer. I was dancing with Tricia Paxton. She's cute and Houston says she's got a great sense of humor to go along with those pretty blue eyes and black hair." He pulled out the seatbelt and fastened it around himself.

His stepmother flashed him her patented 'don't sass me' glare and he fell silent. She'd been giving him *the look* since she married his dad when Riley was ten. It meant business. Sue Flint might be kind hearted and generous, but the entire town knew not to mess with her when she was upset; mainly because it took a lot to break her cheery attitude. His stepmother always smiled, except tonight. Her shoulder length, salt and pepper hair usually curled neatly under, but was uncharacteristically disarrayed tonight. Not bad, but anyone who knew her well would know she was out of sorts.

She looked tired. Her shoulders drooped. Her thin frame, normally strong and upright, bowed like she carried the weight of the world on her shoulders. His dad had been battling a bug for weeks. Was it more serious than they let on? Stubborn as always, his father insisted he was fine. If it was dragging Sue down, it must be serious. He made a mental vow to find out exactly what was going on. Sue's blue eyes narrowed as she looked at him over the seat.

What the heck had he done to annoy her? He wracked his brains for an answer.

Whoa! wait!

"You said there's a baby? No way. No how. I've never had unprotected sex. Somebody's trying to pull a fast one. I'm not a father. I guarantee it."

"You mind your manners, Riley Robert Flint. No more back talk."

He groaned and covered his eyes with his Stetson. He knew when to argue and when to shut up. If there was a baby, it wasn't his. His mind flashed to the past, for a short time, probably six weeks or so, he'd dated a waitress in the city. Mona had been great fun, but in the end, they'd wanted different things. He wasn't ready to settle down and she was. They'd argued about it during their last evening together, after their condom had broken. She'd assured him for months there were no repercussions. She'd told him she wasn't pregnant. It was over six years ago. Way too long ago to leave a baby behind.

He followed Sue and Constable Baxter through the front office of the police station, past some closed doors, and an interrogation room and into the staff room. A couple who appeared to be in their mid-sixties sat perfectly upright on the couch, their faces marred by sad frowns, their eyes damp. They were the only people in the room.

"Mr. and Mrs. Able. This is Riley Flint. You've already met his stepmother, Sue Flint. Why don't you go ahead and tell Riley your story?"

Riley stared at the couple. Mr. Able's fists clenched against his thighs, his jaw was tight and his short-cropped hair stood in disarray, like he'd been trying to pull it out, but he met Riley's gaze with a watery stare. Mrs. Able twisted her hands together and stared at the wall.

"I believe you were acquainted with Mona Able? In Edmonton?" He waited, his tapping toe tearing strips off Riley's conscience.

"Mona Able?" He paused. "Yeah, we dated for a while. Years ago. I thought this was about a baby?" His pulse thundered in his ears and his breath caught. Had she lied to him? Had she been pregnant despite her reassurances to the contrary? Had he failed to live up to his responsibilities? Bile rose in his throat.

"It is about a child. Mona's child. Your child." Mrs. Able looked at him, her eyes brimming with tears. "We expect you to do right by her and her child now that she's gone."

"Gone?" He looked from one person to the next until he'd made the rounds of the room. A tiny squeak came from beside him. He looked in the direction of the sound, a small girl huddled under the table, hidden behind the chairs. She clutched a well-used backpack and a pink stuffed animal. She peeked at him and buried her head in the animal's fur. Holy shit! That was no baby. This was a full-fledged child. She was scrunched way down, but he guessed her to be forty inches tall and very slight. Her blonde hair was a rats' nest of tangled curls.

Mr. Able's angry voice dragged Riley back to the conversation.

"Yes, gone. Dead. Our Mona passed away six months ago. Cancer." His voice cracked on the word. "She left her precious daughter with us. But my wife is ailing. We can't take care of her properly. You fathered her. Mona would want you to take responsibility for her. You are her next of kin." How could one man's voice carry so much recrimination, shame, and hurt all at once? Something in his voice told Riley the strength behind the man's words was mostly bluster. His chest tightened and he shifted to ease the tension building in his shoulders.

The broken condom. Crap! He felt—gob smacked—was the only word he could come up with. His knees wobbled, forcing him to grab the back of a chair for stability. Blood drained from his face. He didn't dare look at Sue, she'd read his guilt in a second.

"I did date your daughter, for a while. But I can't believe she'd want me to look after her child after telling me she wasn't pregnant. She hid her pregnancy from me." Damn! "It was a long time ago. I was maybe twenty-one, twenty-two. We went our separate ways." His mind shifted into overdrive. He glanced at the child under the table. No way! The wee one was *not* his. She couldn't be. He had called Mona to ask and she'd promised him, repeatedly, she wasn't pregnant. He'd have accepted responsibility if she had been. But now, coming out of the blue like this… "Whoa!"

Pain sliced through him. Holy crap, Mona was dead. Shit. Shit. Shit. They hadn't dated for long and now she was gone. He sucked in a breath; his hands fisted. He raked his fingers through his hair, trying to make sense of the situation.

"I'm sorry for your loss," he mumbled, blinking away a tear. "I don't know what to say. You want me to take your grandchild?"

"Yes. You admit she's yours?" Mr. Able asked, his voice shaking.

"I admit she could be," Riley agreed cautiously.

"Now we're getting somewhere," Constable Baxter declared.

"Mona put your name on her daughter's birth certificate. She says you are her father."

"Her? You keep saying her. I assume she has a name?" The man's refusal to call her by name made Riley's hackles rise and his left eye twitch.

"Daisy," he whispered, seeming to choke on the word. "Her name is Daisy. Mona said you were, are, Daisy's father.

She's told Daisy, and us, all about you. How you were in veterinary school when you met at the diner where she worked. How you had a short-term relationship that ended amicably. Mona was sick for months before she passed. We know all about you. She wanted us to have custody of Daisy, but said if anything should happen, you were to get her." He swallowed hard and wiped the tears from his cheeks. His wife buried her face in her hands and sobbed.

"Okay," Riley said, his knees still wobbling and threatening to pitch him to the floor. "Assuming I am Daisy's father, and I want a paternity test. I'll help with her upbringing. I'll pay the bills. I'll do what I can." His body went cold, then hot. Crap. He didn't have the time to look after a child. He had a flourishing veterinary practice to run. He had to help out on the family ranch until his father recovered from the bug ailing him. Money he could spare. He had some savings and he made a good income. But time? Not so much.

"We don't want your money. We need you to take custody of her and be her father. We don't want to give her up. It's killing us. But my wife is sick. She's got rheumatoid arthritis and they can't get it under control. The meds lower her immunity and she's exhausted all the time. I need to devote myself to her care. I'm almost seventy. She's seventy-five. We can't do this without you."

Riley paced the room. "I need to think. Give me a minute. One minute." He crossed the room and went into the hall. Out of sight of those he left behind, he rested his forehead against the cool cinder block wall. Holy sheep dip. Crap on a cracker.

He could barely form a coherent thought, let alone figure out what to do. How did this happen to him? He was careful, always so careful. Yeah, he dated. A lot. But he never, ever had careless sex. He'd followed up. She'd said she wasn't pregnant. He'd believed her.

Dammit. She'd lied.

The walls closed in on him, stealing his breath. He cussed a string of words that would have Sue whopping his backside. As much as he was loath to admit it, he had to face the music. Straightening his spine, he strode back into the room.

Riley scanned the room. The Ables sat on the couch clutching each other. Sue was on her backside, halfway under the table, smiling at Daisy.

Riley kneeled beside the table and slid a chair aside. He motioned to the girl "Come on out sweetheart. There's nothing to be afraid of here. Grampa says your name is Daisy. I'm Riley."

"No!" She shuffled further away, cowering into herself.

Tension ratcheted up his body. Any traces of alcohol left in his blood evaporated like water under a blow torch. She was scared, terrified.

Mr. Able jerked to his feet. "She's upset we can't keep her. She's already lost her mother. Now we have to give her up. This has to be killing her. Lord knows it's ripping our hearts out."

With a brisk nod, Riley turned his back on them and sat on the floor facing the table. "Daisy? Why don't you come on out of there?" She shook her head, her green eyes looked out at him before she buried her head again. He felt sucker punched.

She had his eyes. The room wobbled and his head went light. Two deep breaths restored his physical balance but mentally he remained unstable. "Daisy, darling, the nice lady beside you is my Mom. She's got eight children and four grandchildren. She's sweet and kind and loves everybody. Constable Baxter, do you still give out blankets and teddy bears to kids?" He kept his gaze on Daisy.

"Yes. We've got a cabinet full in the squad room. One of the other officers will show your mom where they are."

"Daisy, how about if you go to the squad room with my mom and she'll get you a new teddy. You can keep your things with you if you like, or Constable Baxter can protect them for you. She's good at protecting things."

"No." Her voice quivered with fear and his heart broke.

"Come on darling," his mother coaxed. "We'll just leave the grownups to talk and we'll get you a blanket and a toy. Why, I made some of those quilts myself. There's one with a Sun Bonnet Sue you might like. Come, let's have a look." She held out her hand, palm up and waited.

Riley's chest clenched; he could barely breathe. Slowly, Daisy inched toward his mother and crawled into her lap. His breath shuddered out in a tense sigh as they walked out of the room together, Daisy clutching her pack and toy in her skinny arms. The door closed behind them and he leaped to his feet. Why wasn't she clinging to her grandparents?

He spun a kitchen chair around and sat backward on it, the back clutched in a white knuckled, death-grip and faced the Ables. "Tell me everything," he demanded through clenched teeth.

Constable Baxter's comforting hand landed on his shoulder.

Slowly, with plenty of tears, they related Mona's story. They'd helped Mona care for Daisy from the moment she was born, watching her while Mona was at work. Then, when cancer struck, Mona and Daisy had moved into their home. Pancreatic cancer had taken her fast, but not before she'd told them, and Daisy dozens of stories about Riley. How he was a good man, one who could be trusted. How she'd lied to him about being a father. How before she'd become sick, guilt had eaten her alive and she'd decided to tell Riley about his child.

Mr. Able lifted a box from beside the couch and handed it to Riley. Inside was Daisy's birth certificate, a stack of DVD discs, some sealed letters, some photographs and a letter to Riley. He tore the letter open with trembling fingers.

Riley,

I'm sorry you have to learn this after I've gone. I promised myself I'd tell you about Daisy, she's yours. Before you, it was almost a year since I was with anyone else. After, there was no one. She's your child and I swear that I was going to call you. I was wrong to hide the truth from you. Please, dear Lord, I beg you, help my parents care for her. She's my heart, my life. I can't stand knowing I'll never see her grow up. I've left letters for her, to be opened on her birthdays, with things I think she'll need to know. I've left videos of my life with her and with advice. Share them with her.

There are no words for the pain I feel for my lies. I regret them.

They say stress can cause cancer. I'm not sure I believe it, but if it's true, I deserve this cancer for my lies and keeping your child from you.

Take care of my baby. We didn't have a fancy life, we had a simple, but good life. She doesn't need things, she needs love.

Your love, Mona.

His fist clenched around the letter. Shit. He smoothed it against his leg, trying to flatten the damage he'd done. Whatever she'd done, no matter what lies she'd told or what truths she'd left unsaid, Mona hadn't deserved to suffer through cancer. She hadn't deserved to die. She deserved happiness with her family, with her child. He blinked back tears. They should have been a family.

There was no doubt he was Daisy's father. Even if the letter and birth certificate weren't enough, she had Flint-green eyes. He had those eyes, as did his father and all of his brothers. Piercing lawn green with shades of brown and gold, the sure sign of Flint genealogy. Paperwork proved she was about to turn six. The timing matched.

"We'd keep her if we could. But we can't. We're getting on in years. But we want visitation. Lots of it."

"Please help us. Look after our baby." Mrs. Able whispered tearfully.

How could he not? Family was everything and if Daisy was his, he'd do his best by her. He buried his face in his hands and closed his eyes. With the birth certificate, and the letter but mostly from looking at Daisy herself, she was his daughter. He'd do the right thing.

Panic squeezed at his chest. What did he know about raising a child? He didn't even know where to begin. Thank God for his huge family, they'd help. And thank God for the internet. He'd be researching forever!

"Daisy is my daughter. I'll do right by her." His whole world was unravelling, his life imploding, but there was no way in hell he'd ignore his responsibilities. Life without one parent was bad enough. Without two, it would be intolerable. Yeah, she had her grandparents, but they were exhausted and he didn't see how they could keep up with an active child. "How do we handle this? I believe she's mine, but I do want a paternity test to be sure."

"Are you saying we lied?" Mr. Able asked.

"No. I'm saying knowing I missed so much of her life is killing me. I want to be certain, to be sure we aren't depriving another man of his child." He paused. "I can't explain it. I just want... Oh hell, never mind."

"It's okay son." Mr. Able stood and patted Riley on the shoulder. "This is a shock. Mona said you'd be shocked but you'd do right. The least we can do is give you one final reassurance. Once the test is done, and you're satisfied, our lawyer will work out the custody arrangements. Promise us we'll have visitation until then."

Riley stood and shook the man's hand. "Mr. Able, Mrs. Able, I swear I'll keep you involved in Daisy's life. But I have to know, why now? Why today? Why didn't you come during the daytime? Why not approach me and give us time to get to know each other rather than springing this on me unprepared? Why wait so long to come to me if she died six months ago?" The questions bubbled out one after another until he clamped his jaw tight to stem the flow.

"Call me Bruce. This is Ruth. The truth is, despite believing Mona about your reputation and suitability as a parent, we had you investigated. There's no way we'd give our only grandchild over to someone unworthy."

"Shit." Riley stared at him. They'd had him investigated? Good Lord. He should be angry, he wanted to be upset, but frankly he didn't blame them one bit.

"Nothing personal, Daisy is everything to us but we needed to know who you were. We'd planned on doing this differently, slowly. But besides Ruth's health issues, I have a growth in my intestines. They don't think it's serious, probably not cancer. But the post-surgical recovery is six weeks. They called yesterday. I go into the hospital tomorrow. I'm in early due to a cancellation. We had no choice except to approach you this way. Can you handle this?"

A simple question, laced with so many layers. None of which he had an answer to. "I'll do my best." He clenched his fists, banking down the urge to scream. He was a father! Of a six-year-old girl he knew nothing about, besides her first name. Crap. Holy crap.

The taste of beer and nachos rose in his throat. Hell no, he wouldn't puke. His guts clenched and he swallowed hard, Daisy needed him calm and rational. His brief encounter with the Ables left no doubt they loved her and they had no other options. Like it or not, he'd just become a father. *Pass out the fricken cigars!*

He could see his life swirling around the bowl, about to be flushed away. No more carefree bachelor nights in the bar. No more impulsive trips to the city. Okay, that might be a blessing, at twenty-eight, it was time to consider growing up.

"Our lawyer says if you agree, you need to sign this document." Bruce produced a sheaf of papers from inside his jacket pocket. "It grants you temporary custody and full parental rights for ninety days, or until the test results come back. It doesn't take away our rights, just ensures your rights and protects Daisy if anything happens to Ruth or I."

Riley scanned the document. He signed it, Constable Baxter witnessed his signature, and handed it back to Bruce.

He shouldn't feel proud. All this was the result of a mistake and his failure to follow up on his responsibilities, but dammit, it felt good to take control and do the right thing.

THE DOOR OPENED and Sue and Daisy came back in, hand in hand.

"Daisy, we have to go. Grampa has to go to the hospital tomorrow. Riley will take good care of you and he'll bring you to visit us. Okay?" Ruth hugged the child tightly and Bruce hugged them both.

"I don't want you to go!" she wailed.

"Sweetie, we talked about this. It doesn't mean we don't love you. We do, and we'll see you lots. Your mom told you one day you'd meet your daddy. She wanted this. We'll see you soon. Stay with your daddy, and we'll call you, a lot. Love you to bits." Their eyes filled with tears, they gave her one last hug and hurried away. Constable Baxter followed them out.

"Hi." Riley greeted his new daughter quietly. "Welcome to the Flint family. I'm Riley, your dad. That's my mom. She's your grandmother. Is it okay if I call you Daisy?"

Her nod was barely a tip of her head and she shifted closer to his mom. "You can call me Riley, or Dad." She shook her head in disagreement. The tiny negative motion slammed into his chest like he'd been gored by a bull. She was like a dog who had been kicked too many times; beat down by life and uncertainty. She was scared to death. He had seen this kind of behavior as a vet and it always tore his heart strings. One of the things he abhorred as a vet was seeing an animal hurt. Maybe his vet experience with injured animals would help him with Daisy. He sure hoped so. One thing he knew about kids, probably the only thing, was they needed love and acceptance.

"Well, you don't have to call me anything, if you don't

want to. You don't have to talk at all. We can be silent friends."

His mom gave him an encouraging smile. He was used to taming and calming frightened or stray animals, how different could this be? Okay, a lot. But he'd start there and blunder his way through. He sat on the couch as far away from them as he could. "I see you picked a quilt. I recognize it. I remember taking mom into the city to buy fabric for it. She needed the perfect pinks and purples for Sunbonnet Sue's hats. We have a fabric shop here, it's called Marcy's, it's in a bright yellow building. But Mom wanted something different, so we drove all the way to Edmonton, where you lived with your mom. Your mom was my friend a long time ago."

Daisy's shoulders dropped a bit. Relaxation? Sadness? He couldn't tell, but she'd reacted which was a good start. "Mom, come sit. It's late, you need to rest your feet." She didn't, it was barely ten o'clock and she was a night owl, but she sat on the opposite end of the couch. Daisy stood beside her, her hands struggling to hold her meager belongings and his mother's hand.

"Look," Riley exclaimed. "There are cookies on the table. I could use something to eat. I'm starved. How about you, Daisy? Would you like a cookie?"

She nodded shyly.

"I'll bet there's milk in the fridge too," his mother added. "Let's sit at the table and have a snack." She tugged Daisy gently toward the table.

Riley rummaged through the fridge and pulled out some milk and an apple. He'd find out who to repay later. Right now, comforting Daisy was his first concern. Since Sue joined the Flint family, food had meant comfort. Maybe that would work with Daisy "Look at this. An apple and milk. And, an Aero bar. This is practically a feast."

Daisy's shy smile told him he might be on the right track. He rinsed the apple and passed it to her. "Apple first, then we'll eat the treats."

After looking at Sue for permission, Daisy bit into the apple with a loud crunch and slurping sound. He'd never seen anyone gobble an apple so quickly.

Later, after Daisy finished her snack, Constable Baxter drove them back to the bar to pick up his truck. She showed him how to install the booster seat the Ables had left at the station and loaded a suitcase and a small box into the back of his truck along with the box the Ables had shown him. "These are Daisy's belongings. I guess they split her belongings, they kept some, you get most of it." She turned to Daisy in the back seat of the truck. "Buckle up sweetie. Here's my card with my phone number. Call me if you need anything. Anything at all. I promise you Riley is a good guy. He won't hurt you. He saved my friend's dog once. He's a good, kind man and your grandparents trust him." She tucked the card into Daisy's backpack.

"Now, you better go, tomorrow is your new grandmother's birthday. She needs to get home to her family. You'll be living with Riley. So, take your grandmother to her house and Riley will take you to your new home. Remember he was your mom's friend. She wants you to be with him. Her letter said so." She buckled Daisy in and kissed her on the forehead. "You'll be safe and you'll like your new family. I promise."

She cut Riley with a glare that was almost physical. "Right, Riley?" Constable Baxter dealt guilt almost as well as his stepmother.

"Your mom was a wonderful lady. I'll keep you safe for her. You're my daughter and we're going to find a way to be friends." He paused. He hadn't wanted a child, but one look at this wee one, and his heart tripped.

Daisy almost smiled and the pressure on his chest eased. The tiny curve at the corner of her mouth made him feel like a superhero. Holy crap, he did love this little bundle of fear and timidity. He didn't know her, or anything about her and she'd already wormed her way into his heart. Love at first sight. Who knew it was even possible?

"After we drop Grandma off, we'll go home."

"That's a great plan," his mother enthused and climbed into the back of the truck and secured her seatbelt. "Tomorrow I'll show you the kittens. We have a new batch of kittens; in a few weeks they'll be big enough to go to their new homes. Maybe your daddy will let you have one."

One look at the glimmer of hope in Daisy's eyes and he'd acquired a cat. He'd probably have to let the thing live in the house too. He was a vet, but he hadn't owned a pet since he left home. He hadn't allowed himself to get close to any of the farm dogs since his birth mother's favorite cattle dog died when he was ten. The dog had been his last link to his mother and losing him had broken Riley's heart. He was in and out all the time. Animal emergencies didn't run on normal work hours and pets needed attention. His busy career and pet ownership didn't mesh well.

Damn. He'd have to figure out how to look after Daisy when he worked. He couldn't drag her with him. He couldn't just foist her off on anyone, not even his parents. His mom was running about double-time to ensure his father rested. He'd have to push them for the truth about his father's protracted illness. At sixty, his father should still be fit and healthy. Sure, he carried a bit of extra weight, but he'd been under the weather for months. Riley should have manned up instead of letting them push his questions aside.

They dropped Sue off and headed home. Daisy was on the verge of sleep but refused to let him carry her into the house. She clutched his hand as he led her up the sidewalk and inside. He led her past the living room, empty except for an enormous television, a rickety side table and two recliners. He made a mental note to buy furniture. At least he had a kitchen table and chairs, even if he didn't have much for groceries besides coffee and junk food.

Daisy was quiet as he helped her into the pajamas they'd found in her box of possessions. She stood, uncomplaining as he worked a comb through her hair. He chattered away about his job as a vet and told her about his brother Ken's children, her new cousins.

Her hair was silky soft, the blonde strands curled against his fingers when he finally worked all the knots out. She was all bony elbows and knees, the pajamas half a size too small. She had the adorable gangliness of a child who'd just endured a growth spurt. No wonder her nightwear was too small.

Hopefully, she had some that fit properly. He'd check it out after he helped her bathe tomorrow. Good lord, he'd never bathed a kid before. He shrugged the thought aside. He'd bathed plenty of animals and he'd ask his folks for some tips.

Riley spent an uncomfortable night sleeping propped in the corner of his bedroom, letting Daisy have his bed. His backside was stiff and his neck ached. He shifted around on the plush, grey carpet, thinking ahead to all the things he'd need to do. His house was enormous. Four bedrooms, three baths, a living room, family room, dining room, kitchen and small office and an undeveloped basement. His bedroom furniture was new. He'd replaced his old, well worn bed when he returned to Coyote Creek to start his veterinary practice. His living room and kitchen furnishings were well used.

Furniture. He'd have to buy some for Daisy. His was the only bedroom with anything in it. For all its shiny newness, his house was nothing more than a bachelor pad. He should have spent more time setting up his home and less time socializing. Too late now. He could almost see his bank account dwindling. He sighed. He'd made this mess and he'd deal with it the best he could.

His bladder was fit to burst by the time Daisy woke in the morning. He debated sneaking out of the room to relieve the pressure but didn't want her to wake alone.

"Good morning, sunshine." He spoke as soon as she peeked open her eyes. "I hope you slept okay. I expect you need to use the bathroom. I sure do." He chuckled. "Come, I'll show you where it is in case you forgot while you slept.

Sometimes it's hard to remember where things are in a new place."

She climbed out of bed and followed him to the bathroom. He gave her a toothbrush and toothpaste and stood outside the door talking about his job and his family. When she was finished, they traded spots and she waited for him.

"Okay, now we have a problem." Her face fell and she turtled into herself. "Oh, no. Not that kind of problem. Come with me. I'll show you something." He led her down the hall to the biggest of three empty bedrooms. He opened the door and showed her the room.

"This is your bedroom, unless you prefer one of the others. You can have your pick of any of them. Except mine. But, none of them have furniture. We'll have to get some and you need new pajamas. Plus, we need to buy Grandma a birthday gift." He lowered his voice conspiratorially. "I forgot to get her something. Can you help me pick out something nice?"

She nodded. "Yes." She spoke so low he barely heard the words, but she'd responded without hesitation. "I like her."

They toured the empty rooms and she settled on the one he'd shown her. Large enough for a bed and play area with a window seat and a bank of bookcases. With effort, he convinced her to leave her meager belongings in the room while they went to town. "You can bring one thing with you." She clutched her tattered stuffed animal and Constable Baxter's card. "Okay, two things," he conceded. "We're making a quick stop at Grandma and Grampa's for breakfast before we go shopping. I'd like you to meet the cousins I mentioned last night."

He paused. "I guess we better buy groceries too."

He helped her buckle into her seat and climbed into the front of the truck for the three-minute drive to his parents' ranch. "We're going to the house I grew up in. It's pretty big. I think you'll like it. It's painted yellow and white. The color's kind of like butter; but don't call it that in front of Grandma. She calls it pale egg yolk." He laughed. "It's just yellow to me. It has seven bedrooms. My family has lots of kids." He glanced in the rear-view mirror; her eyes were as wide as saucers.

"I have four brothers and three sisters. Each girl had her own room. I shared with my brother Carl. Jason and Ken shared a room. Justice, he's the oldest, had his own room. Having your own room is special. Don't worry, you don't have to remember their names. Look. There it is." He pointed toward the imposing two-story house as he turned into the long driveway. It always seemed happy to him, its many windows reminded him of eyes and the wide, white porch reminded him of a big smile.

Riley was fourteen months old when his mother passed away leaving him bereft of memories of her. His only connection had been her dog. Riley had been ten when Robert married Sue. His stepsisters had their mother, his brothers all had memories of their mother. His father loved him, unconditionally, as did Sue, but somehow, he'd always felt a bit like an outsider. It wasn't that he didn't love Sue, he did. It was more about fitting in. Still, every time he pulled into the yard, it felt like he was coming home. The Bar Three Ranch would always be his home. Especially with his new family. God, he had a kid. Just the idea thrilled and terrified him.

He pulled to a stop in front of the house and unbuckled. "Here we are. Let's go eat." He rubbed his hands briskly and helped Daisy out of the truck. "Remind me to get you some books when we're in town. We'll want to read bedtime stories." He doubted she would but was optimistic asking her for help would make her feel more comfortable, like he needed her. Sue always said kids, like some dogs, needed to feel useful.

"Look over there," Riley said, waving down a gravel lane toward a classic red and white barn. "The big red building is one of Grampa's barns. He keeps cows and equipment in there. He's got two smaller ones right behind it. One for cows, the other for horses. I'll teach you to ride horses. That building," he pointed to a steel Quonset, "is where everyone works on tractors and cars. It's like the biggest workshop you've ever seen and it has a play area upstairs."

They turned in a slow circle taking in the cattle dotted rolling fields and the distant tree line. "Those are special cows, Simmentals. There are lots of types of cows, like there are lots of types of dogs. Huskies, boxers, chihuahuas." He smiled when Daisy nodded solemnly.

He explained all the outbuildings and their uses. The wood shed, the garden shed, an old and refurbished cabin used as a guest house. He talked about the rows of corrals standing empty and how in the spring they'd hold dozens and dozens of calves.

A barn cat wandered close and paused to sniff their legs. "That's Boots. I think. There are lots of cats here. They eat mice and the food Grandma gives them. Most of them are friendly. You can pet them, if they come to you first, but don't chase them. Come on, let's go inside and get some breakfast."

"WHO'S SHE?" Riley's eight-year-old nephew, Gary, pointed at Daisy where she hid behind Riley in his mother's kitchen.

"This is my daughter and your cousin, Daisy. She's new to town. Play nice."

"You don't have kids," Zander, his seven-year-old nephew added, backing up his brother.

"You boys stop it." A petite red headed girl stepped in front of them and smiled at Daisy. "Those are my stupid brothers. They're mean. I'm Jane. Uncle Riley is my uncle. Ken is my dad. He's in Edmonton trying to talk some sense into Mommy. I don't know what that means, except we get to sleep over at Grandma and Grampa's all weekend. Even Sunday, 'cause school doesn't start until Tuesday. I'm gonna be in Miss Tricia's class this year. She's the best grade one teacher in the whole school. She's so pretty. She's got black hair and blue eyes and she wears pretty skirts with flowers and sometimes," her eyes went wide, "she wears high heels."

She stopped speaking and looked at Daisy. "Hey, you look like me. You have green eyes like me and Daddy and Uncle Riley, and my other uncles. Who's taller, Uncle Riley?" She tried to stand back to back with Daisy.

"I think you're close to the same height," Riley stated. "You do look alike, except your hair is red and Daisy's is blonde. You're both thin and tall and you do have the same eyes. You look like cousins."

"I think we look like sisters," Jane declared. She looked up at Riley. "If you don't have a wife, like Daddy, how come you have a kid? Kids need mommies and daddies. Didn't Grandma tell you? She told Daddy. She said 'Get off your high horse and apologize.' She made Daddy sad. I don't want you to be sad. Uncle Riley, you need a wife."

Listening to Jane chatter was like hearing his stepmother's voice in his head. She even had her grandmother's mannerisms down pat. The raised eyebrow. The hands on her hips.

Riley sputtered, torn between laughter and paralyzing fear. Dear God, he did not need a wife. Did he? A wife might know how to raise a daughter.

Whoa! What the devil was he thinking? He didn't need a wife.

But a woman's perspective might help.

"Hi." He kissed his stepmother on the cheek as she poured him coffee. "We came by to say happy birthday; and for Daisy to meet her cousins. Daisy starts school next week. I thought it might be nice if she knew some other kids."

Sue gave him the 'I know what you're up to' look. "And?"

"And, I thought you might like to help us shop for the things Daisy needs. I'm not sure what to get." He slid into a chair at the kitchen table. Daisy climbed on his lap. "After breakfast. I've got nothing to eat at my place." He smoothed her hair, pleased she was trusting him.

Sue busied herself at the stove. Her shoulder length hair was neat and tidy. She had a few lines in her face but looked much younger than her fifty-eight years. She was almost as tall as his father, but considerably thinner.

She smiled at them over her shoulder. "Blueberry pancakes?"

"Yes. Please." Riley glanced at Daisy who nodded in agreement.

"I'll cook and help you make a supply list, but there's no way I'm going to drag these three hooligans shopping. You have to learn to do these things. You should probably stop at the bookstore and do some research on raising children." His stepmother was a huge fan of books. Fiction, non-fiction. mystery, romance. Autobiographies and self-help, she had them all. She'd converted an empty bedroom into her own personal library.

"I'll do that on the internet. As soon as I have a chance."

"Uncle Riley," Jane piped in. She'd retreated to a small table in the corner to color. "Maybe Miss Tricia would help you be a daddy. She's the best teacher ever. She knows lots about kids."

"Oh. I don't know honey. I don't know Miss Tricia very well."

"But, she's really nice and she loves kids. She tolded me."

"Good idea." His stepmother grinned at him. "You were with her last night when we interrupted; and judging from the projected class lists for this year, Daisy is likely to be in

Tricia's class." Even though Sue no longer had children in school, she still volunteered there regularly. She slid a plate of pancakes and fresh fruit in front of Daisy who stared at them suspiciously before tasting them. After one bite, she dug in and gobbled her breakfast right up.

"Her name is Miss Tricia," Jane corrected.

"Come on, Mom. Can't you help? Between the two of us, we can wrangle four kids." He hated begging, but he couldn't do this alone. No way.

"Why don't you call Miss Tricia and ask her? If she can't, we'll discuss options."

"Or we could just go." Why was she being so stubborn? She was usually quick to help out. He stifled a groan. She was trying to teach him a lesson. His stomach churned. There was no way she'd help if she was in lesson mode. He chugged his coffee, nearly burning his mouth.

"Let's make a list and I'll call her. I assume you have her number?"

"Daisy, why don't you go play with Jane? She can show you the toys in the playroom downstairs." His stepmother smiled her best smile. "You might be in her class at school."

Daisy refused with a shake of her head and burrowed closer to Riley's side. "No school," she whispered.

"Well, sweetie; school is not debatable. All kids go to school." He stroked her hair.

She shook her head wildly.

"Didn't you go to kindergarten?" Jane stared wide-eyed at Daisy who shook her head again. "I love school. We read and play and I can even write my name!"

The terror and dismay on Daisy's face cut through Riley. "Tell you what, pumpkin; I'll see if Miss Tricia will help us shop today. She's a teacher and she knows everything about school. Plus, not all kids start school at the same time. The big boy who was here when we got here, Gary, is going to start his third year in school. Four, if you count kindergarten. School is a good place. I think you'll like it." He wondered why she'd missed out on kindergarten and vowed to ask the Ables next time they talked.

Daisy pressed up against him. If she snuggled any deeper, she'd disappear inside his skin. Her whole body trembled. He let the subject drop for now. So much upheaval must be hard to comprehend. Her mother had only been gone a couple months. Now she had a new father, she'd lost her grandparents, if only temporarily, and she was starting school. The list made him queasy, he could only imagine how it felt to someone her age.

Heart thundering in his chest, he called Tricia and asked for help. Terror she'd refuse him battled insane hope she wouldn't. He was losing his mind. Twenty-four hours ago, he'd been a carefree bachelor. Now he was a frightened, useless father. Only Robert's years of reminders that family came first kept him from bolting.

CHAPTER FOUR

Tricia nearly fell off her chair when he called. Riley Flint calling her? She never thought she'd see the day. At least he wasn't asking for a date. He had asked for her help and they'd agreed to meet at Watson's Furnishings. It was mid-morning Saturday. The shops on Main Street had been hopping when she walked past on her way to meet him. She'd debated driving down and parking in the grocery store lot across the street but with the sun shining so brightly, she slipped into comfortable walking shoes and set out on foot instead.

Jane Flint came up with the idea of her helping Riley. He told Tricia that Jane had recommended her for the job. Kids suggested the darnedest things. But Jane was a Flint through and through, and like her father and uncles, she had confidence to spare. With just over five hundred kids in the school, she'd heard dozens, maybe hundreds of startling ideas and insights from students. Sometimes they saw things adults didn't even notice.

Tricia paused in front of Coyote Creek's only furniture store. She admired the two-story red brick front and the massive display windows featuring idyllic room settings. The second floor housed small efficiency apartments, the type she'd always known as bachelor suites. One big room containing kitchen, living room and bedroom. The only separate space in each suite was the bathroom. She'd lived here until she signed the lease for her current suite. Having space to move about was a luxury she no longer took for granted.

She was strolling through displays inside when the door opened and Riley strode confidently in. A small girl with long blonde hair curling past her shoulders, wearing too small clothing clutched his hand like a lifeline. Her other hand clasped a tattered stuffed animal to her chest. Her gaze darted warily back and forth. Tricia thought her sad eyes had seen too much pain and heartache. Empathy shook Tricia to her core; she blinked back tears and reached for her happiest expression.

Riley greeted the teenage clerk by name. "This is my daughter, Daisy. We're going to need a few things for her new bedroom." A slight shake of his head warned the girl not to ask questions. "We'll look around a bit and see what we find, okay?" He looked down at the small blonde girl with bright green eyes.

Flint eyes. He smiled. "Come on, let's see what they have. You tell me what you like."

Daisy hadn't spoken since entering the store. They walked in silence and looked at everything. Oh boy, Riley Flint speechless? From what she'd heard about him, speechlessness was unusual. Tricia wandered toward them.

"This one?" Riley sounded puzzled. "It's pretty plain. Don't you want something nicer?"

He was floundering badly. Time for an intervention. She didn't hesitate, stepped forward, kneeled in front of Daisy and offered her hand. "Hi, I'm Tricia Paxton. I'm your daddy's friend." She glanced up at him prepared to warn him not to contradict her. He grinned like he'd won the lottery.

"Tricia, this is my daughter Daisy. She came to live with me last night. She's almost six. She'll start school this week. Shake her hand, Daisy. Like this." He shook Tricia's hand. His large hand dwarfed hers and sent warmth flooding through her. The man packed a punch even with a handshake.

She kept her hand out until Daisy shook it. "Nice to meet you Daisy, I'm a grade one teacher. I think you'll be in my class. Your cousin Jane will be in my class too. What are you guys looking for today?" Tricia's heart melted when Daisy stepped back a bit and looked up at Riley, as if asking permission to speak.

"She's a bit shy; but that's okay." He ruffled Daisy's flyaway hair. "She's in a whole new place with new people. We're thrilled you agreed to help us shop. I'm glad Jane suggested it. Daisy needs furniture for her bedroom, and clothing and school supplies. We also need to get groceries and a present for Grandma's birthday party which is after lunch."

She read the panic and fear behind his enthusiastic response. He was way out of his element. She'd seen him with his brother's children at school, they got along famously. But, having a child thrust on you out of the blue would unsettle anyone. She gave him credit for stepping up to his responsibility; some men wouldn't.

"I'd love to help you. I'm glad you called." God help her, she couldn't resist the urgent plea in his voice. "Is there a budget?"

"No budget. Daisy can pick whatever she wants."

"Oh, then you don't want this plain old bed. Come, look at this! When I was a girl, I always wanted one like this." She led them to an ornate white and gold canopy bed. She slipped off her shoes and climbed up. "Come on, let's test it." Riley looked reluctant but climbed up and lay beside her, their bodies touched from shoulder to toe on the narrow mattress. His body heat warmed her. Good gravy, she was in bed with Riley Flint.

"Come on up, Daisy. What do you think?" Tricia blurted.

She declined until Tricia patted the mattress. "You can't buy a bed without testing it."

Daisy climbed up and sat at their feet, tattered stuffed animal in her arms. She stared at the canopy, a look of longing so intense Tricia wanted to cry and embrace her. She glanced at Riley who nodded.

"How about this one, Daisy?" Riley prodded gently and climbed off the bed.

"Mama says fancy beds cost too much."

"She did?" Riley's smile wobbled. "Well then. You pick

another if you want. But I have enough money for this one. If you want it." Riley stood. "I really like this one. Maybe I should get it for me. What do you think?"

A giggle escaped Daisy and she slapped a hand over her mouth.

"What? I think I need this one and some pink sparkly sheets." He put one hand on his hip and tapped his lips thoughtfully with one finger.

"Pink would be perfect, but sheets with sparkles aren't very comfortable. Shall we get this one?" Tricia asked.

Daisy looked hopeful and then sad. She shook her head from side to side. Riley kneeled beside the bed and grasped his daughter's hands. "Daisy I know you're worried, and frightened and don't know me really well. But your mom was my friend and she'd want you to have this. To have nice things. It would make her happy to see you in this bed. She's probably smiling down from heaven already. What do you say? It's okay if you don't want it, but I have enough money to pay for this bed and everything else you need."

He paused for a moment and looked right into Daisy's eyes. "Your mom left me a letter. She was sad she couldn't give you extra things, she'd be thrilled to see you in this bed. Let's make Mommy happy, okay?"

Oh gosh. Tricia's hand covered her heart. Riley Flint had a heart of gold. She never would have guessed. Perhaps it explained why his old girlfriends still liked him. She leaned in to whisper in Daisy's ear. "I'd take it. Your mom would love it."

Daisy nodded and smiled from ear to ear.

"Great! Now, we need bedding and a dresser." He waved the clerk over. We'll take the entire bedroom set. The dresser, the desk and chair, the bed, the canopy, the nightstand and the white toybox too."

"We don't have it in stock, sir. We can deliver it in a week."

"I'll take the floor model and pay a bonus if you can deliver and set it up by five today."

"Um, let me check with Dad." The girl hurried away and returned a few minutes later wearing an enormous grin. "You've got it; no bonus needed. Dad knows where you live. He'll deliver it this morning. Did you want the pink or the blue cushion on the toybox?"

"The pink, please. The back door is unlocked. It goes in the biggest empty bedroom. The one on the back of the house, directly across from the only bedroom with furniture." They finished the transaction, tipped the girl generously and headed down the street to find linens. Tricia accompanied them. There were at least a thousand questions thundering through her head about Daisy's history but she knew enough not to ask them in front of Daisy. How in heaven had he ended up with a child? Had he known about her? He'd floundered last night when his mom mentioned a baby and he still looked shell-shocked; but he was trying hard to connect with Daisy.

The question foremost in her mind was why he had no furniture. Though she'd never been inside, she'd seen his brand new, enormous house. It was a question for another day. Along with a couple dozen others, all directly related to his daughter, her prospective student.

Linens, clothing, books, toiletries, school supplies. They purchased bags and bags of necessities and lugged them back to the truck. They shopped for groceries, placing the perishables in a cooler in the bed of the truck.

Shopping complete, they strolled down the street toward the diner for a snack; Daisy in the middle, Tricia on one side, Riley on the other. For a magical moment, she felt this man and his child were hers, as if they were a family. Even though it would never be, she savored the sentiment. This was a day worth remembering. Both for the good deed she was doing, and for the pleasant companionship with a handsome man and his child.

As they walked, Daisy tugged on their hands and planted her feet.

"What is it, Daisy?" Riley asked. She nodded at the elegant grey façade of the jewelry store. "Grandma's birthday?" She nodded and smiled shyly. "All right then. Let's check it out." He smiled conspiratorially at Tricia and her blood surged.

Oh man, last night she barely found the courage to dance with him and today she was helping him with his newfound daughter. If they didn't put Daisy in her class, she was going to request it; this timid child needed as many heroes as she could get. Riley had managed to whisper a few details of Daisy's home life when the girl was distracted. Tricia had seen children from broken homes before. Divorce was hard on children. But to be raised by a single mother and then lose her and then your grandparents? Heartbreaking. Tricia knew rejection and loss all too well, her parents' betrayal and fiancé's rejection still cut deeply almost two years after it happened. This child needed someone to stand up for her. She needed family and friends.

They toured the jewelry store. Riley suggested a dozen things, all of which Daisy declined with a shake of her head. Over and over, she returned to the same display. "What do you see?" Tricia squatted down beside her. "Tell the lady which tray."

The clerk set the tray on the counter. Riley lifted Daisy so she could see clearly. She clung to his neck like a monkey. "That." She pointed to a set of two gold necklaces. Two hearts joined together to make a double heart. Each heart was engraved.

"They say, I love you. One for you and one for Grandma?" Riley grinned. Daisy smiled back. "We'll take it. Please gift wrap it."

"The little one has good taste. They're solid 24 karat gold and those are top quality emeralds. It is one of our better pieces, and quite costly," the clerk cautioned.

"Today, it doesn't matter. Today is Daisy's, my daughter's, day. If she wants this for her grandmother, then we'll buy it. Budgeting is for another day." He smiled at the clerk and kissed Daisy on the nose. "We don't get everything we want all the time, but today's a special day. It's our first day as a family."

Daisy nodded solemnly and buried her face in his neck.

He barely winced when he handed over his credit card. Gift purchased, they doubled back and popped into a squat white stucco building known as Allie's Diner. Built in the early seventies, it had a retro feel with red and white vinyl stools perched up against a long counter. The tables were vintage Formica and chrome. It was a blast from the past and served the best stew and biscuits in town.

Tricia debated the stew but settled on tea and a roast beef sandwich. Riley and Daisy shared a cheeseburger platter and a mile-high chocolate cake. Daisy chose milk, Riley had coffee. An hour later, Tricia found herself agreeing to Riley's invitation to attend his mother's birthday party. He'd written the invite on a napkin while they ate. If he kept going the way he was, he'd be a great father, he already knew not to get Daisy's hopes up.

"I think I better get something for your grandmother for her birthday too; and I know the perfect thing. A picture of you and your dad together. Let's go to the park. I'll take some pictures with my phone and we'll get them printed at the drugstore."

After a brief stop at the truck to change Daisy into something pretty and to comb her hair, the pictures were taken, printed and three sets framed in triple frames. Each set held a photo of Riley, one of Daisy and one of them together. She handed Riley one set and one to Daisy for her room while they gift wrapped the other. "This will help you remember your first day together."

"Then we better get one of all of us."

The clerk took the picture with Riley's phone.

"I'll have it printed later."

Tricia followed them home to his acreage which bordered his parents' ranch on one side. Riley kept to the speed limit and obeyed traffic laws. Was that normal for him, or was he driving special because of Daisy? She wasn't prepared to ask her questions, yet, but hoped the time would come when she could. She was beginning to like Riley Flint. She'd travel to the party with them and head home from Riley's after it was over.

He turned the corner off the highway to a long, paved driveway. His house was as impressive as she recalled. It was large, painted grey and had white trim. Two stories with an enormous attached garage and wrap around porch. She'd heard his clinic was connected to the back of his house though she couldn't see it from this angle. It was one heck of a house for a family, but way too much for a single man. It was built on the acreage beside his parents' place and she wondered why he'd built such a big house.

The furniture truck was pulling out of Riley's driveway as they pulled in. She parked her seven-year-old, green Honda CRV beside Riley's pickup. She wasn't much on vehicles, but she was pretty certain his navy-blue Ford wasn't more than a couple years old. Aside from a little mud, it was virtually new.

Daisy climbed out of her booster seat, hopped out of the truck and raced toward the house.

"Daisy, come help with the bags please," Tricia called out, opening the back door of Riley's truck.

"Let her go," Riley said.

"She needs rules too. All day we've given her everything she even hinted she wanted. She needs to know you expect things from her."

"She's a kid." He made a face like a kid. "She's been through a lot."

"As a teacher, as your friend, albeit a new friend, I'm telling you to set some ground rules right away. She should help with small chores." Boy, did she sound like a teacher lecturing a student.

Daisy heard them and walked back to the truck.

"Thank you. Daisy, you can help us carry in these bags and then we'll check out your new room." Tricia waved at the packages.

Daisy frowned. Riley frowned, but they pitched in to carry the mass of bags and the cooler. They piled everything in the kitchen and Daisy took off.

"Shoes off, please," Riley called. "We don't wear shoes in the house. That's why we bought slippers."

Tricia set her shoes neatly by the wall, Riley and Daisy followed suit.

"Thanks, Daisy," Riley praised her compliance. Together, they put Daisy's new bedding in the washer.

"Come on, show me your room." Tricia grabbed Daisy's hand and they raced upstairs, Riley hot on their heels laughing and demanding they wait for him.

The furnishings were already assembled and set in place. "I think the bed would be better over there." Tricia waved to the opposite wall. "Then Daisy can see the stars out the window.

Riley groaned but immediately started moving furniture. Before long, they had the room arranged to suit everyone. Daisy walked from the bed to the dresser and then to the window, a small smile on her face. She opened and closed the toybox and looked inside. She straightened her new books on the shelves and placed her backpack beside the bed. She placed the teddy bear she'd received at the RCMP office in the center of the bed, propped up against her new pillow. Her eyes sparkled with wonderment as she wandered around the room running her slender fingers over everything.

"Tell me again why I'm doing extra laundry?" He asked as they transferred her sheets from the washer to the dryer and put a load of light-colored clothing in to wash.

"Because unwashed sheets are like rocks and scratch like the dickens. All clothing needs to be washed before it's worn. The fabrics contain dyes and stiffeners. They can cause rashes. Some things are laced with chemicals if they're shipped from overseas. Didn't your mother teach you washing ensures everything is clean and ready to wear?"

"I thought I bought ready to wear?"

She laughed at his puzzled expression. "Now you know better." She patted his cheek and he turned to press a kiss on her palm. She jerked her hand back and tucked it into the pocket of her jeans to keep him from seeing her hand shiver at his casual touch.

"Thank you for today. For helping me break the ice with Daisy. I might need your help, a lot." His grateful smile warmed her to her toes.

Oh no. Heck no. Her frown morphed to a grin. Wait until he figured out how hard dating was as a single parent. As a teacher she'd witnessed how difficult it was to be a single parent, for both men and women. She pitied his learning curve. Adapting to being a parent with an infant would be challenging enough but inheriting a six-year-old would test any adult's mettle. Daisy might be meek and agreeable now, but in time she would adjust to her new situation and start acting like a normal, six-year-old child. Luckily, he had a close-knit family to help him out.

She didn't know the details beyond understanding Daisy had lost enough already. Tricia couldn't, no wouldn't, get involved and be another in the line of adults who left Daisy. She'd go to the party today, and then she'd walk away before Daisy grew attached.

"I think you'll manage fine without me," she offered rather than an outright refusal to assist him in learning to parent.

CHAPTER FIVE

Riley unfastened his seatbelt and stared at the vehicles in his parents' driveway. Everyone was here. All three sisters, three out of his four brothers, a bunch of friends and neighbors. Unless he missed his guess, there'd be fifty people here. He squeezed the steering wheel until his knuckles went white. His best friend Houston's truck was parked on the lawn beside several other vehicles.

"What's the matter?" Tricia's hand touched his forearm, easing his tension.

"Look at the cars." He groaned. "Half the town must be here. The place is going to be a zoo. Daisy doesn't need this."

He peered at his daughter in the rear-view mirror. She didn't look worried, she looked almost excited. "There are going to be a lot of people. Are you okay with this, Daisy?" He had to ask, thinking of timid animals who had a hard time around a lot of people. Maybe he would be lucky and she wouldn't mind being around people. Or, better yet, she'd balk about going and he could head home and avoid the endless rounds of questions he knew were coming.

Daisy nodded but just slightly. It was a fraction of a motion. This was too much for him, how would she handle it? How was she in crowds? So danged many questions, so much to learn.

"Listen, Daisy. We'll go in and talk to people. You can stick with me and Tricia, or play with the kids. If it gets too busy, we can leave, you just have to let me know. Everyone is going to want to meet you. You're a special girl, and part of an enormous family now. We'll get through this. Besides, it's Grandma's birthday and she'll want to see us."

Tricia squeezed his arm and turned to face Daisy. "I'm not sure how things were with your mom, I don't think you had a big family. But, around here, in, Coyote Creek, pretty soon you get to know everyone. It's like a huge family. Tons of people, but nice people. There isn't anything to be afraid of in there." She looked surprised. "I guess that's true for me too." She laughed lightly. "These people are my neighbors, and might become friends, if I'm brave enough to talk to them."

"Yup. Nothing for either of you to be afraid of, just the noise." Riley laughed. "Grandma and Grampa's house is always loud. This morning with your cousins was quiet." He puffed out a breath. "You can unbuckle your seatbelt, Daisy. Ready or not, here we go." He slid out of the truck and hurried around to open the passenger doors to help Tricia and Daisy out.

"Thank you, Riley." Tricia smiled broadly, sounding surprised when he opened her door.

"Thank you." Daisy reached for his hand.

"You've got this, kiddo. Let's go wish Grandma a happy birthday."

As they walked past the endless row of guest vehicles Riley stared at the yellow and white house he'd grown up in. Two stories tall, it had miles of trim. How many times in his life had he painted the miles of trim?

"So many times." He groaned.

"So many times-what?" Tricia paused mid-step.

"I was trying to figure out how many times I helped paint this house. The first time, I was ten, it was just before dad married Sue and she moved in with her girls. My stepsisters. We painted every three years. Even after I left home, I came back to help. It's a huge job."

"You have stepsisters?" Daisy whispered.

"I do." Riley laughed. "And a stepmother."

Daisy's eyes went wide. "Is she evil?"

He caught himself before he laughed at the naïve question. He knelt beside her and looked her right in the eye. "My stepmother is the kindest woman you'll ever meet. My mommy died when I was a baby. I didn't have a mom until I was a few years older than you. Sue, your grandmother, became my new mother. You met her this morning and last evening. She's a wonderful lady with a big heart and she loves you and I to bits. You never have to be afraid of Grandma."

"'Kay."

"Let's go say happy birthday, and you'll see for yourself." Riley slipped between Daisy and Tricia and grabbed their hands. "She'll love you just as much as your mom and I do," Riley said.

"Oh. I forgot her present." Tricia pivoted back toward the truck.

"I'll get it." Daisy raced back to the truck, her ratty backpack bouncing against the Sunny yellow cotton of her new summer dress. His niece, Jane, would have called it a twirly dress. The skirt was full and would fly out flat if she spun around quickly. Why did girls like that? His sisters had loved twirly dresses too.

"She's so sweet and so scared," Riley murmured, pitching his voice low. "I'm not sure I have what it takes to be her father."

"Yes, you do. Be kind, show her love and discipline. Watch your brother and remember how you were raised. That's all it takes."

"And if I screw it up?"

"You'll make mistakes, everyone does. Sometimes you move on and sometimes, you apologize. It all depends on the situation. Just love her and try not to act in anger when she tests you. All kids test their boundaries and I expect her cousins will have her testing your limits in no time flat. They're little rapscallions. You're a smart man. You must be or you'd never have passed veterinary school. Think before you act."

"Why do I feel like you're in full-on teacher mode?"

Her lips pursed and she laughed. "Because I am?" Her eyes lit with mirth at her own actions.

Daisy returned with Tricia's gift and her own small

package. They crossed the wide front porch and wiped their shoes on the wicker mat. "Today's special. It's a party and it's summer. We get to wear our shoes indoors. If they're clean. Check the bottoms." They inspected their shoes and walked inside, right into a massive wall of noise.

Daisy cowered and covered her ears.

"Holy heck! This is worse than I expected," he said.

Tricia chuckled. "Do you blame them? Bachelor Riley Flint brings home his new daughter. The gossip grapevine will be overheating tonight."

He buried his face in one palm. "Ugg. Don't remind me. Come on, Daisy. Let's go find Grandma." He pushed his way through the crowd, offering greetings and dodging questions, Daisy and Tricia huddled against his back, following closely until they reached the relative sanctuary of the kitchen. As always, the familiar red and white décor was comforting, like he'd slipped back into his childhood where love was unconditional. Where remonstrations and praise were given freely along with hugs, kisses and Band-Aids.

"Hey, Sue. We're here."

Sue whirled around, a wide smile on her face, joy in her eyes. "I thought you'd never get here. Hi, darling Daisy. Oh, Tricia, so glad you could join us." She stepped over and embraced them all.

"Happy birthday, Mom." He kissed her cheek. "Who invited all these people?"

"Good grief, your father, bless his heart. Although I think a few may have invited themselves. I sent your father to town for more burgers and hot dogs. Jason went with him to keep an eye on him. I don't want your father straining himself. We never planned on this big of a crowd." She chuckled.

"How's he feeling?" Riley asked.

"We can talk about it later." Sue brushed his question off and avoided his eyes.

"Mom, we need to talk about it." He really should have pushed for answers sooner. He was a vet. He knew how important health was. Prolonged sickness wasn't something you could ignore. Guilt clawed at his stomach. He'd ignored the issue way too long.

"And we will. Later." Her firm tone put the discussion to rest, though Riley knew he'd have to press for answers and he would - first chance he got.

"How can we help?" Tricia handed Sue her gift.

"There isn't much left to do. Just crowd control, they're swarming me and have a million questions. Mostly about you!" She poked him in the chest with one finger. "You've got a lot of fast talking to do."

Ugg. He should have stayed home. Who did he think he was kidding? He'd never miss his mother's birthday, even if it meant facing up to his mistakes in front of the entire town.

"This is for you." Daisy held out her tiny, gift wrapped box. "Riley and I got this for you. I picked it out. Happy birthday, Grandma."

Holy crow! That was practically a speech and it came without coaxing. Riley peeked at Tricia; she was grinning from ear to ear.

"For me?" His mother's hand flew to her heart. "How sweet. Come over here and help me open it." She set Tricia's gift on the table and sat facing Daisy. "Thank you so much. Help me with the ribbon?"

The tremble in Daisy's hand as she reached out to help nearly floored Riley. Excitement? Fear? He couldn't tell. "Go ahead, help Grandma. It's okay."

Her wide smile at the permission was heart wrenching. How had they celebrated her birthdays? Quiet family dinners or big parties? Another question to ask her grandparents. Her birth certificate had a date on it, but for the life of him, he couldn't recall it. He'd double check and make sure her first birthday with him was something special. His mother's voice drew him back to the kitchen.

"I have a better idea. Why don't you open it for me? I'm quite tired. I could use the help." A blatant lie designed to pull Daisy further into the family. Sue was brilliant.

Daisy accepted the offered package and carefully picked at the ribbon.

"Should we cut the ribbon?" Tricia took the words right out of his mouth.

"Uh uh." Daisy shook her head. She fumbled for a bit and looked at her grandmother.

"Let's see. Maybe if we tug here, and here. Ah, that's it. You try now." The tears in his mother's eyes mirrored the ache in his heart. He swallowed the lump in his throat.

Together, they unwrapped the package. Daisy handed the unopened box over and stood watching her grandmother, her small body trembling with anticipation.

"I'm so excited. This'll be the best present ever, because it came from you." She cracked the hinged, black velvet box open and gasped. "Oh my." Tears rolled down her face. "This is beautiful. I'm going to share it with you. Half for me, half for you. Because I love you so much. I am so glad you are here." She placed one chain around Daisy's neck and the other on her own. "This is exactly what I wanted. A perfect gift to remind me of my beautiful new granddaughter. Thank you."

"Do you like it?" Daisy said, clutching her necklace in her hand.

"I love it, it's beautiful." She smiled widely at Daisy. "I'm crying because you picked the perfect gift." She pulled Daisy into her arms and hugged her tightly. "You're a wonderful child." She kissed the top of Daisy's head.

Riley glanced at Tricia, tears rolled down her face, she had one hand over her mouth, the other over her heart. He realized he had both hands over his mouth and had shed a few tears of his own. He dashed them away and slung his arm around her shoulders. "Thank you. You did this."

Her smile was watery. "We did this. All three of us."

He nodded. He wouldn't argue, but she'd done this. She'd realized Daisy knew what she wanted to buy. He'd have spent the next two hours offering suggestions, oblivious to the fact his daughter kept returning to the same display. Was he even observant enough to be a father?

The kitchen door opened and his father stumbled through, laden with grocery bags. "What's with all the waterworks?" He teased.

"Oh, Robert. This is Daisy. Look at the beautiful necklace Daisy bought me. It goes together with hers to make a double heart. Isn't it perfect?" She sniffed loudly. "It's so beautiful, it made me cry." She laughed lightly. "Daisy, this is Riley's father and my husband. He's your Grampa."

Daisy ducked her head and slid closer to Sue.

His father set the bags on the counter and kicked off his shoes. Moving slowly, he knelt beside his wife. "It's beautiful. You made your grandmother very happy. It's the perfect birthday gift. Almost as perfect as getting a new granddaughter. You're the best gift ever."

Daisy's face glowed with the praise, her face alight with joy.

"And you son, I'm proud of you. You did the right thing." He stood and patted Riley on the shoulder. "Welcome to the Bar Three Ranch, Miss Tricia. I'm glad you could join us. Now, you three come help me fire up the barbecues before the crowd gets too hungry and decides to lynch the cook. "Come with Grampa. We've got cooking to do." He held out his hand.

Daisy glanced from his hand to the paper and ribbon on the table and then to Riley.

"Do you want to keep the paper?" Riley asked.

She nodded.

"I'll get you a bag." He dug a zippered plastic bag out of a drawer and helped her fold the paper and slip it inside. "We'll tuck it into your backpack."

"You adults go outside. Daisy and I will find Jane and join you." His mother made a shooing motion with one hand and his dad wandered back outside. Daisy in hand, Sue went searching for Jane.

A moment later, alone in the kitchen with Tricia, Riley

breathed a sigh of relief. "Oh my gosh, that was—I don't even know what to say." Words and emotions tumbled through his head and he couldn't form a coherent sentence.

"It was beautiful. And sad." Tricia swallowed hard. "She's so young and she's been through too much. Your mother gave her such a gift. Oh Riley, letting her choose the present was brilliant. I'm so proud of you." She rose up on tiptoes and brushed a light kiss across his cheek.

He froze, terrified of scaring her away. Sweet heaven, Tricia Paxton kissed him. Yesterday she barely wanted to talk to him, today she kissed him and she was proud of him. Why did her approval seem so important? He felt a grin spread across his face. He could get used to this. He hugged her tight to his side. "We did this. You and I. I can't thank you enough."

"Did you see her go with your mother? She didn't hesitate."

"I could hardly believe it. I thought she'd refuse." It was fabulous that she was already stepping out of the timid box they'd found her in.

"She's adapting already. Incredible."

CHAPTER SIX

"Tricia, will you fill the cooler while we get the barbecues going?" Riley's father, Robert Flint, waved a work roughened hand toward a stack of bagged ice, sodas and beer alongside an enormous plastic tub. He stood in front of three massive propane grills.

Sneaking glances at the pair, she started her task. There was no doubt they were related. Tall, strong and muscular without being bulky, and those incredible Flint-green eyes. They moved with the same fluid grace that spoke of bodies accustomed to hard work. From the back, it was difficult to tell them apart in their Wranglers, Stetsons and plaid shirts. With their hats covering their hair, you'd swear they were brothers. Their age difference wasn't apparent until they turned toward her. Robert's face was an intriguing road map of sun and smile lines. Riley's face was smoother, but she could see he was going to improve with age. He was only going to improve with age.

She'd seen all the brothers around town. With their dark hair and green eyes, there was no doubt they were Flint men. They looked like their father, but with slight variations. Robert had one dimple; his sons had one, two, or none. The brothers were all close to six feet tall. Kendrick was a bit taller, and Carl was shorter and stockier. Even Riley's nephews had the unmistakable Flint look.

Riley was fitter than his father, who was developing a rounded middle. It didn't show from behind, but his belly bulged forward in a testament to aging and a love of his wife's legendary cooking.

"What's up with your health, Dad?" Riley asked. "You should be over this bug by now, not teetering on the fence between health and sickness."

"That's not a discussion for your mother's birthday. We'll talk about it later."

Riley sighed. Getting the brush off about something so important must be frustrating, but Tricia silently agreed with Robert, now probably wasn't the time to discuss it.

"So, you've got a daughter." Robert handed Riley a stack of burger patties. "Put these on the grill. You gonna tell me why this is the first I'm hearing of you having a child? We raised you better than that."

Tricia turned away to hide a smile as she filled the cooler. Riley's father had used almost the exact phrase his stepmother used in the bar last night. Funny how families often shared the same speech patterns; she saw it a lot as a teacher. Not only ways of speaking but thought patterns as well. The Flint family were devoted to one another and took their familial duties seriously. Even Riley's niece and nephews had pitched in to help out their new cousin by suggesting Riley call Tricia for help.

"I swear, I didn't know Daisy existed."

"Hmph."

"Really, Dad? I've never had unprotected intercourse with anyone. As a rancher's son, I know semen's a valuable commodity and you don't just spread it around willy-nilly."

Tricia couldn't help laughing. "A commodity?"

"It's a ranch thing. Bull semen isn't cheap you know." Riley said.

"Yeah, but bull crap is," Robert grumbled.

She really shouldn't listen to their private conversation, but they'd started it with her here, so she stayed. She placed a few cans gently into the slowly melting ice.

"No bull crap, Dad. God's truth. Never. I've never even considered unprotected sex. I wouldn't be so disrespectful to a woman. Too many things can go wrong. Once, a condom broke, but I swear to God, I swear on my truck and my business, I followed up with her. Several times. She told me she wasn't pregnant." His shoulders were tense as he slapped a burger on the oversized grill. It sizzled and popped as he added more.

"My relationship with Mona was short. Having a child without knowing isn't something I'm proud of, but I called her repeatedly about the consequences. She promised me there were none. I had myself tested for disease afterward too. In hindsight, I should have gone to see her, but I had no reason to doubt her word. If Mona hadn't gotten sick and died, I'd never have known about Daisy. I'm glad I get to know my daughter. I didn't want Daisy to lose her mother, but I'd never leave a child to be raised without me. I'd have done the right thing if I'd known and I'm doing the right thing now." He eased the barbecue shut.

"Pass me a beer, please." Tricia handed Riley a chilled Pilsner. He popped the top and took several long swallows.

"This isn't where I wanted to be right now. I'm years away from wanting a family, but here we are. I've got a daughter and I intend to raise her as best as I can. I'll raise her to know right from wrong and she'll always know love. I'm as nervous as a ten-point buck in hunting season, but I'll do right by her."

Who talked like that? Sperm as a commodity and a ten-point buck in hunting season? Boy when things went south, the cowboy in Riley Flint came out, big time. She'd have laughed if he wasn't so serious about the whole matter.

"Would you like a beer, Mr. Flint?" She glanced at Riley's father. Like his son, he was the quintessential cowboy. While his son belonged on the cover of a western romance novel, Robert would be right at home on the cover of a western movie or novel.

"Can you have beer, Dad?"

"Doc says two drinks a week. I've been dry for a month. One beer won't hurt me." Robert grumbled. "Pass me a beer, please, Miss Tricia. And call me Robert. We don't stand much on formality here at the Bar Three or in Coyote Creek. I'll take anything, except a lite one." He chuckled, his smile carving deep grooves in his cheeks and around his eyes. "No self-respecting cowboy would be caught dead drinking lite beer."

"Indeed." She raised one eyebrow in challenge. "But you bought lite beer; and please, if we're going to be casual, call me Tricia." She passed him a can.

"Well, Tricia. Some of those town sissies like their low alcohol beer; I'm just being accommodating. Take those coolers for example. My Sue loves those danged things. Like drinking watered down syrup if you ask me. She likes 'em. I buy 'em. Happy wife, happy life. You mark my words, Riley."

"Not planning on having a wife any time soon, Dad. I've got one little girl to deal with. I expect she'll keep me on my toes."

"What are you going to do with her when you work?" Tricia stood and wiped her hands on her jeans. "Doesn't a vet get a lot of calls outside of ordinary working hours?"

His jaw dropped and he froze, his beer half way to his mouth. "Hell's bells. I thought of that last night but with everything today, it just left my mind. Now I'm going to have to interview nannies."

"Ones old enough to drive at night, if you expect them to come to your place in the wee hours. It's a good thing your place is only fifteen miles outside of town. Distance could rule out a lot of candidates. Or you might have to hire a live-in nanny." Tricia watched the realization of his predicament dawn in Riley's eyes. In less than twenty-four hours his perfect life had turned to shambles. He was putting up a brave front, but his rigid posture and wrinkled brow gave him away.

"Son, you better talk to your mother. She'll know who's

available for night work. Your mother and I'll take a few shifts, but we're not giving you any more than we give to your brother Kendrick, and his wife's run off."

"I appreciate any help you can give me. I knew this wouldn't be easy, but I had no freaking clue how complicated it would be."

The screen door banged shut and Daisy and Jane barreled out on the back deck, hand in hand. Daisy stopped abruptly and looked at Riley. The girls stood side by side, looking eerily similar and strikingly different at the same time. Both were tall and thin for their age with Flint-green eyes sparkling beneath too-long bangs. Daisy's hair was curly blonde, Jane's red hair hung straight to her waist.

They looked at each other and smiled conspiratorially. Anyone could see this duo would become fast friends and a force to be reckoned with.

"Can we play in the treehouse? Grandma says it's okay." Tricia's chest constricted at the hope and fear in Daisy's expression. Not fear of Riley, but of having her request denied; as if she was accustomed to disappointment. With her mom sick and dying, she'd probably missed out on a lot.

"Sure thing, kiddo. Be careful on the ladder and come back when we call you for dinner. And don't forget to say please next time." He ruffled her hair. "Grandma's a stickler for manners."

"Grandma's not a sticker." Jane laughed. "You're funny."

"Stick-ler. It means she really wants you to use your manners. Go have fun in the playhouse with your cousin."

They raced across the lawn and scampered up the wooden ladder and into an enormous treehouse.

"Wow. Nice treehouse." Across the perfectly groomed lawn, seventy-five feet from the edge of the deck, was the most enormous treehouse she'd ever seen. It stretched between four enormous pine trees. It had two ladders, two solid walls, two half walls. The roof overhung a railed porch and the entire thing was painted green and brown to match the evergreens it was suspended between.

"We built it when we were kids. Dad did most of the work. I suspect we hindered more than we helped. But it was fun; except the times I hammered my thumb." Riley laughed. "We had a lot of good times, and a lot of fights up there. Camping out was the best."

"Camping out." Robert chuckled. "The lot of you never made it through the night more than once or twice. Too cold. Too windy. Too many bugs. There was always an excuse; until you got old enough to try sneaking out of the yard."

"But if it wasn't a school night, you always let us try."

"I can't even imagine." Tricia studied the treehouse. "You'd never even consider sleeping in the yard in the city. I would have loved it."

"You can always come out here and the three of us can have a sleepover," Riley suggested.

A sleepover with Riley? Her heart zinged into action; her pulse raced. She resisted the urge to fan the heat from her face. Yikes. She hadn't thought she'd be interested in a cowboy.

Yeah, but the fantasy. Riley, a treehouse and a sleepover.

"I'm going to see if Sue needs any help in the kitchen." She bolted inside before her mind got any more carried away with the fantasy. Riley Flint was not for her, no matter how stimulating he was. She was a teacher and she'd lost her last position because she'd been implicated and assumed guilty when her parents, both accountants, were caught embezzling from the private school they all worked for. She wasn't about to risk this job for a fantasy.

She paused inside the door to calm her racing heart. Riley was entirely too attractive and so kind to his family. He was a great guy. But being around him brought back painful memories of being burned by family. She'd had nothing to do with her parents' crimes, but they'd dragged her down with them. She'd been fortunate. Only time, money and a good lawyer had proven her innocence.

CHAPTER SEVEN

Riley fired up the second barbecue and loaded it with smokies. He was placing hotdogs on the top rack when Robert spoke.

"Tricia's one heck of a gal. Good of her to help you out."

Riley jerked in surprise, burning his finger on the grill. "Ouch. Did you have to bring her up?" he chided, sucking his finger before sticking it into the icy drink cooler water.

"Well, you brought her here." Robert chuckled.

"She's—nice."

"Who's nice?" Riley's oldest brother Justice asked.

"Mind your own business, bro."

Justice laughed. "I heard you were strolling around town with the pretty grade one teacher and a little girl on your arms. Rumor has it you're a family man now."

"I was with my daughter, Daisy. Tricia was helping us shop for the things Daisy needs." Great, he knew better than to hope to get through the day without divulging the intimate details of his life. Especially with his brothers.

"How'd you come to have a daughter? How old is she?" Justice persisted.

"Daisy is almost six. Her mother died of cancer."

Justice's mouth gaped open. "How'd you keep her a secret this long?"

"Can we do this later? In private?" He should have called a family meeting and gotten this over with all at once. He wasn't exactly ashamed of what he did, of how he ended up with a child. He'd been in a monogamous relationship which resulted in an unexpected child, but it hadn't even been twenty-four hours and he was already on the hot seat.

"Nope. You sure she's yours? You gonna get a paternity test?"

"Yes. I'm sure she's mine. Yes, I'm going to get the test. Let it go."

"She's got Flint eyes," Robert chimed in. He nodded toward the treehouse. "She's over there with Jane. Except for the hair, they're identical. But you leave them be. She's as skittish as a newborn colt. Give her time to adapt before you start trying to fix everything."

"I don't try to fix everything. I just look out for my family."

"You're always trying to fix our lives." Riley squared his shoulders and braced for a fight. "You're my oldest brother, not my father. Stay out of my business."

Justice clapped him on the shoulder. "Chill, dude. Just making sure you know what you're doing. Parenthood is a tough gig. I know." His teasing grin morphed into a frown. He slumped like a deflated balloon.

"No news on Hannah?"

"Nothing. It's been twenty-one months since she vanished. I could kill Ellen for letting her run away." He raked his fingers through his hair. "I don't know why I ever married her. She doesn't even care that her daughter's missing. She's off to Paris with her fourth husband."

"Any clues?" Riley persisted. His brother looked like hell. He was unshaven, his shirt was wrinkled and his boots dusty. Since Hannah disappeared, he'd had his ups and downs. Today was obviously a down day.

"Nothing. The RCMP are calling it a cold case, but I think I may try to convince Amy Baxter to look into it. I heard some rumors of kids going missing in Whitecourt around the same time. I'll spend every waking minute searching for her, in person and online. I won't quit until I know what happened to her." He cursed under his breath and smiled weakly.

Riley recognized the smile for the brave front it was. There was no happiness in Justice's eyes. Anger, disappointment and determination resided there now. As they had since his teenage daughter ran away.

"Who's missing?" Tricia stepped onto the deck with a stack of empty platters.

"You don't know?" Riley asked.

"If I knew I wouldn't have asked. Is there anything I can do? Do we need to start searching for them?" She looked from Robert to Riley to Justice.

"I guess she was gone before you arrived in town. Tricia,

this is my oldest brother Justice. His daughter went missing almost two years ago. I'm surprised you haven't heard about it."

"Oh my gosh." Her hand clutched her chest. "That's so awful. You must be devastated. Is there anything I can do?"

Her offer seemed to touch Justice. He shook his head. "No thanks. Unless you hear any rumors of missing kids in the area. I keep searching and hoping." He patted her on the shoulder. "Look, I'm going to say hi to Mom and hit the road."

"Son, it would make your mother very happy if you stuck around," Robert suggested.

"Yeah, but it would kill me knowing I wasn't searching." He held up a hand before anyone responded. "I know, I'm slacking on my ranch work. I'll pick it up. I'll run the west fences out to the old campground and mend any breaks. After I check the campground for signs of Hannah, I'll come back. Maybe the crowd will have thinned enough I can visit with family. The piteous looks are more than I can tolerate. I have to do something. Standing around is killing me." He nodded solemnly and went into the house.

"Holy crap," Tricia whispered. "I had no idea."

"You're probably the only person in town who doesn't. Nobody talks about it, but everyone's got their eyes and ears open."

"She disappeared from Coyote Creek?" Bewilderment filled her voice.

"No, from Edmonton. She ran away from Justice's ex-wife Ellen's place," Robert said. "She was gone two weeks before her mother noticed. She was wrapped up in her new husband and believed Hannah when she said she was going to stay with a friend for a few days. Turns out the friend knew nothing about it. I should have paid attention when Hannah missed calling me. She called Sue and I every weekend. Ellen had an excuse for that too."

"How could she fail to notice her child was gone?"

Tears streaked down Tricia's face and gouged Riley's heart. He thought he'd shed all the tears he had for Hannah. He swallowed hard.

"She was fourteen," Riley said. She'll be sixteen at the end of November. She was coming to live with Justice the next summer. Our best guess is she got impatient and started home before Christmas. Nobody knows what happened for sure. We all pray she's okay. Anytime I'm up late with an animal or can't sleep, I search the internet for clues."

"We all do," Robert chimed in sadly. "Pass over those plates. We better get the food on before Sue notices us slacking. She can't find out we were talking about this; it would ruin her birthday." He forced a laugh. "Not a word of this discussion to anyone."

His warning landed hard on Riley. Dear God, what if something happened to Daisy? How would he handle it?

"Shit," he mumbled.

"Watch your mouth, son."

"What?" Tricia asked.

"I never really got it until now. I knew I had no idea what

Justice was going through; but I think I just got a glimpse. He's holding up way better than I would and I've only had a child for eighteen hours." He turned toward his father. "I'll pick up more chores around here. I can teach Daisy about ranch life while I work. I can handle a bit extra so Justice can search." It wasn't enough and didn't make up for not doing more earlier. It felt a lot like too little, too late. The optimist in him reminded him of better late than never.

Tricia set the plates on the table and patted his arm. "You're a good man, Riley Flint."

Robert announced dinner by banging on the metal triangle hanging from the eaves of the house. Moments later, a parade of people streamed outside, each one laden with a platter of food. They placed the food on the long line of folding tables stretching across the yard before trooping away to return with folding lawn chairs.

Robert joined Sue at the head of the table and welcomed everyone. Only after they filled their plates and seated themselves at the family picnic table did anyone else approach the buffet dinner.

With Tricia, Jane and Daisy in tow, Riley joined the queue for food.

"I'm going to have dessert first," Jane declared.

"You'll do nothing of the sort," Riley countered with a laugh. "This is early supper. You'll have a proper meal. Meat, vegetables and a carbohydrate. All the things to make you grow."

"What's a car go hi grate?" Daisy wrinkled her nose at him.

"Car-bo-hy-drate. It's pasta, rice, potatoes, bread. You should try your grandmother's rye bread. It's delicious with butter."

"It tastes gross," Jane whispered. "But sometimes you gotta eat it so you don't hurt Grandma's feelings."

Tricia snickered and Riley feigned a glare at her. "Today, you don't have to eat it. Come on girls, I'll help you fill your plates." He let them make a few selections, vetoed a few more and added small portions of vegetables. He settled the girls on a blanket and sat with Tricia on nearby chairs.

"Well done."

Tricia's praise felt good. "Just channeling my brother Ken. He'd make all his kids eat properly."

"He's not here?" She looked around the crowded yard.

"No, he's in Edmonton wooing his wife. Trying to get her to come back. It's an ugly situation but he still loves her. I guess Mom told him she'd rather he went after his wife than stick around for the party." He shrugged. "My family is —complicated."

"Aren't they all?"

"What about you? Is your family complicated?"

"Beyond belief." Her words were heavy with unspoken emotion.

He waited for her to say more, but she focused on her plate and avoided his gaze. He debated pressing the issue, his curiosity was overwhelming. He pushed the thought away. They were barely friends; he had no right to pry into her personal life. Maybe after he got to know her better…

"We ate everything!" Daisy and Jane chimed in unison, skipping up to Riley brandishing their empty plates.

"Can we have treats now?" Jane added.

"Nobody gets dessert until we sing happy birthday to Grandma Sue and she cuts her cake. But you can put your dishes in the plastic bin by the back door and go play for a while. Just don't go far."

He watched to ensure they deposited their semi-disposable, reusable plastic plates in the bin to be washed. "I don't know where Mom got these plates. I carried them in the day she bought them two years ago. They're strong, sturdy plastic. We use them for every large gathering and most of them are as good as new. Safer than ceramic or glass, not as wasteful as paper and you don't have to worry if one gets broken, and the plastic silverware is dishwasher safe. We found that out when I accidentally put one into the dishwasher."

"They're ideal," Tricia agreed. "Although I wouldn't want to wash them all." They laughed together.

"No worries there. Neighbors will sneak in and wash most of them while Mom's busy visiting. She'll pretend to be offended, but everyone knows she'll be thrilled. It's a game."

"So, who else here is your family?"

"Well, you met Justice." He pointed to two men standing near the treehouse. "Those two are my brothers Carl and Jason. Carl's the shorter, stockier one. He's thirty. Jason's thirty-three. He's the tall one who looks like me."

"I know Carl from the garage. Jason does look like you.

You could be twins." She turned to grin at him. "Except Jason doesn't have your dimple."

"You noticed my dimple?" The idea tickled him.

"Well, I kept seeing this guy all over town. I thought I was losing my mind. I'd see him in a western shirt in one store and ten minutes later in a T-shirt." She chuckled. "I figured out there was more than one of you when Ken's son Zander talked about all his uncles during our family unit in school. And you have sisters too, right?

He groaned. "I have three pesky sisters. Beth, Candy and Jenn."

"Where are they?" She scanned the yard.

"Jenn's in the treehouse. She's the youngest. She dresses like a gypsy. Beth is twenty-two. She's the one in scrubs hovering over Dad. She's a nursing student. "

"They've got Sue's features. Their hair looks like Sue's must have when she was young."

A petite blonde stepped in front of them. Her fatigue style pants were cotton, with lots of pockets. She was tanned golden and her green eyes sparkled with happiness. She thrust out her hand.

"Hiya. I'm Candy. Riley's sister."

Riley groaned. "Candy's our little eco-warrior. She's twenty-four and gonna save the planet from the evils of man."

"Man is not evil," she quipped, shaking Tricia's hand. "Just careless of Mother Nature's gifts. I wish everyone paid attention, reduced waste and took care of our planet. It's the only one we've got."

"Nice to meet you, Candy. I'm in your camp. We could do a lot more to protect the earth."

Candy tipped her head and gave Riley a mocking grin. "See, I'm not a crazy person."

"I never said you were a crazy person. I said you're twenty-four years old. Maybe it's time you got a job. A paying job. Stop sponging off Mom and Dad."

"Yeah, I need to stop borrowing money from them. So, can I borrow a hundred bucks and your kitchen?"

"Okay, the money I understand but my kitchen?"

"Bake sale. I need the cash for ingredients and your kitchen for baking." She mocked a curtsy and winked.

Riley laughed aloud.

"Riley," Tricia chided him.

"Candy has never, ever baked anything edible."

"Come on, that's not true." She rolled her eyes.

"If you give me one example of you making a successful dessert, I'll *give* you the money and loan you my kitchen."

"Two years ago. Your birthday cake." She held out her hand and waggled her fingers until he put the cash in her hand.

"I'll give you the win on this one, but I'm pretty sure Beth made the cake and you took credit. There is one condition. No cooking alone, you need a chaperone and clean up when you're done."

"That's two conditions, Riley." Tricia chimed in. "And, I'd love to help you bake. I read about the bake sale in the paper. It's a great cause. Does Riley have baking pans or should we do this at my place? What are you planning on baking?"

"Riley is sitting right here and he does not have baking pans, or any baking ingredients. Give me a list and I'll go shopping."

Candy bent over and kissed him on the cheek. Thanks bro, I'll text you." She skipped away with his money in her hand.

"She's sweet," Tricia laughed.

"Wanna bet I get stuck buying everything and she donates my money to the bake sale?" He sighed. "Some day, she is going to have to grow up."

"Come on, she's living her passion. We should all be so lucky."

"Can't she find a job doing her passion?"

Tricia patted his hand. "She'll get there, she just needs time to figure out where she's going. You're good to her, it's nice you support her dream. I've noticed your family seems to pull together a lot. For school plays, the entire family shows up. At last year's Christmas Bazaar, everyone came. You're like a herd all by yourselves. This summer, you guys took half of the prizes in the fishing derby."

"Are you stalking us?" He teased, not hiding his pleasure to learn she was up to date on their lives.

"Not stalking, exactly, your family is hard to miss. The love and support you share is—it's incredible." She sounded almost envious.

"They're all a colossal pain; but I love them dearly." He did have a great family, despite feeling like he didn't fit in very well. Even his daughter found an ally immediately in Jane. Everyone watched out for everyone. Sometimes it was as if he stood on the sidelines, waiting to be invited in. It wasn't that they didn't love him. They did, he didn't doubt it for a second. But his brothers all had the camaraderie of knowing their mother. Riley was so young when she died, he had no memories of her and felt left out when they shared theirs.

And the girls, his stepsisters…they'd all lost their father, but they still had their mother. It was only Riley who felt like he didn't have a place. He wondered if he'd ever get beyond the pain of being motherless and move on.

They took a short visit to see the kittens. Daisy adored them, but they were too young to leave their mother. Riley promised to think about letting Daisy get one when they were old enough to find new homes. Much later, after the cake was served and most of the guests gone, Riley, Tricia and Daisy climbed back into his truck to head home. He'd barely started the engine when Daisy dozed off.

"Did you know your mom?" Tricia asked out of the blue.

"No, she died when I was a toddler. Dad married Sue when I was ten."

"That's terrible." She paused. "I mean how sad to spend so long without a mother. But how marvelous Sue stepped into such an enormously all male family and pitched into raising you boys."

"She kind of evened the odds. Instead of six men alone, we're six men and four women. Although the males don't stand a chance against a gaggle of females."

He laughed and feigned injury when Tricia mock slapped his arm.

"Be nice to your family, it's clear they adore you."

The depth of his family's caring struck him anew. Their relationships were far from perfect, but he wouldn't trade his family for anything. Especially now that he had a daughter of his own.

CHAPTER EIGHT

Tricia stood in the doorway to her classroom staring at her dusty desk and naked walls. At the end of the school year last year, she'd taken everything down for painting. The walls were institutional beige; a universal not-quite-cream color, more a cream with hints of sour green. It was duller than dishwater and threatened to suck all her joy for the new school year right out of her. Who picked these colors?

Well, first things first. She grabbed a trolley from the storage room to haul boxes of supplies into the school. Inside, she dusted down the desk, the round student tables and their multi-colored chairs. She rooted through her boxes and sorted items into two categories. Things to use now, and things she'd need later in the year; those she placed into the oversized metal storage locker she'd had to empty to facilitate moving it for painting.

She outlined the chalkboard behind her desk with a

scalloped paper border of sunflowers which matched the airy curtains she hung on pressure mount rods over the utilitarian venetian blinds in the windows. Next, she designed a display for the bulletin board over the open shelving for student supplies. The science curriculum had some flexibility; she'd start the year with a science unit on insects. First to go up were the diagrams of insects labeled with the names of body parts beyond the students' ability to read. Being able to read the words didn't matter, they'd discuss them. Most children had a knack for memorizing and pronouncing big words. She'd seen it over and over again, her students easily picked up Canada's second national language in French class.

On a side table she set out insect models and books about insects. She designed and shifted and rearranged items in her classroom until a soft knock sounded on her door.

She turned toward the sound. Joanne Mahoney stood in the doorway, her long red hair piled high on her head in a messy bun, her oversized purse draped over her shoulder. Her jeans were tattered and her T-shirt proclaimed she was a well-educated woman who cussed a lot. Not appropriate attire for an elementary school teacher but perfectly Jo. "Jo! What are you doing here on the weekend? And why didn't you call me?"

Her best friend and fellow first grade teacher laughed. "Same as you, restoring my classroom to order after they painted. Have to get a head start or the first week of school will be a mess. Are you going to keep working, or do you want to go grab a bite to eat? It's nearly noon and I hear Tammy has a new cook from Newfoundland. The special today is fish chowder with fresh baked sourdough bread…" she trailed off enticingly.

"Oh man, you're cruel. A good friend wouldn't taunt someone on a diet. You do know that, right?"

"A diet?" Jo looked surprised. "You're what, a buck twenty soaking wet?"

"One thirty-five. I'm not walking as much as I used to in the city. I need to work out more."

"Fine." Jo grinned. "Let's walk over for lunch and back. You could join me Tuesday and Thursday nights for cross training. Come with me. We do something different every class. It's close, it's in the rec space above the curling rink. Right across the street from your apartment."

Tricia winced. "I don't know, I'm more of a walking person. I'm not very coordinated."

"Come on, give it a shot. You can't be any worse than Mrs. Adelson. She's pushing seventy and she comes every night. She rocks yoga classes."

"You want me, a klutz, to work out in front of the town's number one gossip? Fat chance." She grabbed her purse and after looking at the sun streaming down outside her window, left her jacket behind. "Come on, let's go eat. I skipped breakfast."

"Breakfast is the most important meal of the day," Jo sing-songed.

"True enough, but I was busy all day yesterday and forgot to go for groceries."

"Funny thing about being *busy*, I heard you went shopping

with a certain attractive veterinarian." She smirked and raised one eyebrow.

Tricia ignored the comment, locked her classroom and they headed out on the ten-block walk to Tammy's. Tricia paused to breathe deeply the moment she stepped into the fall sunshine. "I love the smells out here." She inhaled again. "Pine, fresh air, fresh-cut grass, flowers…it really doesn't get better than this. The city never smelled like this."

Fifteen minutes later they stood outside Tammy's. The building was midway between Bar None and the hardware store. It was a blue, utilitarian, cinder block box with a flat roof and enormous display windows. Years ago, it had been a hardware store. The door opened and an elderly couple strolled out drawing the enticing aroma of fish chowder and fresh baked bread with them.

"I might have been mistaken; this is the best thing I've smelled in weeks. I haven't had fish chowder in months," Tricia exclaimed as she hurried toward the door. Inside, fourteen of fifteen vinyl booths were filled. They settled into the only empty booth. Their waitress, Honey, was beside them in an instant, her blonde spiral curls bouncing as she jingled up to them.

"What can I get you ladies?" Her charm bracelet chimed as she slid two menus on the table and poised her pen over her coil notebook.

"Coffee and the fish chowder special for both of us," Jo chimed in. "It smells delicious."

"Best batch yet," Honey enthused. "Chef found a new seafood distributor and his cousin works here now. He's won awards for his bread. Prestigious awards. You're going to *love* this bread." She sighed blissfully and skipped away.

"That girl is the most upbeat person I've ever met," Tricia commented, her eyes following Honey until she disappeared through the swinging doors into the kitchen.

"She's always so happy. And her clothes. I've never seen anyone pull off those gypsy skirts and peasant blouses like she does. Not even Riley's youngest sister, Jennifer," Jo added slyly. "Speaking of Riley—I heard you were with him all day yesterday; including at his mother's birthday party. And don't even try to change the subject. I'm on this like a Pit bull on a pork chop."

"I was assisting Riley with," she stalled for a moment, "with a project."

"A project? I'd hardly call his illegitimate daughter a project." She chuckled.

Honey slid two coffees and two glasses of ice water in front of them. "Now don't you girls be gossiping about Riley. The Flints are a fine, upstanding family and you two, being teachers, should know better than to tell tales out of school." She looked furtively around. "At least wait until there aren't so many eager ears hanging around. There's nothing faster than the Coyote Creek gossip system." She grinned and walked away, her anklet of silver bells chiming with every step.

"Honey should be a teacher. She can deliver a rebuke in the kindest tones and you want to agree with her." Tricia lowered her voice. "She's so beautiful and such a free spirit.

She brings sunshine wherever she goes. I don't think I've ever seen her down in the dumps."

"Enough delaying tactics." Jo shook her slender finger under Tricia's nose. "I want the scoop. Leave nothing out."

"Mrs. Flint's birthday was lovely. There must have been a hundred people there. Some dropped in for a quick hello. People came and went like the place had a revolving door. Tons of people were there when I arrived and still there when we left."

"Aha! When *we* left?"

"Riley called me yesterday morning. He needed help shopping for his daughter. I helped him out and he invited me to his mother's birthday. I wasn't going to go, but Daisy seemed to want me there."

The tables around them emptied, leaving them alone in the corner. Honey brought their lunches. "Enjoy, ladies. I'll be over there if you need me." She waved at the tiny table reserved for staff members.

Tricia stirred her chowder. Chunks of fish, potato and carrots in a thick white broth. A shrimp, a clam and a couple scallops floated to the surface as she stirred. The rich, thick aroma tickled her nose, she couldn't wait to dive in. She spread a thin layer of butter on her still-warm bread and watched it melt in before tasting it.

"Oh man," she groaned. "They better not have this special often. I'd weigh a ton. This bread is to die for."

"And the chowder, I'd kill for this chowder." Jo eagerly scooped another spoonful into her mouth. They ate in silence until Tricia finished. She set down her spoon and wiped her mouth on her napkin.

"So, why'd you ditch me at the bar?"

"You're kidding, right?"

Tricia shook her head. "Nope. Friends don't leave friends alone in a bar."

"Come on, this is Coyote Creek. It's, like, a five-minute walk to your place. I arranged a ride for you. Besides, I've been chasing Houston since he came to town and he finally noticed me. No way was I passing up a chance to go for a starlit walk with him." She sighed blissfully.

"I could have walked you home," Tricia joked. She wasn't angry at her friend, just disappointed she hadn't taken the time to say she was leaving.

"Yeah, I like you, but you're no Houston Jackson. Besides, I sent Riley to take you home." She finished eating and pushed her plate away.

"And, his mother and Amy Baxter dragged him away to meet his daughter. I walked home. I knew I wore my walking shoes for a reason," she teased. "Seriously, I don't like being dumped on other people. Next time, can you tell me yourself instead of making me some charity case?"

"You think you're a charity case?" Jo's mouth hung open for a second before she snapped it shut. "You're my friend, my best friend. I couldn't leave you alone, I know you're uncomfortable in the bar. I apologize. Next time, if there is a next time, I'll tell you in person." She made an X over her chest. "I cross my heart. Now, tell me all about yesterday."

Careful not to let anyone overhear, Tricia related her day

with Riley and Daisy. She concluded the story with, "I checked the class lists and I've got one less student than you. I'm sure Daisy will be in my class this year."

"Sweet, you'll be able to see Riley all the time. Maybe parent-teacher conferences will take on a whole new meaning." She wiggled her eyebrows and winked suggestively.

"I would never fraternize with a student's parent." Did Jo really think she would?

"One day you'll realize this is Coyote Creek and nobody cares. If you're discrete in front of the students and parents, dating is allowed. In a place this small, a girl has to be open to possibilities. Even Principal Keller, king of the uptight, knows people need personal lives."

"Well, I'm not looking for a relationship, so the point is moot."

"Look, you told me about your jerk of an ex, but don't hide because he was a tool. The Flints are great. Riley is Houston's best friend and business partner. He's honest and trustworthy. I'm just saying, if you guys were dating and we were dating—it could be good."

"You're dating Houston?" They rose in unison and headed for the cash register to pay their tab.

"We're going out on Friday. Sammy's Steakhouse."

"Sammy's has the best peppercorn steak. Get it with the deep-fried mushroom caps and shredded onion ring topper. It's to die for," Honey injected, joining them at the counter.

"That sounds like a lot of food." Jo grimaced, clearly torn between the amount of food and the desire to order it.

"It warms up like a dream. I get three meals out of it. It's *so* good. Now, if I had a date to take me…" she trailed off and giggled. "Look at me, dreaming in color. I came here three years ago to escape the city. I didn't realize there wouldn't be any eligible bachelors. Oh well, that's life. The universe will provide."

"You don't even sound upset," Tricia pointed out.

"I'm not, not really. Sometimes I think about it, but I don't really worry too much. Life's short. Focus on the positive and be happy, darlings, be happy. Enjoy this beautiful universe." She waved expansively and her bracelets chimed their agreement.

They settled their bill and strolled back to the school. The warm sun and cool breeze blew away the cobwebs caused by the delicious lunch. They parted outside their adjacent classrooms and returned to their decorating. The rest of the weekend passed in a blur for Tricia as she spent her time in the school, prepping her classroom for the influx of new students.

ON THE FIRST day of each school year, Tricia was always up early, and in her classroom long before she needed to be there. Seeing all those eager faces was a thrill that never got old. In all her years of teaching, she had never slept in on the first day of school.

Until today.

Unable to sleep for thinking about Daisy, Tricia paced the

floor in her apartment until she finally dozed off on the couch at three a.m. Startled awake by a car horn, she showered in record time and raced through the streets to the school, barely stopping at stop signs, risking a ticket. She had to be there for the morning staff meeting at seven-thirty. She skidded into the staff room as the principal called the meeting to order.

Her mind was so caught up in worries over Daisy she almost missed Principal Keller calling her name.

"Sorry, sir. I was thinking ahead to my new students."

Hands on his ample hips, he cast a dubious glance her way. His round belly stretched the buttons on his shirt, his nearly bald head glistened in the fluorescent lights. After a moment he smiled.

"After talking to Mr. Flint, I've decided to place his daughter, Daisy, whom I believe you've already met, in your classroom. As it happens, Daisy has been through a lot and is extremely worried about what's going to happen in school. She was home schooled for kindergarten. She'll be with her cousin Jane in an attempt to reduce her stress."

"I'll be cautious and watch for issues," Tricia reassured him, wondering what he was leaving out of the conversation. How had Principal Keller learned so much about Daisy's situation over the weekend? Grapevine? Or, had Riley called him? She shrugged the questions off, the answers didn't really matter.

"As you know, this school has an open-door policy. Parents are welcome to visit their child's classroom for short periods at any time. After a long discussion with Mr. Flint, I'm permitting him to be in your classroom for the entire day.

For the entire week if necessary. Normally, this would be more than we permit, but considering the exceptional circumstances, I'm prepared to allow it. Are you?"

Riley Flint in her classroom all day? A flitter of nerves ran through her. Normally, she was confident in her teaching skills, why did the thought of Riley watching her every move make her nervous? She resolved not to think about it.

"I welcome his presence. I don't know all of their story, but I do know Daisy is frightened and probably has a fear of abandonment. Mr. Flint is welcome to visit until Daisy is settled." Silently, she hoped Daisy would settle in without difficulty. Something about Riley's sudden and absolute dedication to his new child reached inside her and squeezed her heart. Family should always be there for each other.

CHAPTER NINE

Riley stood in the doorway of Tricia's classroom, Daisy clung to his hand, her nails digging in painfully - those nails needed a trim. Great, another thing to add to his mental to do list. If it got any longer, he'd have to write it down. For half a minute, he watched Tricia putter around the classroom. He cleared his throat.

She whirled around to look at him. "Hi. Daisy, Mr. Flint, please come in." She waved them forward.

"We're a bit early," Riley explained. "I thought Daisy might like to see the classroom before the others arrive. If it's okay with you."

"Okay? It's perfect. I was sorting out who would sit where and I could use some help. I've got these name tags. The yellow ones are for boys and green are for girls. I'd like a mix of boys and girls at each table. Can you help me set them out?"

He admired the way she looked Daisy in the eye and

talked to her like an adult. It was the way Sue talked to all her children and grandchildren, with respect. Daisy nodded and Tricia passed over the yellow cards with instructions to put two on some tables and three on the others.

"I'm putting you and Jane at the same table. You'll be together, but there will be someone in between you. You'll be able to see her and talk to her. But most importantly, you can play with her at recess and sit together at lunch, if you stay for lunch."

"We packed our lunches. We've signed up for lunchroom supervision starting tomorrow. Today, I'll hang around and visit."

"Can he sit with me?" Daisy asked in a small voice that wrenched Riley's guts.

"Well, I think the other kids might be jealous if you get to sit with your father and they don't. So, I think we'll have him sit in a chair by the back door. He'll be close by if we need him."

Daisy's brow wrinkled and for a moment Riley wondered if she'd rebel. He held his breath, waiting. After a long, thoughtful moment, she nodded and he felt himself relax. One hurdle overcome.

They finished setting out the name tags when the bell rang. "Come on. We line up outside. I'll show you where we meet to come into the school and where to place your shoes if they're dirty." Hand in hand they followed her out of the classroom, down a short hallway and outside.

The morning sun shone brightly, bringing highlights of reddish gold to Tricia's nearly black hair. Riley took a moment to admire her welcoming smile as she called out, "Grade one students, over here please."

"Morning, Riley," Joanne Mahoney greeted him as she joined Tricia. "This must be Daisy." She squatted gracefully in front of them. "I'm Miss Mahoney, I'm the other grade one teacher. You'll be in Miss Paxton's class."

Daisy looked wildly around, her gaze finally landing on Tricia.

Jo chuckled. "Just so you know, Tricia is Miss Paxton. At school, we use titles like Mr. Mrs. or Miss to show our respect. One or two teachers prefer to be called other things, but you'll learn about that later." She smiled and rose to her feet.

Riley was fascinated by the speed Tricia and Jo organized the group of parents and children, splitting them into two groups. Everyone trooped inside to the classrooms they'd been assigned. Aside from Daisy, he didn't notice any unfamiliar faces. Hopefully, the established groupings of cohorts would welcome a new friend.

"Uncle Riley? Daddy says you're supposed to bring us home after school and stay for supper. He has to talk to you about something. I think he's upset. He's been grumpy since he got home from visiting Mom." Her voice wobbled on the last word before she brightened. "And I can show Daisy my new room and the playhouse and the puppies."

"I can do that. We'll wait out front by my truck. You know which one, right?"

She nodded and Tricia called the class to order.

"By now, most of you can write your own name and know

what it looks like. If you don't know, don't worry, we'll have you writing your name in no time. Say goodbye to your parents and find your name on the shelves at the side. You can put your backpack in the cubicle labelled with your name."

Everyone rushed to obey, even Daisy. She found her cubicle with no effort. Thank goodness she recognized her name in print. The idea that she'd need to know hadn't even crossed his mind. Fatherhood was tougher than he ever imagined. So many small things to trip him up. Daisy took Jane by the hand and led her to the table closest to Tricia's desk.

Brilliant planning on Tricia's part. Daisy would be comforted by her nearness and by having Jane close. Riley was impressed by her thoughtfulness and consideration.

"Mr. Flint, you can take a seat at the back of the classroom by the reading corner, please. You can raise your hand if you have any questions or if you need to go to the washroom."

The classroom erupted in snickers and outright laughter.

After a moment, Tricia put her hands on her head and called, "Hands on top."

"That means stop," the students chorused, then slapped their hand on top of their heads and stood quietly in place. Daisy quickly mimicked them.

"Take your seats." She waited until everyone was settled. "Today, we're going to start with a game. We're going to play get to know you. I'll go first. Hi, everyone. I'm your teacher. You can call me Miss Paxton or Miss Tricia. I like puppies and chocolate cake. Ahmed, you're next."

"I'm Ahmed and I like fishing and puppies. I pick Mr. Flint."

"Um, what?" Riley floundered, surprised to be chosen.

"Would you like to go next, Mr. Flint?" Tricia smiled broadly.

"I'm Mr. Flint and I'm a veterinarian and I love animals and pizza. I pick Jane."

Jane wiggled in her seat, excited to be chosen. "I'm Jane and I love my new cousin Daisy. I pick Daisy."

Daisy's cheeks turned pink and she stared at the desk. Riley's chest hurt watching her agony and fear. He was about to intervene when she spoke.

"I'm Daisy. I'm new." Her voice warbled a little. She swallowed hard and looked up at her cousin. "I love my cousin Jane and Grandma's new kittens." She paused. "I pick him." She gestured to a blonde boy across the room. She looked at Riley and smiled shyly. He gave her two thumbs up and grinned back, his cheeks aching from the smile's stretch.

His daughter was amazing, he was so proud of her. The boy started speaking.

"I'm Kyle. I like horses and dogs." Kyle Broderbund wasn't the type of child who'd ever be popular. His family had arrived in Coyote Creek about three years ago. They were dirt poor, his father was a heavy drinker, his mother supported them by working at Bar None. She was a fabulous waitress and a good mother. Unfortunately, she barely made enough to survive on and Kyle dressed in hand-me-downs from the church. They lived in a trailer on a rented half-acre property across the road from Riley.

What made Daisy choose him? Perhaps she recognized something in him. Did she see his poverty and identify with it, or was he just a random choice? Either way, Riley would encourage his daughter to be friends with Kyle. Living close together outside of town would facilitate a friendship and benefit them both.

Kyle chose another child and so it went until all the children had spoken. By the time they were finished, children were shifting in their seats and fidgeting with items on the tables.

"That was great." Tricia applauded. "I'm so pleased you're all in my class this year. I couldn't have chosen a better group of children. Now, I know you're all used to being outside and playing, so instead of starting work right away, I think we'll do some painting."

The room erupted in cheers.

"Some of you have new family members. New moms or dads. Maybe a new pet or sibling. I'd like you to paint your family." She passed out paint trays, brushes and large sheets of thick paper. "Don't forget to put your name on the paper. If you have trouble, Mr. Flint or I can help you, just raise your hand."

Several hands shot in the air. Riley glanced at Daisy who picked up a pencil and meticulously printed her name on the bottom of her paper. Relief flooded through him. He had no idea how to teach printing. So many things to learn about parenting, for a moment he was overwhelmed. He pushed the feelings aside and hurried to assist those who needed it. He watched how Tricia wrote each letter on a scrap of paper, allowing the students to copy on their papers. Another lesson learned. Who'd have thought he'd be back in elementary school and getting an education?

The day passed in a blur of activity; Riley was exhausted by three-thirty. The bell rang and the children hurried to their compartments, grabbed their backpacks and headed for the door. Tricia stood inside the doorway saying goodbye to each child and found something positive to say to each of them.

"May I see your picture?" Riley asked Daisy while waiting for a chance to talk to Tricia. Daisy nodded and led him by the hand to her seat.

Riley stared down at the picture and barely hid his frown. A little girl dressed in pink stood alone in the middle of the page. To the left, a tall, thin woman stood wearing a halo. The woman and child had matching blonde curls. On the right, barely on the page, was a man wearing what clearly was meant to be a cowboy hat. The adults were as far away from the image of Daisy as they could without being off the paper.

"Is that your Mom?" He asked kindly.

"She's gone to heaven," Daisy said solemnly.

Her soft words broke his heart and stole his breath. "Yes, she is, but she'll always be your Mom and she'll always love you, and I'll always love you." He swallowed hard. "I see you've painted the dress we bought you on Saturday. You've done a great job. Is this me?" He tapped the cowboy and Daisy nodded.

"I'm pretty far away from you." He reached out and tugged on one of the curls it had taken him so long to untangle. "It's okay that we're not close yet. I hope some day you'll feel close to me, and you'll love me as much as I love you. You're a special girl, Daisy and I'm proud to be your father."

Tricia let out a soft gasp, drawing Riley's attention away from Daisy. Tricia had one hand over her mouth, the other rested on her chest. For a second, he thought he saw a tear in her eye, but she blinked and it was gone. Her hands dropped and she flashed him an enormous smile.

"That's a lovely picture," she spoke as she joined them. "I see your mom and your new dad. It's a pretty picture of both of your families. It's going to look nice hanging on the wall with the others. After a few weeks, we'll take it down and you can hang it up at home."

Riley recognized the advice for what it was, a suggestion to display her art in a prominent place. He stifled a grin. He was an uncle after all, he'd seen ten million pictures and projects created by his nieces and nephews. He even had a few hanging on his fridge.

"I think," he said, "we better go shopping soon. We're going to need a bulletin board for your projects. I can't wait to show them off to everyone. Especially my friend Houston. He doesn't have a daughter to make him beautiful pictures. He's going to be so jealous."

"Houston, Mr. Jackson, works with your daddy. Maybe one day you can go to work with them." She left the words hanging in the air.

"That's the plan for today. We'll go home and have a snack and then I'll take you to my clinic; the place where I work with animals. I've got some things to do and you can help me if you want."

Daisy nodded eagerly.

Riley's spirits soared. Victory! He'd take any sign of enthusiasm he could get.

DAISY DOZED off in the truck on the way home. Riley suspected she was exhausted from not sleeping well. She went to bed without complaint. Last night he'd heard her crying but when he entered her room, she feigned sleep. He wasn't going to force her to talk, so he sat on the edge of her bed holding her small hand in his until she finally slept.

He smiled at her reflection in the rear-view mirror. She was a pretty little thing. So strong, so fragile and so broken. He hoped he had what it took to help her heal. He'd give it a few days and then he'd ask Tricia or his mother who he could call on for assistance. Surely Daisy would need counseling to recover from the loss of her mother and being separated from her grandparents.

He turned his attention back to the road. He was carrying precious cargo and didn't want to take any unnecessary risks. Life was so different now. He floundered mentally. How was he going to learn everything he needed to know about child rearing?

The advice his mother gave his brother Ken popped into his head. "Go with your gut. Never act in anger and don't be afraid to admit you're wrong or have made a mistake. Set rules and stick to them." At the time, he'd thought she was over-simplifying things. Now, he knew she was, but the advice was sound anyway and it gave him a place to start.

He'd emulate his mother and Tricia. They were both great with kids. Handing out praise generously and being kind with remonstrations. Kind of like training a dog.

"Oh boy," he chided himself. He better not let anyone hear him relate child rearing to dog training. People would flip their lids; but the similarities did exist.

He pulled into the private part of his yard, pausing just off the main road. To his right his driveway split, curved in and went straight to the small clinic parking lot.

He looked at his home. His grey and white house sat in the center of the broad lawn with plenty of room for flower beds if he ever found the time to work on them. It had a double attached garage on the left and attached clinic slightly behind and on the right. He'd designed and had the house and clinic built when he graduated veterinary school. Thankfully, his parents had encouraged him to save as much money as he could through high school. They'd taught him budgeting and the importance of savings. He'd gotten through university with part of his savings intact. A small inheritance he'd received from an uncle had also helped with the purchase of his home.

The clinic was a joint venture with Houston. Riley provided the land and building; Houston bought the equipment. It was an equal partnership and they were busy enough to consider hiring an assistant. Maybe a receptionist or veterinary-tech.

Riley and Houston had met in university and had clicked immediately. The idea of starting their own clinic rather than buying into another vet's practice had been a dream at first. With careful planning they'd made it a reality.

Now, Houston's truck was parked alone in front of the clinic's reception area. Fortunately, today had been an unusually quiet day, there were almost no appointments, which allowed Riley to spend the day at school while Houston caught up on the bookkeeping.

Riley pulled ahead, parking in front of his double garage and climbed out of the truck. When he opened her door, Daisy climbed sleepily down and holding hands they went into the house.

Houston met them in the kitchen, arriving through the walkway connecting the house to the main part of the clinic.

"Daisy, this is Houston, Mr. Jackson. He's my friend and we work together."

Houston knelt and offered his hand. Daisy looked at it and backed up to hide behind Riley.

"This is what we do when we meet someone new," Riley reminded her. "Nice to meet you." He shook Houston's hand. "Now you try."

Daisy reached out and touched Houston's hand without stepping from behind Riley's legs. "Nice to meet you," she whispered and turned her face into Riley's thigh.

"Nice to meet you too. I know we'll be friends." Houston stood and rummaged in the cupboard, extracting a plastic container. "Aha!" He crowed triumphantly. "Come on Daisy, this is going to be a treat. Your grandmother makes the best oatmeal raisin cookies on the planet." He sat at the table and patted the chair beside him.

"Go ahead," Riley guided her forward. "I'll get us some milk." He paused until she climbed up to the table across from Houston.

They sat and chatted while they had their cookies, Houston filling them in on the day at the clinic. They included Daisy as often as possible, though her answers were often just nods or head shakes. Riley called it progress; she wasn't cowering from them and she even smiled once. It gave him hope that she'd open up eventually.

"I'm going to take Daisy out to the wild pens and show her the animals." Riley informed Houston. "Can you watch the clinic until I get back?" Houston nodded and Riley continued. "Sometimes, people bring us injured wild animals and we fix them up and set them free. We don't keep them in the clinic, we keep them in special cages out in the trees. They feel safer there, away from people. You won't be able to touch them. We'll feed them and look at them. Right now, we've got a Snowy Owl and a red fox. You'll like the fox, but he's shy. It's almost time to let him go, he's well enough to look after himself now."

The joy in Daisy's eyes mirrored the joy he'd felt as a boy when he brought home injured animals and strays for healing. Saving an animal's life was why he became a veterinarian. It had been his calling since he found his first injured bird when he was six. Later events had only reinforced his decision. He couldn't wait to share his passion with Daisy.

They finished their snack and changed into work clothing.

He asked Daisy to dress in her old clothing. She looked like she might defy him until he mentioned they might get dirty. "I have work clothes and nice clothes," He said. "I keep my old, worn out clothing, for wearing to work with animals. I get dirty, a lot. We don't want to ruin your pretty new things, so let's get changed and go to work."

He helped her choose some clothing and showed her the hallway where he and Houston stored their work wear in the passageway between the house and clinic. A dozen hooks lined the walls with boots and shoes lined up neatly below the clothing and lab coats. The corner held a wash-up sink and an apartment sized washer and dryer.

"The hooks are pretty high," he said. "I'll put a few down low so you have your own. And I'll get you a white jacket like mine to wear in the clinic, if I can find one small enough." Her happy grin told him he was on the right track.

CHAPTER TEN

Friday, Tricia and Daisy worked together to tidy the classroom while they waited for Riley to arrive. He'd phoned the school shortly before dismissal to let them know he was running late. He was going into emergency surgery to save a dog hit by a car. The school had no before and after school care program, so the receptionist, a close friend of Riley's mother, had agreed to supervise Daisy until he arrived. Somehow, in the busy shuffling at day's end, Tricia found herself volunteering to watch Daisy until Riley showed up.

"How are you enjoying school?" Tricia asked.

Daisy shrugged and focused on wiping the chalkboard clean as high as she could reach; while Tricia wiped down the whiteboard.

Tricia studied her for a moment. She was quiet in class, only speaking when called on, but the other children seemed to have taken her under their wing. She was always surrounded by girls during recess and everyone wanted to be her partner. Part of that stemmed from growing up in Coyote Creek's welcoming atmosphere. Part of it was simply because Daisy was a novelty. Someone new to play with. This age was so much kinder than teenagers who were more interested in being the top of the heap rather than part of the pack.

Tricia suppressed a shudder at the memories. Being a bit of an introvert had made starting a new school in grade ten a brutally painful experience. She'd survived it, but her ego had taken more than one damaging blow. Arriving in Coyote Creek had been less painful, but still awkward.

The residents of town had been eager to welcome Tricia; but her reticence and reluctance to put herself too far out there had gradually turned them away. They weren't friendly, but over time, they'd stopped trying to include her. She wondered if she'd made a mistake in keeping her distance. Maybe small-town living wasn't as cutthroat as city life. She pushed the thoughts aside for consideration later.

"The other kids sure like you," she said. Daisy nodded. "What's your favorite part of school? Do you like gym class? Library? Recess?"

"Libary," Daisy said. "I like books."

"Do you read with your father?" A silent nod. Glory be, getting answers out of Daisy was like pulling hen's teeth.

"Daddy reads, I don't know how. Jane can read." Her eyes brimmed with tears and she drew in a shuddering breath.

"Is that why you don't know if you like school? Are you worried you can't read?" Her sad nod cut straight through Tricia. "Did you know everyone learns to read at different times? I was almost in grade two when I learned to read. I had to go to special school in the summer to learn. I was so worried I'd never be able to read, but here I am, a teacher. You can do this. You know all your letters, and the sounds they make. Next week, we start phonics. That's how to sound out words. You'll be reading really fast. Come over here, I'll show you."

Daisy set her eraser on the ledge and followed Tricia to the storage cabinet.

Tricia grabbed a phonics workbook and sat at the closest table. She patted the chair beside her and Daisy hopped up.

"Some words, we learn what they look like and memorize how they sound, that's sight reading. But most words, we can figure out by sounding out the letters. Look at this one. What letters are these?" She pointed to a word.

"A and T.

"Very good. Now, what does A sound like?"

"Ay or ah." Daisy grinned.

"Both are right. This time, it is ah. And what sound does T make?"

"Tuh."

Tricia high fived her. "Perfect, you're getting it already. Now put it together."

"Ah…ah…ah tuh."

"Perfect!" Tricia exclaimed. "Now say it fast."

"Ahtuh."

"Faster."

"At." Daisy hopped up and down in her chair. "I read it."

"You sure did, Daisy," Riley chimed in from the doorway.

"That was amazing. Learning to read already. You are very smart. I can already see you're going to be a great reader. Are you ready to go?"

"Can I do one more?" She looked from Riley to Tricia and back, her expression filled with hope.

"It's okay with me, if it's okay with your father."

Riley nodded his approval and joined them at the table. They worked their way through cat, sat, rat and bat before Tricia suggested they stop. "If you'd like to do more at home, I can let you borrow this book for a few days, if you remember to bring it to school everyday."

"Can I, please?"

"Sure thing. We can read more tonight. Put the book into your backpack. It's time to get going. It's almost supper time." He paused. "You know what, learning to read your first words is a very important event. I think we should celebrate. How about we go out for dinner?"

"Yes, please." She jumped up and down. "Can we have pizza? Mommy loved pizza." Her happiness dropped into a frown.

"It's okay to talk about Mommy. I know she loved pizza. We shared lots of pizzas. Pizza it is. Miss Tricia, would you like to join us?"

"Um," Tricia floundered for an answer. She didn't really like to socialize with parents outside of school. How could she say no and not put another chink into Daisy's already dented heart? She was already in deeper than she wanted to be. Dinner with Riley? She mentally shook her head. No, dinner with Daisy, to celebrate.

"You know what," she said at last. "I'd love to come with you. Learning to read is a special thing, it's worth celebrating. You go ahead, I'll lock up and meet you there. Oh, where are we going?"

"Tuscan Gardens. Best pizza in town." Riley chuckled. "Come on, Daisy, let's go celebrate. Miss Tricia, we'll meet you there."

Tricia watched them walk away, hand in hand. Her emotions tangled together, almost tripping her up. Riley was so great with Daisy; he was learning to be a father. His kindness was touching, but spending time with him, with them, might be a mistake. She wasn't sure she wanted to become further embedded in their lives. Being Daisy's teacher was commitment enough.

"You made it," Riley exclaimed twenty minutes later as Tricia stepped inside the dimly lit restaurant.

"For a minute, I didn't think I would. I was cornered by another teacher who wanted to chat. I had trouble breaking away." She laughed. "Sometimes it's tough to choose between friends." Especially when a new potential friend had offered a hand of friendship. She'd had to beg off with a declaration of other plans and a promise to meet after school next week.

Tuscan Gardens sat on Main Street across from the chocolate shop. Its exterior was dark wood with a red and white striped awning. Inside, it resembled an indoor Italian garden with light grey stucco walls accented with sunny yellows and golds. Terra cotta flooring and statues of ancient heroes, gods and goddesses gave a classic feel. Solid wood tables were adorned with budding flowers in small vases. The room was divided into sections separated with high walls for a private, grotto-like feel. Seating was a mix of free-standing tables and booths of various sizes. Faux grape vines clung to the lattice roof and were accentuated with live lemon trees in the small front windows. The three of them stood by the brick and wood hostess station, waiting to be seated.

Tricia breathed deeply, pulling in the scents of garlic, spices and fresh baked bread, making her stomach growl. "It smells incredible in here. I've walked by hundreds of times. The smell always makes me hungry, but I've never eaten here."

Riley laughed. "It doesn't look like much on the outside." He referred to the plain dark-wood siding on the one level, box-like building. "But the food is heavenly."

"I've wanted to eat here but I'm not much for dining alone. Thank you for inviting me to join you." She smiled warmly.

"Thank you, for helping Daisy learn to read. She did amazing." His pat on Daisy's shoulder was a proud-father gesture.

The teacher in Tricia wanted to compliment him on his efforts to be a good father, but

she knew better than to embarrass him in front of Daisy. Perhaps she'd bump into him when he was alone one day. For now, she'd let her wide smile show she recognized his hard work.

The hostess led them on a wandering path to the back. They passed Principal Keller and the physics teacher having dinner. Keller raised one eyebrow in question as they went by.

Riley stopped beside the table. "Principal Keller. Nice to see you. We're treating Miss Tricia to dinner tonight as a thank you for staying late with Daisy when I was delayed by an emergency surgery. In that short time, she got a great start on teaching Daisy her phonics. We're celebrating the first of many victories in learning."

Tricia hid her smile. Something in Riley's voice virtually dared the principal to say or imply anything improper was going on. Was he protecting his reputation as a father, or hers as a teacher? Did it even matter? Either way, it felt chivalrous.

"That's—nice. We've been quite pleased with Miss Paxton's work. She's a benefit to the school and the community."

"Indeed, she is," Riley replied. "My brother was impressed with her teaching skills last year, and Jane already adores her." This time, there was no denying the soft warning in his words.

She'd heard the Flint family stuck together but she'd never imagined being lumped under their protective umbrella. Their teenage hostess looked intrigued by the exchange. No doubt the high school kids would hear about the conversation in short order. The gossip grapevine, alive and well with the teenage set.

"Nice to see you Principal Keller. Have a nice evening." She nodded politely and followed the hostess to their table. She slid into the booth and Daisy climbed up beside her. Riley sat across from them, a slight frown wrinkling his brow. He set his Stetson on the seat beside him. Tricia suspected he'd been hoping to sit with Daisy. If the opportunity came up, she'd remind him part of parenting was learning to let children make their own decisions. This was a small one but would lead to Daisy's self-reliance and independence. With a mental frown she reminded herself it wasn't her job to teach Riley how to be a good parent. She had to stop thinking it was or she'd become irreversibly involved in their lives.

Their hostess set menus in front of them, gave Daisy a coloring book and crayons. She took their drink order and walked away.

"What would you like to eat?" Riley asked his daughter who shrugged and looked longingly at the crayons. "After you look at your menu and decide what you'd like to have, you can color."

She flipped open the menu and pointed at the first thing she saw.

"Hmm." Tricia looked at the selection. "Pasta with spicy chorizo sausage and shrimp. I don't know if you'll like that. Do you eat spicy foods? Maybe pick something from here instead." She flipped open the small children's menu. "But it does look delicious."

She looked up; Riley grinned at her.

"Sorry, sometimes the teacher in me takes over. I didn't mean to step on your parental toes." She shrugged. "I'll try not to get in your way again." Riley's low-throated chuckle tickled across her skin like a physical caress.

"It's not like I don't need the help. Although I suppose if I never take the lead, I'll never learn. This is all so new to me. I feel a bit like an animal taken away from their home. Out of sorts but weirdly hopeful too." He leaned closer to read the children's menu. "Let's see. There's spaghetti, grilled cheese, pizza, soup, salad and hotdogs. Hotdogs? In an Italian restaurant? They really want to cover all the bases. What do you feel like?"

Daisy shrugged and glanced at the crayons.

"I think I feel like pepperoni, mushroom, ham and pineapple pizza with fresh tomatoes on top and a side salad," Tricia offered her suggestion. "Would you like pizza? Maybe, if your dad likes the idea, we could all share one pizza."

They agreed to share a pizza and each have a salad. Their drinks arrived. Tricia had mint tea, Daisy was thrilled to be allowed a clear soda in honor of learning to read, Riley had a beer from Mulligan's, a local micro-brewery.

They watched Daisy carefully color the first page of the tiny safety-themed coloring book. The silence between them wasn't companionable, nor was it uncomfortable and Tricia found herself battling the urge to blurt out something to break the silence.

"I have a question," Riley spoke after several long moments of silence.

"Go ahead, ask. As long as it isn't too personal." The protective barrier of words came out before she realized she was worried about personal questions. She bit back the need to add a qualifier or retract the statement.

"I've done some reading. A lot of reading. I can't figure out what time a kid needs to go to bed. I'm used to dealing with animals, they don't need the set bedtime a child does. How much sleep should Daisy be getting?" The words blurted out in a rush, as if he couldn't say them fast enough.

"Well, it does vary, but typically, six-year-olds need about ten to twelve hours a day. Some need more, some need less. Why?"

"Little Missy here," he gestured to Daisy. "Is having a bit of trouble sleeping. I try and put her to bed between seven-thirty and eight, we get up at seven. But sometimes, and it's not a problem, but sometimes, I find her in my room at night. I want to help her get the best night's sleep she can. Could she be getting too much?"

"She's bright and alert in class, so she's likely getting enough. Do you have a bedtime routine?"

"You need a routine?" He blurted and scraped his fingers through his thick dark hair leaving it standing on end.

"Everyone does. You probably don't even know you have one. I'll bet every night you do the same things before you go to bed." And, here she was, wrapped up in parenting advice when only moments ago she'd vowed, not for the first time, to keep her distance.

He looked thoughtful. "I guess so. I have a cup of tea and read a bit, wash up, brush my teeth..." He trailed off and smiled. "Yup, definitely a routine."

"Daisy needs routines. When I was growing up, after supper, I finished my homework, I played quietly until bath time. I brushed my teeth, read with my parents and then I went to bed. Same thing virtually every night. You could try something like that." She turned to Daisy. "You wake up at night sometimes. Do you know why?" It was almost a rhetorical question; children rarely had the cognitive skills to understand the thoughts and worries plaguing them.

She nodded and ducked her head.

Riley looked helpless.

"Your father might be able to help if you knew what was wrong."

She shook her head.

"When you want to talk about it, I'm here to listen," Riley advised.

Tricia gave him a discrete thumbs up. They shared small talk as they ate, carefully including Daisy in the discussion and encouraging her to speak and have opinions. They didn't determine the cause of her late-night wanderings, but eventually they managed to get her to admit she preferred a different cartoon than Riley.

Tricia and Riley shared a look of victory. It would be so easy to get used to being a part of this small family. She'd have to be on guard or she'd get too close. Every minute spent in their company put a chink in the brick wall she'd built around her heart.

There was a rumble of male laughter and a spate of light-hearted female complaints and several of Riley's siblings strolled into view. Carl and Jason pushed their way into Riley's side of the booth. An extremely thin girl stood beside the table looking at Daisy. She wore a floral print broomstick skirt and an orange and yellow lace top with tiny pompoms around the bottom. The outfit was sixties meets gypsy, but it worked. Her hair was tightly braided against her scalp into blonde-brown dreadlocks, complete with clinking beads on the ends.

"Hi, Daisy. Remember me? I'm Jennifer. Everyone calls me Jenn. I'm your dad's baby sister. Can I sit with you?"

Tricia scooted over and Daisy followed, pulling her precious crayons and book with her.

"What have you done to your hair?" Riley blurted.

"They're called dreads. I like 'me. Thought they'd make a nice change."

Carl laughed, making his dimples show. "They look a shi-er-crap load better than the green and orange she had last month."

"My hair, my life, my money." Jenn taunted her brothers. "I'm thinking of an uber-short pixie cut next. You know, like, three inches long all over."

"No!" Daisy blurted.

Everyone froze and looked at her. "Why not?" Jenn asked softly.

"I like it. I like the beads and it was pretty and long and curly at Grandma's birthday." She reached up and fingered a couple of beads before her hand dropped to her lap.

"Well then. Next time I change it, I won't go short. Maybe some crazy colors, just for you. But," she shook her finger at her brothers, "I'm not promising not to cut it all off if I get the urge."

The resulting chorus of male groans made all three females laugh.

The guys thanked Daisy. "Thanks for getting her to see reason, at least for now," Jason said. "What is it with women and hair? They're always cutting and coloring and curling and primping."

"We want to be beautiful," Tricia offered, though her own hair was subdued, falling dark and straight past her shoulders.

"And you are beautiful," Jason offered gallantly, with a dimple-free smile. He grunted when Riley elbowed him in the side.

"What are you guys doing here anyway?" Riley demanded, turning his brother's attention from Tricia.

"Same as you," Jenn laughed. "Eating. What are you guys doing here? Is this like a date or something?" She raised one eyebrow at the same time as Jason and Carl lifted theirs.

"Not. A. Date." Riley stated. "A celebration. Miss Tricia taught Daisy several words today. We're celebrating her learning to read."

"Congratulations. Give me five," Carl held up his hand and another round of high-fives ensued. "This calls for dessert." When the waitress returned to take their order, he added chocolate cake for Daisy.

"This is a party, so I'll let it go once. But in the future, please ask before you feed my child junk," Riley warned.

"Dude, look at you going all parental on us," Jenn teased with a wink. "I never would have thought you'd turn adult. Another one down in flames." She sobered. "But you're right. Kendrick makes us obey the rules with his kids and Justice did too until—" She looked at Daisy. "Well, you all know what I mean."

It was astute of an eighteen-year-old to realize the potential issue of mentioning missing children in front of a child who'd recently lost her entire family. Tricia saw the gratitude in Riley's eyes when he smiled at his youngest sister.

"How's the record business?" He asked.

"Great," Jenn enthused. "We sell almost as much vinyl as we do CDs. It's great having a job where there's music all the time. Although the boss won't let me sing when we have customers."

"Thank heaven," Carl teased. "You have the worst singing voice on the planet."

"She's not so bad." Tricia laughed. "I've heard her. I won't say she's talented, but I've heard worse." She clapped a hand over her mouth. "I mean…"

Everyone roared with laughter.

"Don't worry about it," Jenn offered. "I suck, but it doesn't stop me. I love music and I love singing and I'll keep on singing. Maybe I'll take some voice lessons so I can sing at the town Christmas concert."

"I'll give you fifty bucks not to." Jason reached for his wallet.

"I'll take that deal." They laughed and he put his wallet away without paying.

Tricia watched the family banter, not feeling included, but not feeling left out either. Daisy leaned against her and after a few moments slumped over.

"Riley," Tricia injected into the first quiet spot in the conversation. "I think you better take this little one home. She's sound asleep."

He glanced at his watch and groaned. "Crap. Seven-thirty.

We should have been home ages ago. I better get her to bed. Shoot. She didn't get a bath."

"She's fine for a night or two," Tricia advised. "I'll walk you out and help you with her."

Riley pulled out his wallet.

"I've got the bill," Jason and Carl proclaimed in unison.

"Thanks guys. Great to see you. Even you." He tugged on one of Jenn's braids. She popped out of the booth and hugged him. Tricia scooted over, bringing Daisy with her.

"Night, brother dear. Say goodnight to Daisy if she wakes up and bring her by the shop so we can talk music. Nice seeing you again Tricia. You should come by soon; we've got a whole new collection of 90s boy band music. You'll love it."

Everyone gaped at Tricia. "Boy bands?" Riley laughed.

"As it happens," she adopted a faux haughty air, "Boy bands influenced generations of youth, it's for research purposes. I am an educator after all." She couldn't contain her smirk.

"You know it," Jenn cheered.

"Nice to see everyone again. Thank you for the company and for dinner. Jenn, I'll come by and check out those albums. Thanks for the tip."

As they walked away from the table Tricia heard Carl say, "I can't believe we horned in on their date."

"They said it wasn't a date," Jason countered. "If it was a date, we'd have left them alone.

Somehow, Tricia doubted they would have. She was learning the Flint family didn't hesitate to stick their noses in each other's business. They didn't seem to have many secrets.

"Can you grab my keys? They're in my front pocket." Riley hoisted Daisy, still sound asleep, higher and cocked his right hip toward Tricia.

Her hand in his pocket? It felt deliciously over-personal, but she carefully extracted the keys and unlocked his truck.

He settled Daisy inside and fastened the belt on her booster seat before turning toward Tricia. "Thanks for watching her today and for helping with her reading." He paused. "My family seems to like you."

She didn't know what to say, she wasn't good at handling praise, so she avoided answering. "It was a pleasure to help you out. She's a sweet girl."

"She's coming around more everyday. No real issues yet, but from what I've read, I can expect them to show up anytime. I'm trying to prepare. Thanks again."

He rested his hand on her shoulder sending warmth flooding through her.

"I'll stay here, with Daisy, until you get in your car. I'll follow you home to make sure you get there safely. Then, I'll take sleeping beauty home."

"You don't have to. I'll be fine."

"A gentleman always sees his date home. If I wasn't with Daisy, I'd insist on seeing you inside and knowing your door was locked."

"I appreciate the gesture, but that's not necessary."

"I'll follow you home. Once you're inside the building, I'll leave." His tone left no room for rebuttal.

"Good night, Riley. Thanks for dinner and a nice evening out." She turned toward her car and pivoted back. "You're doing great with Daisy. Be patient with the sleep issues. They'll either come to a head or go away. If they get worse, you might want to see a professional."

"Sue suggested getting help. I'll cross that bridge when I come to it. Thanks though. Now go," he waved toward her car, "I'll follow you."

She saluted and went to her car and grinned the whole way home at the comfort of Riley's headlights in her rear-view mirror. Troy, her ex, would have let her go home alone at night, in the city. She could get used to the gentler, more caring attitude of small-town life and a man like Riley Flint. Even if he was a bit pushy about it.

She turned down the alley and pulled into her designated spot in the horseshoe shaped lot behind her building and climbed out of her car. She hurried to the back door and unlocked it. She waved at Riley. He pulled into the parking lot and stopped as close to the steps as possible.

"Take care of yourself and have a good night. I'll see you later in the week. Goodnight, Tricia."

"Goodnight, Riley. Drive safe." She slipped into the building and let the door close behind her. Contentment rolled through her as she climbed the stairs to her suite. Riley was a good man and trying hard to be a good father which seemed at odds with his reputed fun-loving ladies man persona. Which was the real Riley Flint?

"Come on, Daisy. It's time to go, before we're late," Riley called up the stairs. Dresser drawers thumped open and closed. He heard Daisy's voice but couldn't make out her words. He wondered if he was meant to, or if she was talking to her toys again. She seemed to whisper to them a lot. He suspected it was a girl thing but wondered if she shared her deeper feelings with her trusted stuffed animals. It could be tough to talk to people about feelings; he often found himself working out his emotions by talking to the animals in his care. Perhaps she was doing the same.

Finally, she strolled downstairs, her favorite toy in her arms. She wore her blue jeans and a pastel T-shirt rather than the dress he'd expected.

"Hey," he said, "Weren't you going to wear the pink dress Miss Tricia helped us pick out? This is a party. We dress up for parties. I'm wearing my best shirt, my nice boots and my cleanest hat." He grinned to show there was no pressure about her clothing choices.

"Kyle says you don't wear shit-kickers with dresses." She crossed her arms over her chest defiantly.

"Well, Kyle doesn't know much about dresses then, but he is a boy. Auntie Jenn and Auntie Beth and Auntie Candy all wear cowboy boots with dresses. A lot of ladies do. And, we don't call them shit-kickers. Shit is an impolite word, please try not to use it." He was pleased when she nodded. "Now, about the dress. Do you want to wear it with your boots? You can wear those jeans if you prefer. You can wear the dress and boots, jeans and boots or put either with your white shoes with the bows. Or with your tie-ups."

He waited, hiding his impatience, while she considered her options. She stood motionless, thinking for several long minutes. Was this a kid thing or a chick thing? He didn't have any trouble making decisions. Clothing wasn't important to him; he knew when to dress up and when to dress down. Maybe she didn't. He'd need to research this. If he spent any more time on line reading about kids, he'd have to buy shares in his internet provider.

"Do you want to wear the dress or jeans? We'll pick shoes after."

"The dress. Auntie Jenn wears dresses." Her response was decisive.

"Run upstairs and put on the dress. Call me if you need help." He smiled when she turned and raced up the stairs. She was back in record time with the dress on. She whirled around showing him her back.

He zipped up the pretty floral dress. "Spin around, let's see how it looks." One thing his sisters had taught him was they liked to show off their clothes. She spun in circles spinning the wide netting skirt until it lifted high and flat with her motions before she slowed to a stop. "A very pretty dress," he praised. "You look lovely. You changed quickly. Thank you."

She beamed at the compliment. Relief flooded him. Crisis one solved. Now for shoes. Women and shoes. He sighed soundlessly.

"You have runners, dress shoes, sandals, and cowboy boots. I'm okay with all of them. It's up to you. Let's get our shoes on and head out before we're late." He picked up Jane's birthday gift. Poorly wrapped and sealed with half a roll of tape, it was the best he and Daisy could manage. He was proud of their joint effort. He never wrapped gifts, he stuck them in a gift bag and taped it shut. They'd laughed at their ineptness as they sealed the doll in multi-colored polka dot paper and topped their creation with an enormous yellow bow.

At the door, she stood in front of their new shoe rack and studied her options. Riley waited patiently. He didn't know if it was only Daisy, or if all kids had this much trouble making decisions. For now, being a few minutes late didn't matter; even if he despised tardiness.

"Well?" He asked kindly after a few minutes.

She picked up her red and black cowboy boots and looked at him, uncertainty and questions in her eyes.

"Those'll be great." He stepped into his boots as she put

hers on and they were out the door. He glanced at his watch and made a mental note to allow more time in the future. Daisy climbed right into her booster seat and he watched her buckle up. She'd never complained about the seatbelt, despite her initial fumbling attempts to fasten it.

"Did you and your mom have a car?"

"No, we rode the bus and sometimes the train. Grampa has a car. I like your truck."

"Our truck. We're sharing it, and when you're old enough I'll teach you to drive."

"When I'm eight?"

"Probably when you're sixteen."

She sighed. "That's so far away. I'll be old."

"Now you have something to look forward to." He was optimistic that referring to a future together would reinforce the idea he wasn't going to go away like her mother or grandparents.

The ride to town was quick and they talked about the cattle grazing in nearby fields. With every trip they made, Daisy spoke more freely. They pulled to a stop outside of Allie's Diner, claiming the last spot for several blocks. Saturdays were always busy downtown.

Allie's was as busy as usual. Riley waved toward the back where dozens of helium balloons floated over two tables pushed together. His parents were there as was his brother Ken and all three of his children. Jane leaped off Sue's lap as soon as she noticed them. She grabbed Daisy by the hand and tugged her toward the others.

"I love your dress and your boots. Those are the best

boots. Mine are just plain black." She raised her boot long enough for her cousin to catch a glimpse before they hurried forward. Riley trailed behind.

"Look Daisy! Look at all the presents," Jane exclaimed, clapping her hands in excitement.

Daisy thrust the poorly wrapped gift she'd carried from the truck into Jane's hands. "Happy birthday."

"Thanks." She dropped the gift gently on the table and grabbed an enormous package and shoved it at Daisy. "Happy birthday. Grandma says it's your birthday too. Except mine is tomorrow and yours is today. I always have a special party with my cousins and Grandma and Grampa. Grandma says she doesn't like kid parties, they're too noisy." She leaned in close to Daisy and whispered, "I think it's a fib, 'cause she comes to my party every year."

"Daisy, darling." Sue stood and embraced both girls in a hug. "Your dad told me today is your birthday. Tomorrow is Jane's. This party is for you and Jane. Isn't it lucky you get to share your special day with Jane?"

Jane interrupted to declare, "Half the presents are mine and half are yours. We have four each. It's so great." She jumped up and down.

Daisy blinked and looked down at the gaily wrapped gift in her hands. She glanced up at Riley with tear filled eyes, refocused on the gift and burst into tears.

Shit. This wasn't what he expected. She was supposed to be thrilled and excited like Jane. Didn't she want to share her birthday? He knelt and embraced her. Pain shot through his heart. Parenting was so difficult. He didn't even know where to start.

"Are you okay?" He asked quietly.

Daisy shrugged.

"Want to talk about it?"

She shook her head sadly. "Mommy can't come to my birthday."

"Oh sweetheart. Mommy's in heaven, she's looking down, watching you. She'll be happy you're with your new family who loves you and gave you lots of gifts. She won't be sad. Why don't we sit a minute?"

He eased the gift from Daisy's hands, set it on the table, pulled out a chair and sat with Daisy on his lap. She snuggled in close and closed her eyes. The mixed blessing of snuggling in for comfort conflicting with her unsettled emotions wrenched at his heart. Was parenting always like this?

Jane came close and tapped her on the shoulder. He glanced at his mother for guidance. Her shrug seemed to tell him to let Jane speak.

"Daisy? My mommy is gone away too. Daddy says he's bringing her back, but it makes me sad. You don't have to share your birthday with me. You can have it all for yourself."

"That's very generous of you," Ken praised his daughter.

Daisy sniffed and wiped her face on Riley's shoulder. *Gross. Kid snot.* Animal messes he could deal with, but kid boogers? Not so much.

She straightened up and turned to Jane. "Your mommy is gone, too?"

"Yes," Jane replied solemnly.

"You can share my birthday." Daisy reached out and hugged Jane close. "We can be family and friends," she added wisely. "Mommy said it's good to have friends."

"She's right. Friends are wonderful," Sue enthused. "Come now, climb up here. You in this chair, Jane in that one and we'll order some lunch. After we eat, it's presents and then cake. Happy Birthday, darlings!"

Lunch was burger and fries all around, except for Robert. He got his burger, but Sue insisted he have salad instead of fries which reminded Riley to talk to them about Robert's health. Learning to live with a daughter had distracted Riley from his concerns over his father's pallor. How did family men deal with having problems on multiple fronts?

Daisy gobbled her burger and most of her fries when Riley noticed she'd slowed down. She chewed each fry with agonizing care, paused and reached for another.

"You don't have to eat all your fries if you're full," he advised.

"Mommy says no dessert if I don't eat all my food. I like dessert…"

"That's good advice, and usually it's true. Today, because it's your birthday, we won't worry about it. This restaurant, Allie's Diner, serves enormous portions. Too much food for one small girl."

"Can I eat 'em?" eight-year-old Gary asked hopefully.

"Sure thing, if Daisy's had enough." At her nod, Riley pushed the plate to his nephew. "Enjoy."

"Thanks. I need to bulk up for lacrosse," Gary mumbled

around a mouthful of fries. "Coach says I need more muscles. I'm too skinny."

Riley choked back a chuckle. "Good plan, you're thin like your dad was when he was a kid." All the Flint men had been scrawny lads until they hit their teens and grew six or seven inches and bulked up. As adults they ranged from five-foot-nine to six-foot-two. Ken was the tallest, he was thin but broad shouldered and strong. Carl was the shortest and bulkiest. One thing they all shared was muscles honed from hard physical work. Even Jason, who owned the butcher shop, hefted crates of meat all day, keeping him fit. All of them bore a striking resemblance to Robert with their dark hair and green eyes.

Riley's sisters, Jennifer, Candice and Elizabeth, were average height, fit and curvy. With Candy and Beth coming in at five-foot-six and one hundred fifty pounds. Jenn was only five-four and slender. They shared their mother's stature and body type.

"Lacrosse? I didn't know you were going to play," Riley stated.

"Either that or hockey and I suck on skates. I can skate, but I'd rather run. Plus throwing the ball around is way tougher than hockey. I can't wait until I'm old enough to play contact lacrosse."

"I'll work with you a bit and teach you some skills. I played in university. Your dad was better at hockey. So, call me when you need help. I can work with you while I teach Daisy." Teaching his daughter a sport was a flash of inspiration. Nothing bonded a family like sports.

"What's lacrosse?" Daisy piped in.

"A sport. A bit like basketball, a bit like hockey. It's played with nets on sticks and a hard ball. It takes a while to learn, but you'll pick it up in no time. Auntie Beth played field lacrosse when she was young."

"Enough of this sports talk. Time for gifts," Sue declared, handing the girls matching gifts. Daisy took her cue from Jane and opened the card from her grandparents. Riley and Ken read the cards aloud. The packages contained matching sweaters. The next packages contained matching shoes. The third contained identical skirts and T-shirts.

Finally, only two packages remained, both badly wrapped.

"I got that one for you," Jane declared, pointing to the large package she'd given Daisy earlier.

"We got this for you," Daisy handed over the gift they'd brought.

"We'll open them together," Jane declared. "One, two, three, go!" Paper flew in all directions as they dove into their last gift. Everyone laughed as they revealed identical dolls, complete with diapers, bottles, clothing and shoes. Daisy's package contained extra clothing.

"I got you extra dolly clothes, 'cause I know you don't have too many and I have lots. Now, we can play dolls together after school."

"Can we play now?" Daisy asked.

Riley suggested waiting until they were home before loosening all the accessories from their protective packaging. It looked like Jane might kick up a fuss but she was defused by the arrival of the birthday cake.

The entire restaurant joined in singing Happy Birthday. They made wishes and blew out the candles.

"What did you wish for?" Jane asked. "I wished for a new bike. Mine's too small."

"I wished for a new mommy," Daisy whispered, almost too low to be audible.

CHAPTER TWELVE

Riley felt sucker punched in the gut. Holy hell. A mother? Well that was one wish destined to go unfilled. It wasn't like he could order a wife and mother from an online catalogue. He ran a mental checklist of single women in town, not that he was looking to get married. None remotely suitable came to mind, except…

"Miss Tricia," Jane exclaimed. "You came to my birthday. Our birthday."

Oh no! No way! Fate was not thrusting a potential wife into his path. Nope.

Tricia grinned at the girls. "Actually, I'm here to pick up my lunch. I was so busy working I forgot to eat. I decided to walk over and pick up lunch and eat it in the park and enjoy the sunshine. I stopped for a minute to talk to a friend, saw it was your birthday, both of you, and came over to say Happy Birthday."

"Thank you," the girls chorused in unison.

"You're welcome."

"What does an elementary school teacher do on a Saturday?" Ken asked, stealing the words right out of Riley's mind.

"I'm refinishing a nightstand. I scraped off a dozen layers of paint and sanded the entire thing smooth. Since it was nice outside, I worked in the parking lot of my building. Now, I'll stain and varnish it in my apartment with the windows open." Her eyes shone with enthusiasm for her project.

"You should get Riley to check it out," Ken suggested slyly. "He's great with wood working. He really knows how to use his hands."

"I wouldn't want to inconvenience him. It's a simple project. I'm learning as I go. I've done a few pieces. I can't wait to start on the antique buffet and hutch I found at the flea market this spring. Trouble is it's too big to haul around. I'm going to have to rent a space to work on it. I can't drag it inside and outside every time mother nature decides to switch up the weather." Her words were light and carefree. "I'll figure it out. For now, it's stored safely away."

"Riley's got an enormous, empty garage," Ken threw in. "He only parks inside in winter. I prefer to park inside where I can keep my baby cool in summer and cozy in winter."

"Kenny-boy, you drive a minivan. I don't know why you even worry." Riley mock punched Ken in the shoulder.

"Boys," Sue barked in the universal mom tone meaning stop that now or there'll be hell to pay. The joking stopped instantly. "I'm sure Riley wouldn't mind one bit if you used his garage, Tricia."

"I couldn't impose."

Riley knew when to admit defeat. "It isn't an imposition. Really. You've helped me a lot over the last while. I'll pick it up for you and give you a key. You can work on it whenever you want."

He watched her as he spoke. Her expression went from wary, to cautious to thrilled. Suddenly an inconvenience made a one-eighty, straight to pleasure. Definitely a feeling he could get used to.

"Let me know when you want it picked up," he concluded.

"We'll work something out," Tricia offered. "Maybe I can trade dinner or something for space rental; because it's a big thing for me to have space to work in."

"Join us for some cake?" Sue suggested.

"Please, please, please," Jane hopped up and down on her chair with Daisy echoing her words.

Riley and Tricia shared a look. Surely, she wouldn't refuse? This was the most excited Daisy had been since arriving on his doorstep.

"I would love to join your party."

"Take my seat," Ken offered. "I have to run anyway. Lindy agreed to meet me in Sangudo for dinner. Sort of a halfway point between here and the city, neutral territory, to discuss—things. I have to run or I'll be late. If she drives an hour and a half and I'm late…" he trailed off meaningfully. "Mom, Dad are you still okay taking the kids for another night?"

"Of course, dear. Go, go. Leave your ego behind," Sue warned.

"Happy birthday, Jane." He kissed her on the cheek. "Happy birthday, Daisy." He patted her hand. "Bye kids. I'll see you tomorrow. I'll pick you up right after breakfast." He kissed them goodbye, waved at everyone and hurried out of the diner.

CHAPTER THIRTEEN

Tricia watched Ken go. He looked like a man heading to his execution, but at the same time he looked strangely optimistic. She didn't envy him one bit. Lindy, his estranged wife, had a reputation for getting what she wanted. The rumor mill said her dream had been her marriage and kids; until she started longing for her old legal career. She'd returned to Edmonton and her old firm when Jane started kindergarten last year. Everyone in town knew how vehemently Ken wanted to win Lindy back. Tricia silently wished him luck, the kids missed their mother, and their family life. Maybe Lindy meeting him halfway was a good sign.

"Would you like to cut the cake?" Robert offered as Tricia took a seat between Daisy and Jane. She accepted the large knife gracefully.

She probably shouldn't have agreed to stay. Being jerked into Flint family life was a little uncomfortable. They were a great family, always sticking together and helping each other out. They were quick to make friends and defend those they loved. Being Daisy and Jane's teacher, she already felt too attached to the family. Becoming a personal friend seemed to exceed the bounds of propriety.

"So how are you liking our small town, now that you've been here a while?" Robert asked between the excited chatter of kids talking and devouring the cake.

Tricia looked down at her plate and pondered her answer. Four layers of light, moist chocolate cake, separated by layers of marshmallow fluff whipped with cream cheese, one layer of cherry pie filling, all of it topped with a decadent whipped cream frosting and princess decorations. Life in Coyote Creek was like the cake, it had more layers than she expected, often surprising her.

"I really like Coyote Creek. Jo and I have renewed our friendship. I can get almost everything I need here. It's been over a year and I've only had to return to the city twice. It's a nice place to live. I'm glad I moved here."

"How does it compare to the city? Do you love it here?" Sue asked.

"I like the quiet and seeing familiar faces everywhere; although I sometimes feel like I live in a fishbowl under constant surveillance." She chuckled. "At the same time, I miss the anonymity. It's tough knowing virtually everyone has a child or a relative destined for the school. Everyone's so casual about it."

"You'll get used to it," Robert piped up. "Most of the people here are good, honest folk. Aside from a few bad seeds, Coyote Creek is a great place. We aren't without our problems. There are a few down on their luck, though I won't mention any names." He waved around the table. "Little pictures have big ears."

"Don't they!" Tricia agreed.

"You'd do all right to date one of my boys," Robert offered. "Except for Ken, they're all single. They've got good jobs, they're respectable. Riley would make a great husband."

"Dad!" Riley's voice rose in warning.

"I'll take that under advisement," Tricia said with a laugh. It was sweet how Robert looked out for his children. "I'm not really looking to date, but when I am, I'll keep them in mind, along with the other eligible men in town."

"You won't find a better man than one of our boys," Sue declared, bursting with pride. "The Flints have been in town since the oil patch first opened up. You could call us one of the founding families. We've lived through a lot of changes and we've contributed a lot to this town. We help organize all the town festivals. The Christmas pageant, the Easter parade, Canada Day celebrations, the Harvest Festival. Maybe you and Riley could join the committee."

Holy cow! These people weren't just family centric; they were town centric and determined matchmakers. Time to divert the conversation before she ended up on a date. "I'll consider it. Thank you." The few bites of cake she'd eaten sat heavy in her stomach. She couldn't decide if it was the conversation or the lack of lunch that was wreaking havoc with her digestion. She glanced frantically around, looking for a diversion. Someone to go talk to, anything. What a time to discover keeping her social circle small also hindered her chances of escaping this conversation. She glanced down at Daisy.

Daisy stared across the restaurant, her brows pinched together, a puzzled look on her face. Her entire focus was on one dark haired man in army fatigues near the window.

"What's the matter, Daisy? Do you know that man?"

"What man?" Riley and Robert asked in unison. Their eyes followed her gaze. Robert scowled at the man.

"Do you know him?" Riley asked quietly. The question aimed as much at his father as his daughter.

"No." She turned her attention back to her cake, took a bite and focused back on the stranger. "But he looks like Riley."

Tricia studied the man. "Maybe a bit, but lots of men have dark hair and green eyes."

"Try not to stare, it's impolite."

Tricia admired the way Riley offered the suggestion lightly, and with a smile of reassurance. "What did your dad get you for your birthday?" She asked Daisy.

"Nothing," she responded quietly, though she didn't seem upset.

"Ah, but I did," Riley commented. "Your gift is at home. I didn't want to spoil the surprise party by letting you know I knew today was your birthday. I'll give it to you later."

"Another present?" Daisy's smile was a mile wide. "I already got lots."

"One more from me. Did you know today was your birthday?"

"No. Mommy just got me a present on my birthday. She never told me what day it was. She said it made the surprise better. But it wasn't as good as this." She beamed.

"I'm glad you're having fun with your cousins," Tricia said and gestured for Riley to follow her. They stepped a few feet away from the table, out of earshot.

"I know this isn't the right time, or place for this conversation, but you haven't been by the school in the past few days. Since we're both here, I thought I'd bring it up. I sent you a note home about teaching Daisy your name, address and phone number and asked you to stop by to discuss it."

"I didn't get a note." He looked puzzled.

"Strange, I put it in her agenda. The one you sign every night. Wasn't it there?"

"I didn't see it. Maybe it slipped out?" He sounded puzzled and his brows pinched together.

"I also called you and you never called me back," she said, keeping her voice low to discourage eavesdropping by his family and the surrounding patrons.

"I didn't get a message. Did you call my cell?"

"No, I called the house and left a message."

"Weird, there wasn't a message on the machine. I still use a machine; the blinking light reminds me to check for messages when I've had a long day and Lord knows I've had a lot of those lately. I wonder what happened."

Tricia suspected she knew what happened to the note and the message. Kids could be devious when they were afraid they were in trouble and it certainly wasn't unusual for a child to act up when they were dumped into strange new situations. "Well, let's not worry about it now. I wanted to make sure you were teaching her the basics. Most of my other students learned it in kindergarten. Daisy can't recite hers yet, but that's not unusual after a move."

"Shit. It didn't even cross my mind."

"Relax, Riley." She placed a comforting hand on his arm. It was warm and strong under her fingers. The light dusting of hair tickled her palm. She dropped her hand to her side. "Just start teaching her those things, and her full name. It wouldn't hurt if she knew her grandparents are Sue and Robert Flint as well."

"But this is such a small town, everyone knows everyone."

"I don't want to freak you out, but—"

"I'm a guy, we don't freak out." He rolled his eyes.

"Look, bad things happen to good people and it's best to be prepared. If she knows who she is and where she's from, she can get help if she's ever taken from town."

Riley gasped. His mouth flapped open and shut. He started to speak and swallowed hard. "Parenting is going to kill me. It's Hanna all over again."

"No, it's not. Hope for the best but prepare for the worst. Don't scare her, make learning these things a game. She's safer in this small town than she ever would be in the city. Take it easy, it'll be okay. And, you totally freaked out. You nearly had kittens." She laughed.

"I. Did. Not. Freak. Out."

"Yes. You did."

His cell phone rang and he pulled it out of its holster. "Excuse me, I'm on call at the clinic. I have to take this."

She nodded and returned to the table. Three minutes later, he rejoined them.

"Mom can you take Daisy home with you? I've got an emergency. It's straight out in the opposite direction from home. It'll save me half an hour if I head right out. I wouldn't ask if it wasn't important."

"Can't Houston take the call?" Robert asked.

"He's on vacation, he's gone all week. We never arranged a replacement. I wasn't expecting the new—situation." Sue and Robert's eyes lit with the realization of his words. Having a daughter thrust unexpectedly in your lap meant an entire life re-evaluation.

"Oh no. We can't, we have the truck," Sue exclaimed. "There aren't enough seats for everyone. Can she go with you?" She looked frantically around the diner as if a solution would magically appear.

"I can take her home for you. I mean to your parents' place. It'll only take a few minutes. I really don't mind," Tricia offered.

"I would really appreciate it, if it's not too much trouble. Daisy," Riley said, to catch her attention. "Miss Tricia is going to drive you to Grandma and Grampa's house. You can stay with your cousins. I have to go to work. There's a horse who's hurt badly. She needs me. It's an emergency. I'll pick you up when I'm done. Okay?"

Tears brimmed in her eyes but she nodded. He moved behind her chair and turned Daisy to face him. "Look, I'm an animal doctor, a veterinarian, which means I look after hurt and sick animals. It's my job. Right now, a horse needs me and I have to go. Grandma and Grampa will take good care of you. I'll be back as soon as I can. I promise. I love you and I'll be back."

She flung her arms around him and buried her face in his neck. "Promise?" she mumbled tearfully.

"I promise. You can play with your cousins, like a really long birthday party!" The pain in his voice was obvious, as was his understanding he had to stay strong on this one. Backing down would add to his burdens later.

"Come on, we'll get your booster seat out of the truck and put it in Tricia's car." He turned toward her. "You did bring your car?"

"I did. Come on Daisy." She offered her hand. "Let's get the seat."

They walked out of the restaurant, hand in hand with Daisy in the middle. Daisy stared at the dark-haired man as they passed. He stared right back; his expression neutral. Daisy must have a fear of strangers. Tricia didn't think he was local, but there was something familiar about him. She shrugged. Maybe he had one of those familiar-type faces, though he did look a bit like Robert.

They quickly transferred the seat into Tricia's Honda and Riley, ever ready with his equipment and meds in a lock box on the back of the truck, took off to save the horse. Daisy and Tricia went inside to help clean up the party mess. Balloons, presents and the leftover cake loaded into the car, they followed Robert's truck back to the ranch.

"Isn't keeping the cake exciting?" Tricia asked, glancing at Daisy in the rear-view mirror. Her head slumped to the side, her eyes were closed and her mouth gaped open. She was adorably asleep, the cake tipped dangerously on the edge of her lap. It would make a huge mess if her grip slackened in sleep. Tricia shrugged. Wouldn't be the first time there was a food spill in her car.

Tricia pulled to a stop in front of the Flint's enormous house. It must have been great to be raised with so many siblings, friends and enemies all rolled into one. Being an only child had been crazy at times; particularly after her parents were caught embezzling. She tucked the sad thought away and focused on the joy of the moment. She loved children and it was nice to do a favor for a friend. In this case, it was extra special. Daisy's need for stability meshed nicely with Tricia's innate desire to help children find their place in the world.

Daisy shifted and Tricia twisted to look at her. She smiled sleepily at Tricia.

"Come on, Daisy. Let's go inside and see your cousins." Daisy frowned and fumbled with her seatbelt, one-handed. "Hang tight. I'll hold the cake while you get out." She hopped out and opened the back door. She accepted the cake thrust into her hands and watched as her charge fumbled with her buckle before freeing herself and climbing down.

"You know what? We better take this cake inside and put it in Grandma's fridge until Daddy comes to get you. We don't want it to get too hot and melt." She turned toward the house; Daisy followed slowly behind. Tricia wondered for a moment if being left here was going to be uncomfortable for Daisy.

Ten minutes later, in the middle of a full on hissy-fit, Daisy proved her right. She clung to Tricia's legs whimpering and begging her not to leave. Her cries altered with pleas to go home to Riley's house. Tricia and Sue shared a helpless look. There was a time to stand strong, the trouble was, Tricia didn't know if this was it, and Sue seemed equally lost. Giving in to the inevitable, Tricia decided to take Daisy to Riley's.

"Daisy, please stop," she commanded gently. "I understand you're upset, but your behavior is upsetting your grandmother. If you apologize to her for your tantrum, I'll take you home and stay with you until Riley gets back." As the words flowed from her lips, she realized abruptly the wiser course of action might have been to stay right where she was. Well, she'd made the decision and now she'd live with it.

Still clutching her leg, Daisy peeked up and whispered an apology. It wasn't graceful, it definitely wasn't sincere, but she'd done as asked.

"You're forgiven," Sue responded politely. "Here are my keys to Riley's house. Just leave them with him when he gets back and I'll get them later." She passed the keys to Tricia, went back to the kitchen and returned with Daisy's half of the leftover cake. Cake in hand they headed back to the car.

With Riley's ten-acre parcel adjoining the enormous Flint ranch, the ride took only minutes, most spent on one driveway or the other. Inside, they put the cake and the lunch Tricia had purchased and forgotten to eat in the fridge.

"Can we read?" Daisy asked, her eyes bright with hope.

"I don't see why not. Let's find the book I lent you."

They sat together in Riley's recliner. As they shifted to get comfortable, his soothing, enticing scent rose to tickle Tricia's nose. Being in his house, his chair, felt way too intimate. She shoved thoughts of Riley away and opened the book.

<h1 style="text-align:center">CHAPTER FOURTEEN</h1>

Riley paused at the stop sign and slapped the steering wheel of his truck in frustration before he pulled out on the gravel road leading back to the highway. He had expected the house call to treat a coyote attack on a horse to be short. The injuries had been much worse than the owner, Rick Rogers, had described. The roan mare had been brutalized and was near death from loss of blood when he arrived. Three hours and nearly four hundred stitches and the once-beautiful mare had a fighting chance of survival, if Rogers kept up with proper follow-up care as instructed.

Doubt nagged at him; the injuries were much more than he'd expect from a single coyote. Had it been a pack of coyotes? More likely the horse had been ravaged by Rogers' dogs. They'd been penned up in a dog run near the house and had snarled, howled and barked continually during Riley's visit.

Rogers had completely ignored them, and Riley followed

his lead. The dogs seemed unusually territorial and somewhat out of control. It was feasible that they'd damaged the newly acquired horse but Riley had no proof. He'd make notes on the incident later to keep the facts and his opinions clear and separate.

He hadn't seen any children on Rogers' acreage, he'd seen his wife, a tiny bit of a woman who'd come outside, thrown some bones at the dogs and scurried back into the house. Usually, most families came out to chat. Perhaps she was shy. They were new to the area. Rogers said they'd moved in a couple months ago and they'd acquired the horse last week. He seemed comfortable around the horse and the stall was clean with food and water readily available. Still, Riley couldn't shake his sense of unease about the man, the horse and the circumstances of the injuries.

He shook his head sadly, cases like this cut deep into his heart. He became a vet to save animals, not to treat egregious injuries caused by neglect or brutality. With nothing but unsubstantiated suspicions, he couldn't even report the injuries. He made a mental vow to keep his ears open for rumors about the area's newest resident and to informally check in with his friends in the RCMP. He knew who to talk to, without filing a complaint.

It didn't seem right to cast doubts on Rogers' character, but it was equally wrong to let the questionable event go unremarked. He shrugged off the unease and pulled to a stop at the end of the unpaved road. His cell phone chimed with a text message.

Night was falling and with no other vehicles in sight, he threw the truck into park and checked his phone.

Haven't heard from you. Thought I'd let you know Tricia took Daisy back to your house. We'll catch up with you tomorrow. Mom.

He chuckled at the way Sue signed her texts; as if he wouldn't know who was texting him. Completely computer and smartphone savvy, she still had some old-fashioned ways about her. For a moment he debated calling her to find out what was up, instead, he shot her a quick thank you text, turned onto the highway and continued his journey. If there was anything important he needed to know, she'd have told him or called.

Driver's window down to let the fresh air wash away his unease, he drove carefully watching for wildlife crossing the highway. He slowed once to let a moose cross the road and twice more when he passed small clusters of deer grazing on the lush grass at the roadside. Deer could bolt across the road in an instant and were notorious for panicking and changing their mind halfway across. No sense risking an accident.

He skirted the outside of town and was home in twenty minutes.

He pulled into the driveway, pausing for a moment to look at his house. With porch lights which came on automatically at dusk and a warm glow behind the light drapes of the living room, it felt like the house was welcoming him home. Funny how the extra light made such a difference. With sudden clarity, he realized how much he missed having a family to come home to.

Before leaving home for university, family had felt oppressive. They watched his every move, all the time. Privacy was a concept at best. Now, sitting here, basking in the enticing glow of his home, he felt—connected. Knowing his daughter was inside brought a glimpse of understanding how his own parents had protected their children. He'd pushed against their rules and boundaries time and again. He owed them a thousand apologies for broken rules, missed curfews and plain insolence. How had they known where to draw the lines and when to flex their rules?

He shook the thoughts aside and pulled alongside Tricia's small car. It was getting late, he was exhausted, emotionally and physically and he was in no shape for the mental gymnastics required to understand the juggling act of good parenting. He parked the truck and followed the sidewalk around the back of the house to the clinic entrance. His cowboy boots thumped quietly on the cement. He'd traded his rubber work boots for cowboys for the ride home. There was no sense dragging farm mess into his truck unless he had to.

He washed up quickly and went into the house, his mind whirling with the comfort of being home, his daughter's welfare, his future, his exhaustion and many concepts he couldn't even fully articulate. Life was emotionally overwhelming sometimes and his had been a roller coaster since Daisy's arrival.

He slipped out of his boots and hung his jean jacket on a hook at the back door and washed up. The house was still and silent. Knowing there was someone inside gave him a sense of welcome. Padding quietly on sock feet, he made his way through the dark kitchen to the living room.

He paused in the doorway, golden light spilled from the lamp beside his recliner, illuminating Daisy and Tricia who snuggled together on the chair, forgotten book on their laps. Daisy was fast asleep, Tricia smiled sleepily at him.

"Hi," she whispered. "I heard you come in." She looked him over, her eyes traveling from his head to his toes and returning to his face. "You look bushed. Tough call?"

"The worst." He made a vague waving motion to dismiss the subject. "How was the afternoon? Sorry I was so late."

"No worries. These things happen. We went back to your parents' place. Daisy was overwhelmed and wanted to come home." She shrugged as if it were no big deal but he suspected there was more to it.

"We came back here, practiced phonics, had some supper and played for a while. She dozed off while I read to her. She was so tired I didn't want to risk waking her by moving her." She laughed lightly; the sound almost inaudible. "My legs are falling asleep; I was just going to try and get her to bed."

"Let me," Riley said and strode forward. He scooped Daisy into his arms. "Thanks for changing her into her pajamas."

"I thought it might be a good idea, in case she fell asleep." She shrugged and wiggled her legs.

"Hang tight, I'll tuck her in and be back in a flash." He smiled and carried his precious bundle upstairs.

Skinny though she was, it was awkward to hold her and

flip the covers back. Somehow, he managed it without waking her. He tucked her in with her two favorite stuffed animals and turned on her night light. He opened the blind to let the moonlight in and turned back to the bed.

So precious, so innocent. His heart swelled with love. He stroked Daisy's hair and kissed her forehead. Was it always like this for parents? He almost laughed at the naïve thought. Of course, it wasn't.

"Goodnight, sweet girl. Sorry I was out so late." He slipped from the room leaving the door open a few inches and returned to Tricia who wandered around his living room stretching and twisting.

"You must be kinked right up from having her sleep on you."

"A bit but I enjoyed it." Her smile was like a beacon lighting up the room. "I love kids and she was wonderful— once we got here."

He winced. "Was she bad?"

"She was adamant about not staying with her cousins. I think maybe the excitement of the party and being left with virtual strangers was overwhelming. She calmed right down when we got back in the car."

"But they're not strangers, they're family," he protested.

"They're *your* family. They aren't hers. Give it time. Her life's been a mess since her mother got sick and died. Small things might really trip her up; but she's strong and she'll get through it. Especially if she knows you have her back."

He thought about his own childhood. He'd never known his mother, she died when he was an infant. Robert had raised him and his brothers with the help of a few part-time nannies. By the time Robert married Sue, she was a familiar face. His trials were entirely different than Daisy's. His childhood wasn't without issues, but he'd known love and acceptance his entire life. Guilt rattled through him over his inability to voice the depth of his caring for his stepmother even though he loved her and knew she loved him.

He dropped into his chair and watched Tricia pace. "I guess I'll have to figure out how to make sure she knows I'm here for her no matter what happens. She's so young to have gone through so much."

"True, but you can help her and show her how this is all going to make her stronger."

"How do I do that?"

"I have no idea. I'm just a teacher, I only took a few child psychology courses in university. But I do know anything you survive makes you stronger. Have you looked into counseling at all? It might be a good idea."

"I've thought about it, but I've barely had time. It's been go-go-go from the moment she arrived. I'll have to make time. In fact, I'll program an alarm in my phone so I don't forget to do it first thing next week. Would you like a glass of wine or some tea?"

She stopped walking and turned to look at him. He saw the indecision in her eyes and realized his offer might be construed as inappropriate, she seemed to have a rigid moral code about socializing with a student's parent.

"Consider it a thank you, for helping me out of a tough

spot." Not entirely true, but not a lie either. He liked having her in his house and wanted to spend more time with her.

"I suppose a glass of wine wouldn't hurt." She held up a finger. "A small glass, I still have to drive home."

"Red or white?" He stood and gestured toward the kitchen. "I have a couple bottles of each. Nothing's open."

She walked ahead of him. "Tea will be fine, no need to open a new bottle."

"Ah, but I'm going to open it anyway. I enjoy a glass of wine now and then and tonight; I have company to share it with." He flashed her a rogue grin when she turned to look at him. What he really wanted was a good stiff drink. A shot of rye or maybe a Scotch. But if she was good with wine, so was he. Besides, he didn't want to get in the habit of drinking away his work stress, nothing good would come from that, but a few minutes in Tricia's pleasant company might be the balm he needed.

"Are you okay?" She turned to look at him.

"What? Oh, yeah. I'm fine. Just tired." He flipped on the kitchen light. "I'll run downstairs and grab a bottle."

"You didn't answer my question. Tough night?"

"The worst." He avoided details by slipping through the doorway and heading to the basement.

Tricia watched him go. His quick avoidance of her question made her wonder what had gone wrong this evening. Had he lost the horse? He seemed upset, but not enough to have lost the animal. She shrugged and settled at the kitchen table. Either he'd talk or not. It wasn't like she was in a position to force information out of him.

He returned, brandishing a bottle of pink wine. "I found a rosé. It's a cheap one, but my sisters, Beth and Candy, both like it. Will this work?"

"I'm not a wine expert by any stretch." She looked at the bottle of Henry of Pelham Rosé. "Oh, I've heard of this, it's supposed to be good; and Canadian too. I like to buy locally where I can. I've been eying up the Field Stone Fruit Wines from Strathmore. I hear their Black Currant is to die for. Too bad the liquor store here doesn't carry it. I'm debating taking a trip next summer and seeing if I can get a winery tour."

"Do they offer them? It might be fun."

"I have no idea." She chuckled. "Just another pipe dream."

"And do you have a lot of pipe dreams?" He opened the wine and poured them both a glass. "Shall we sit here or in the living room?"

"Oh, here please. One of your recliners is comfortable, the other is brutal. It's fit for the pit." She slapped a hand over her mouth. "Sorry," she mumbled through her fingers. She really had to learn to keep some of her thoughts to herself. Around Riley, they seemed to burst forth unwanted. Luckily, he laughed.

"I know, it's dad's old chair. He brought it over when he discovered I didn't have much furniture."

"Have you considered buying something else? Like a couch? Maybe a couple tables? You could turn it into a family space rather than a man cave." She accepted the glass he held out to her. "Thank you. Years ago, we had neighbors from Newfoundland." She changed the subject. "They always had kitchen parties. It seemed like whenever people gathered at their house, we ended up in the kitchen. We sat on chairs, the table, the counters, or leaned against the wall. For whatever reason, everything happened in the kitchen."

"Mom and Dad's place is like that too. I think it's Sue's cooking. We'd hang out in the kitchen and she'd start feeding us. Everything from snacks to cake to full-on meals." He rubbed his tummy appreciatively. "I do miss her cooking."

"You don't go over often?" How could he not visit his parents at every opportunity? They were only a quarter mile away.

"We have dinner about once a month. They invite me every Sunday, but it doesn't feel right to keep eating there." He shrugged expressively.

"So, have them here. Cook dinner for your family. You can cook, right?"

"I'm a decent cook, when I want to cook. Nothing fancy, but edible. Trouble is I don't have enough furniture for everyone and I'd need a kids' table."

"Well, this conversation has come full circle. We're right back to why haven't you bought furniture? And the answer is…?"

"I never felt the need. I guess." He wrinkled his nose.

"Let me see if I have this straight…you won't have your family over because you don't have furniture. You don't have furniture because you don't see the need. I can't decide if you're crazy or hypocritical or lazy. Get off your backside and go shopping." Her words came out as more than a suggestion but less than an order. Surprisingly, he didn't take offense.

"Are all teachers annoyingly logical or is this your superpower?" He chuckled.

"We take special classes in logic and manipulation in university," she joked before sipping her wine. "Oh, this is good. Thank you. You could go look at Watson's and see what furniture they have. I know you know where they are."

"I looked, sort of, while we were there buying Daisy's furniture. Nothing jumped out at me. I need to go to the city and I can't see making the trip for nothing. If there was something here, I could keep my money in the community."

"Ever heard of online shopping? Or, go to the city, test drive some furniture and come back and see if Watson's can order it for you. There's more than one way to slice bread."

"I'll make a deal with you, I'll look again, and if I don't find anything, I'll take Daisy to the city as a treat and we'll find something. I should take her to see her other grandparents anyway."

"Deal." She offered her hand and they shook in agreement. His hand was warm and solid beneath hers. She tugged back when he held on a bit too long. "And you'll decorate for Halloween and Christmas too?"

He gave her a look that screamed 'seriously' and laughed. "You know it's cheating to change the rules after the deal is struck? Right?"

"Yeah, yeah. Whatevs," She rolled her eyes like a

teenager. "Just letting you know kids expect these things and as a bachelor, I doubt you bother."

"I'll have you know I handed out candy last year and decorated for Christmas." He leaned back and crossed his arms over his chest.

"You gave your niece and nephews granola bars for Halloween and you put out Poinsettias you bought from a school fundraiser." She copied his confident motion. "Gotcha."

Riley laughed aloud; the deep strong chuckle stroked down her backbone leaving shivers in its wake. Wow. The man had the greatest laugh. He really should laugh more often. The infectious sound made her grin. She sipped her wine. It was refreshingly cool and the perfect balance of sweet and dry.

"Do you have a wine cellar? This is perfectly chilled."

"No, a cold storage room. Although, I admit, it's rather empty. I suppose I'll have to keep a better supply of food in the house now…" He trailed off thoughtfully and looked out the window to the dimly lit yard. "So much has changed. I'm fumbling to keep up, to adapt." He looked up at her. "Don't misunderstand, I'm trying my damndest to get into this fatherhood thing, but it isn't easy. I care for Daisy. How could I not? But every day brings new stresses and revelations. The questions are never ending. I feel like I'm floundering in quicksand and I'm about to go under. I'm drowning in responsibilities."

"You've had responsibilities for years. I hear stories about how your family splits up duties and chores, they always have. You managed the responsibility of university and vet school while working part-time. You run a clinic with an impeccable reputation. This is just one more." She suspected the source of his unease but wanted him to find it for himself.

He fiddled with his glass, spinning it in slow circles on the table. He rocked it around and around on its base, the wine rising higher and higher threatening to spill over the edges. He released the long-stemmed glass and it wobbled roughly and finally settled upright.

"That's the thing. Up until now, every responsibility I've had has been escapable. I could walk away if I chose to. This time, I'm stuck. There's nowhere to run. My entire life, my lifestyle has changed and not by choice." His brows pinched together and he tipped the chair back on two legs and slammed forward again.

She waited him out despite the myriad of questions rocketing through her mind.

He stood and paced to the fridge, opened it, peered inside and closed it quietly. He walked around the table, and he stopped, staring out the window, his back to Tricia.

"I don't resent her. None of this is her fault. I'm annoyed at Mona for hiding my daughter from me. I'd have done the right thing. I swear it." He raked his fingers through his hair and then drummed them lightly against the window. "I don't know what to do."

His voice rose slightly at the end of the last words and she wondered if he were asking her for advice. It didn't matter, she wasn't going to give any, but she'd sit and let him work it out for himself. She had a hunch he didn't actually want to escape his responsibilities; he just hadn't accepted them. Yet.

"I guess I'm stuck with this one." His vocal groan matched her silent one. "I didn't mean it like that." He glanced at her over his shoulder and pacing. "I'm so jumbled up inside. I regret not knowing her from birth. I didn't want the responsibility but I accept it. She's a sweet kid even if she's mixed up and scared. It just—it changes so much. Every aspect of my life needs to be revisited and altered. My work schedule, the way I drive, dating, time with my family, my eating habits. How much I drink. My freedom to do as I please is gone and I don't know how to deal with it. I only know I have to."

"Why? Nothing has to change. You could give her up for adoption or give her back to her grandparents and let them deal with her as well as their health."

He froze in his tracks, staring at Tricia. His fists clenched and his forearms bunched. Abruptly he laughed, then relaxed.

"Well played, teacher. You caught me. I could never give her up. Nobody needs to be abandoned by their family. Especially not someone so innocent and who's been through as much as she has."

Tricia knew what he meant. He was right, nobody deserved to lose everyone they loved. It sucked from start to finish. She'd been there. Her family had turned on her, forcing her to walk away from their deceit. "You love her?" She pitched her words as a statement and a question, deliberately putting him on the spot.

He frowned and slid back into his chair. After a long, slow

sip of wine he responded. "Honestly, I do love her. Which makes me wonder why this is still so difficult?"

"Life's supposed to be difficult. If we didn't have pain, sorrow or strife, there would be nothing to measure joy and happiness against."

"You sound like a counselor, or a minister."

"Am I wrong?" It felt a little unethical to be putting him on the spot, but she couldn't help herself. She wanted, needed, to be certain Daisy got the best care she could. Besides, part of her knew he'd never give Daisy up. Caring for others and living up to your responsibilities seemed to be an innate Flint family trait.

"Even if you're right, it doesn't mean I like it."

"People seldom like to hear the truth about things they're avoiding." She provoked him further and drained the last of her wine.

He started to speak but a small voice from upstairs stopped him.

"Riley? Are you there?"

The voice was teary and kicked Tricia straight in the heart. Oh man, she was in deep. Way too deep. She had to get out of here before this duo pulled her in further.

"I'm here, Daisy. I'll be right up."

"I'll go now, thanks for the wine." She rinsed her glass and set it alongside the sink.

"You could stay. We could talk more after I get her settled." His eyes pleaded with her.

"I could, but I won't. She needs your undivided attention

until she realizes you're not abandoning her. Thanks for the wine. I'll let myself out."

He placed a hand on her arm as she walked past on her way to the door.

"Tricia? Thank you for being there when we needed you and thanks for the advice. Even if I didn't want to hear it. I'll be in touch about moving the buffet for you. And thanks."

"You're welcome. Goodnight, Riley." She loved the way his name sounded on her lips.

"Riley?" Daisy's voice shook with fear.

"Coming," he called loudly. "Thank you, Tricia." He smiled warmly and hurried toward the stairs.

Danged if she didn't like the way her name sounded when he said it.

CHAPTER FIFTEEN

*R*iley raced up the stairs. Daisy stood outside her room, her favorite stuffed animal clutched in her arms, tears streaming down her cheeks. His heart hurt at the sight of the naked fear on her face.

"What's up, buttercup?" he asked, keeping his tone light.

"I woke up and you weren't in bed. I thought you went away. Where's Miss Tricia?" She sniffed and wiped a hand across her face smearing snot everywhere.

"You fell asleep when you were reading. When I came home, I tucked you in and Miss Tricia went home." A slight mistruth but accurate enough for her needs.

"Oh." She sniffled again. "Where were you? You weren't in bed." The accusation hung heavy in the air.

He knelt in front of her, looking her right in the eye. "I'm older than you. I go to bed later. I was downstairs."

"I thought you were gone." She stared at the floor.

He raised her face to look at him and placed his hands gently on her shoulders. "I promise I won't leave the house without waking you up and telling you first. Not even to go to my clinic." He hoped he'd be able to adapt the rule once she adjusted to living with him. One step at a time. He repressed a sigh.

"Come on, Daisy. Let's wash your face and dry those tears. I'll settle you back in bed and read you a quick story. A short story. It's late and way past your bedtime." He led her into the bathroom. "I'll wait outside while you try and pee. You might need to since you fell asleep with Miss Tricia."

He closed the door behind him and chattered about his drive home and the animals he saw. He kept the one-sided conversation going so she knew he was there. Once she flushed, he helped her wash her hands and face and tucked her back in bed. "What shall we read?"

"*Sneetches*." She sniffed again.

"*The Sneetches* is a pretty long book." The book, his favorite Dr. Seuss collection, was too long for a late night read. "How about one story from the book instead?"

"Two?" she countered.

"Which two?"

"*Too Many Daves* and *Pale Green Pants*."

"Oh, I don't know. *Pale Green Pants* is pretty scary," he warned, making her laugh.

"No, it's not. It's a good story. It's about friends. Miss Tricia told me so."

"Well, I can't argue with an authority like that. You win.

I'll read them both but only because they're short. Then, it's right to sleep. I'll stay in the house. Okay?"

"Can you go to bed?" Her voice was low and pleading, almost as if she were afraid she'd get into trouble, but risking asking anyway. She was a feisty little thing.

"No. But I promise I won't leave the house. I have some important reading to do for work. I'll be downstairs in the living room."

"'Kay." Her agreement was reluctant at best, but he accepted it as a step in the right direction.

"Squish over and make room for me to sit beside you." He snuggled close and opened the book and started reading. She was asleep before he finished the first story. He kissed her on the head, whispered goodnight and after tucking her in, he crept from the room.

With a sigh he returned to the kitchen and fired up his laptop. He had a ton of research on childrearing to get through. First, nutrition. The vet in him knew physical and mental health often went hand in hand and a properly fed body fueled the mind and helped provide emotional stability. If there was one thing he knew, it was that Daisy needed all the help she could get. She was extremely thin, was it the result of a growth spurt, or was she missing something in her diet?

He devoured countless articles on nutrition and turned to family-oriented blogs for discipline advice. So many contradicting opinions. Peace, love, talking. Time outs. Loss of privileges. Chores. He concluded his only option was to find out what worked for him and Daisy. He flipped through some pages until he landed on a child psychology blog.

A whisper of sound woke him. He blinked sleepily and discovered Daisy, chin down on the kitchen table, staring at him. He jerked back in surprise. "Whoa!"

"Morning." She giggled.

"Good morning to you, too." He stretched and twisted the kinks out of his neck and shoulders. "Ugg. I shouldn't have stayed up so late. I guess I fell asleep while I was reading. Which wasn't so smart." He rubbed his face briskly, his five o'clock shadow rasped roughly under his hands.

"What were you reading?"

He pondered his answer before revealing the truth. "I was trying to learn how to be a good dad. You're a special girl, you deserve the best dad you can have. I don't know how to do that, so I have to read and learn how."

Her green eyes went wide with disbelief. She patted his arm and smiled. "It's okay. Miss Tricia says you can do anything if you try hard enough."

"She did, did she? I sure hope she's right." Good gravy, was there no escaping the woman? Everywhere he turned she was there. Even in his dreams. Thank heaven Daisy couldn't read his mind. "Well, Miss Tricia sure was nice to help us out yesterday when she stayed with you. I hear you caused a bit of trouble. Want to talk about it?"

"No." She stared at the table, tracing the lines of the woodgrain with her index finger.

"Hmm. Well, you don't have to talk about it now, but you do have to talk to me later. Okay?" He tried to sound firm and understanding but wasn't sure he hit the mark. He waited for an answer.

He grasped her hands and held them lightly between his until she looked up at him. "I know you're having trouble adjusting to this new life, and you aren't in trouble for being upset yesterday. Everyone gets upset. But we do have some rules you have to obey. First rule is always tell me where you are going and I'll always tell you where I'll be." It wasn't the issue at hand, but an easy rule seemed a good place to start. "And, you need to give me all the notes sent home from school. Okay?"

She flushed but nodded her agreement.

"Second, when you're upset, try and talk to me, I'll try my best to understand and to help you, like I did last night."

Another nod.

"All right then. Shall we have breakfast? What would you like?"

"I dunno."

"How about I start some coffee while you think about it? You can look in the cupboards and fridge at the groceries we bought the other day and see if you find something you want." He dumped yesterday's coffee filter into the compost bucket and rinsed the basket and pot. With fresh coffee brewing he turned back to Daisy. "Have you made a decision?"

"Bunny cakes."

Oh no. What in the world was a bunny cake? He had to think fast to figure this one out. "I'm not familiar with bunny cakes? What, exactly, is a bunny cake?"

Daisy giggled. "It's a pancake shaped like a bunny."

"I don't know." He gave her a funny face with scrunched up eyebrows and wrinkled nose to let her know he was joking. "Sounds pretty crazy to me."

"Mommy made them," she said seriously.

"Well then, you tell me how to make them and I'll try my best."

"First you mix the batter. Mommy measured and I mixed." She said wisely.

"Pull up a stump and we'll get started."

"A stump?"

"That's cowboy or rancher talk for pull up a chair or take a seat." He paused. "Pull a chair up to the counter, you can stand on it if you're careful."

She pushed the chair across the floor, it squealed all the way.

He pulled out the pancake mix and a bowl. He read the instructions aloud and they set to work. He measured, she counted and poured everything into the bowl while the electric frying pan heated.

"Remember not to touch this. It'll get hot. While we wait for it to heat up, we can mix the batter. Spoon or mixer."

"Mixer." Her eyes lit with glee and he had a sudden feeling he was going to regret this. He slid the worry aside. How bad could it be? Three minutes later he had his answer.

Daisy dropped the whirling mixer, twice, sending batter flying about the kitchen. Droplets covered the walls, floor and ceiling. They had batter in their hair and their clothing was covered. He couldn't help but chuckle at the disaster.

"What the devil is going on?" Sue's laughing voice sounded from the doorway.

Riley and Daisy fell into a guilty silence. It took him a moment to realize this was his house and he could do whatever he wanted. His next thought was food fight. He stifled the idea and looked his stepmother right in the eye and said, "Making bunny cakes. Why do you ask?"

Sue sputtered with laughter and Robert let out a loud guffaw.

"What's a bunny cake?" Robert asked when he had himself back under control.

Riley and Daisy shared a look. "Bunny shaped pancakes," they said superiorly, as if everyone knew what they were.

"I'm not sure you've got the technique quite right." Sue smirked. "What do you say we clean up this mess and I'll show you how it's done."

"You can make bunny cakes?" Riley asked.

"Of course, I made them for the girls all the time. As well as unicorn cakes, teddy bear cakes and Christmas tree cakes. You boys were always in too big a rush to wait, so most of the time you got circles. They take less time."

Daisy gasped in delight.

"I know when I'm whipped," Riley declared. "Come on, Daisy. Let's get cleaned up and we'll watch and learn how it's done."

"I've got the kitchen," Sue declared. "Robert, call the other kids in from the truck and we'll get this party started."

By the time Riley and Daisy changed and returned to the kitchen it was spotless. Jane stood on a chair beside the counter, her brothers sat on the floor under the table playing with Lego which must have arrived with them, because Riley didn't own any. Another thing for his never-ending shopping list.

"Hop up beside Jane and I'll show you how it's done. Mind the pan, it's hot." Once Daisy was in place, she placed the mixer into Daisy's hand. "I'll hold on with you until you get the hang of it. Mixers can get out of control if you're not used to them. But I think you already know that." She winked at the girls and they giggled.

Batter safely mixed, she let them watch while she used a spoon to carefully shape rabbit heads with the batter. "They take a minute to cook. Riley, you help the girls set the table. Robert, can you get out the juice please?"

Everyone jumped to obey and she flipped the first bunny cakes over. From the back they hadn't looked like anything special, from the front it was a rabbit, complete with eyes, nose whiskers and pointy ears.

"Wow!" Jane whispered in awe and clapped her hands. "They look like rabbits. Thanks Grandma."

"Thank you," Daisy said solemnly. "They're just like Mommy used to make."

"And now, I can make them too," Riley decreed and set his hand to making the next batch. Everyone had a good laugh when the boys declared his rabbits looked more like monsters.

"Monster cakes," he declared seriously. "I believe I've invented a new thing. I'm killing this cooking thing. I'll be the next *Top Chef.*" The joy on Daisy's face raced through him. It was wonderful to watch her interact and play with her cousins. She even sat on Robert's lap to eat her pancakes. She was warming up to her new family, him included. Life was turning around.

Now if only he could corner his parents without kids around to discuss the issues Robert had been having with his health. How serious were they?

Tricia stood on the front steps of the school and watched Daisy and Riley walk down the sidewalk toward his pickup truck parked half a block away. Daisy had attended school every day this week and as the days rolled by, she was becoming increasingly open and engaging more with her peers. It was like watching a rose bloom in slow motion. It hadn't been without hiccups and setbacks. Occasionally, Daisy had reverted into her shell, especially when the other students were particularly rowdy or crowded her, but overall, her social skills were improving by the day and Tricia could see the remarkable girl she'd become.

Most interesting was the fact that Daisy, and in turn Jane, had become Kyle Broderbund's friend and champion. Today, the dynamic cousins had punched Quinn Rattler for teasing Kyle about his clothing. She'd been too far away to intervene quickly enough to stop the tussle and it had put Tricia in a bit of a quandary.

Quinn was a bully, straight up. He picked on the other kids. Bossed them around and dominated the classroom with glares and quiet threats. When he'd started teasing Kyle, Daisy had stepped right up to him and said, "Stop picking on him. He can't help being poor. He's my friend, you leave him alone." Jane joined her and they stood, elbow to elbow, hands on their hips between Quinn and Kyle.

"Who's gonna make me?" He demanded.

"We are!" the girls declared in unison.

"I dare you. You can't stop me, you're chickens. You even try and I'll punch you in the face."

"It's okay, Daisy," Kyle said quietly trying to move between the girls.

"No. Quinn's a big mean jerk and you're my friend." She hauled back her fist and punched the bully in the nose. Jane added a follow up blow.

Quinn burst into tears and ran to Tricia demanding retribution. She'd had no option but to haul all four of them into the principal's office and call their parents. School policy demanded suspension for physical violence but after a quiet conference between the parents, Tricia, and Principal Keller, they agreed to a week of detention, twenty minutes after school every day. The children would perform any tasks Tricia asked of them and if she ran out of chores, they'd help the janitor clean.

She hoped she'd find some teachable moments with the four and would be able to lead them to friendship and to see the value in kindness. At the moment they stood firmly three against one and although Quinn's mother was astounded to learn her son was a bully, she seemed eager to nip it in the bud.

Riley and Daisy stopped at the corner. Daisy pulled on his hand and when he looked down, she spoke to him. He nodded and she turned and raced back to Tricia.

"Miss Tricia?" she said breathlessly when she skidded to a stop. "I'm sorry for being mean. Kyle's my friend and nobody should pick on him. I won't hit no more." She stood there looking penitent and subdued.

"Apology accepted. Perhaps next time, you could ask for help."

Daisy nodded solemnly. "Okay. Bye." She waved gaily and skipped back to her father.

Again, Tricia watched her go. At Riley's side, Daisy paused and they both waved. Warmth and a sense of belonging flooded through her. How lovely to be worthy of a second wave. She'd had more than one close relationship with students in the past, but something about this felt different.

"Heck of a family, eh?" Jo's voice startled Tricia.

She whirled around to glare at her friend. "Dang. Don't sneak up on me!" She laughed. "I'm too young to die of a heart attack."

"And too old to be single," Jo teased, flipping her wavy red hair over her shoulder. "You really should go after Riley. He's handsome, single, responsible."

"I'm not looking for a relationship. All I want is to do my job and live my life in peace, out of the public eye."

"Girl, this is Coyote Creek. The gossip grapevine is faster than the speed of light. Nothing goes unnoticed here. There's no way to fly under the radar. Get used to it. Live your life. You're way too young to be a spinster. Forget what happened to you in the past. Your ex was a total jerk. Your parents were worse. Get over it. Nobody here is judging you on your past."

"People know?" Panic shot through her and she jerked backward. "Jeepers. Is there no privacy? I thought I was getting away from my rep."

"Not in this small town and certainly not with the internet. I expect half the school board Googled you before you were hired."

"Then why'd they hire me?" She pushed past her friend and into the school.

"Wasn't a big deal at the time. The school needed a substitute, I suggested you. When they asked me about the thefts, I told them you weren't involved and legally, you'd been proven innocent. Heck, I didn't even have to fight for you. You proved yourself and they hired you full-time."

"I'm glad you were there for me, you believed in me when no one else did which means a lot to me." There weren't enough words to express her gratitude. When she'd felt alone and abandoned, Jo was there for her. Full-on support, no questions asked.

"Hon, I've known you since we were dorm-mates. I stuck up for you because there was never a doubt in my mind about your honesty. Now, when are you going to be honest with yourself and realize this hick town isn't out to get you? People like you, they respect you, even if you stick to yourself and don't socialize. It's time to suck it up and go after your dreams. Go after your dream man."

"Riley isn't my dream man." She protested, though part of her, a large part, wondered if she could make a relationship with Riley work.

"I never said Riley," Jo teased as they walked down the hallway, their steps falling in unison.

"You might as well have." She whirled around, hands on her hips to stare at her friend. "I'm not ready to date." Okay, part of longed for male companionship. She wouldn't mind having more female friends either but it was tough to open herself up to that kind of hurt again. In a small town there was no place to hide when relationships or friendships faltered or you made a fool of yourself.

"You are ready to date. You just have to admit it."

"No. I'm not." Tricia sparred back.

"Are too."

"Am not." They looked at each other and exploded into laughter.

Breathlessly, Tricia clutched Jo's shoulder. "You're the best friend I ever had. So many people abandoned me, but not you. You were there for me the entire time."

"Technically," she chuckled, "I was here for you while you were there. Nevertheless, I think you owe me a drink for being so awesome."

"I'll buy that. Come over later and I'll make seafood linguini for us. We can crack a bottle of wine."

"Or, we could go to Bar None and have a greasy burger and fries and you can buy me a drink."

Tricia laughed. "You and your greasy burgers. Okay, what time?" It seemed right to accept her friend's request without putting up her usual fuss. Besides, Riley would be home with Daisy and she wouldn't have to worry about bumping into him.

"Just like that? Without a fuss?"

She shrugged as if her agreement meant nothing. "Yup, I owe you. But I have to hit the grocery store on my way home. I'm out of fruit, yogurt and chocolate."

"I didn't see your car in the lot."

"I walked. I always walk, I'd think you'd have noticed this by now. After all, you're my BFF." She shook her head in mock grief.

"I'll give you a ride, I'm heading out. I need a few things too."

"Works for me. Let me grab my things. I've got some craft preparation to do this weekend for our snake unit next week." They parted in the hallway.

Tricia took a few minutes to write up her report on the day's incident, making sure to include Daisy's apology. The incident was minor, insignificant, compared to some she'd experienced at her previous job, but she wanted complete documentation, including the parents' reactions and the follow-up behaviors. People reacted differently here. There was no denial, no blame game, just acceptance and calls for better behavior. It lent an optimism she wasn't expecting. Maybe she could have a personal life here without fear of reprisal.

Of course, dating meant finding someone to date. How many single men were there in a town of two thousand people? She certainly wasn't going to date the father of one of her students, despite having two single father families. She shook the thought off, powered her laptop down and stuffed it and her craft supplies into her leather satchel for the journey home.

She paused with one hand on the well-worn buckles, the other stroking the butter soft leather. The leather briefcase that once belonged to her maternal grandfather had at one time been stiff and solid. Now, years of aging and use had softened it. Time had turned the color from tan to a warm butterscotch brown and tempered the leather to soft and pliable but still strong. Her grandfather had given her the case when she graduated university. She'd carried her supplies in it every day since. He was gone now, but she'd always remember him coming home from work and dropping the case at the door to wrap her in a warm embrace when she visited during the summer.

"You ready or what?" Jo asked from the doorway.

"I am, but before we go out, you have to promise not to ditch me like you did last time." She waggled a warning finger under her friend's nose.

"Only if you agree to dance with every man who asks you."

"No deal."

"What's up with that? Are you chicken?" The teasing lilt in Jo's voice left the taunt feeling light.

"You know I can't dance. I love to dance, but I've got two left feet. Or more accurately, I have one left foot and one peg leg." She mimed a peg leg walk. "I hate embarrassing myself."

Jo laughed. "You've seen half the people here dance. Some of them are brutal. Nobody. No-bo-dy, gives a crap. Dance. Have fun. Live a little before you settle into spinsterhood."

"You're pushing me into a relationship because you're diving head in with Houston. Just because we're friends doesn't mean we have to do things on the same schedule. You can date even if I don't."

"But what about double dates? Houston and Riley are business partners and best friends. They spend a lot of time together. We could double date."

"Aren't you forgetting someone?" The sudden pressure from the one person she thought understood her was annoying. Riley's life was in turmoil, he wouldn't be dating anyone for a while. Her heart went pit-a-pat when she realized he was safely off the market and away from the women who seemed to follow his every move. At least for now.

"Who could I possibly forget? Riley's single, you're single…" She trailed off questioningly.

"Daisy? Does the name ring any bells? Coyote Creek's newest resident?" She hated the sarcasm and doubt flooding her voice. But seriously, how could Jo forget the adorable girl who'd lost her mother? Frustrated, she walked down the hall toward the exit.

"Shoot. I totally forgot." She paused. "You certainly seem concerned about her. Anything important I need to know here?"

"She's my student, nothing more. She might need a little

extra care to get her through this, though Riley is going to get counseling for them both. To help them adjust."

"And how, pray tell, do you know that little tidbit." She waggled her eyebrows suggestively. "You seeing him on the sly? Visiting him while his precious daughter is asleep? Intimate parent-teacher conferences?"

They'd known each other so long that Tricia knew Jo was joking. Tricia couldn't help but wonder if the rumor mill was putting ideas into Jo's head and if she half believed the teasing accusations. "It isn't like that. I happened on them in the café last weekend having a birthday party for Daisy and Jane. They invited me to join them. Ken had to leave and Riley got called in to work. Long story short, I drove Daisy home and stayed until Riley got back."

Jo unlocked her aging Ford Fiesta and they climbed in, rolling the windows down to release the heat trapped from being in the sun all day. "And you talked?"

"We talked, *just talked*. About Daisy and counseling. Nothing else." Somehow not mentioning the wine felt like a lie. She'd always considered omitting facts a lie of omission. Heat flooded her face and she turned to look out the window hoping Jo would put the car in gear so they could drive away from this conversation.

"Oh. My. God. You're blushing. There was more than talk. Are you seeing him?" Jo raised her hand in a high five. After a moment, she let it drop to her lap.

"I'm not seeing him. I'm not seeing anyone. I adore my single life." She injected as much enthusiasm into her voice as she could. The lie burned on her lips and left a scalding sensation in her gut. She felt like she'd downed four shots of Jack straight up. "I would never date a parent of one of my students."

"But you'd like to," Jo suggested with the unerring intuition of a long-time friend. "I've done it you know. Dated the parent of one of my students. Here. In town. The world didn't stop turning when we ended it, the universe didn't explode. The sun didn't go supernova. The—"

"Stop. I get it. Enough bad metaphors already. Your love life does not impact mine. I won't date a student's father."

"Has he asked you?" Jo probed what turned out to be a sore spot.

"No."

"But you want him to."

"I don't."

"You do," Jo sympathized. "You just don't want to want him to ask you out. Girl, you're seriously messed up." She put the car into gear and backed out of her stall. "Let's get some groceries and hit the bar. I need a drink. Hell, you need a drink. I'm going to teach you how to chill if it's the last thing I do."

"Shut up and drive," Tricia ordered her friend with a regal wave toward the street.

Riley leaned against his truck on the driveway outside their parents' house waiting for the rest of their siblings. Ken rested his forearms on the truck box beside him. They'd hired two teenage girls to babysit for the evening. Daisy had agreed, albeit reluctantly, to stay with the teens when they promised to paint her nails. To keep things familiar, Ken had dropped his kids off at Riley's and the girls had joined them. Tonight was, if everything went according to plan, a sleepover. Daisy's first.

Justice, Carl and Jason arrived together in Jason's pickup. Two minutes later, Beth, Candy and Jennifer arrived in the ranch truck.

"Dad's gonna shit bricks," Beth the twenty-two-year-old middle sister said after embracing her brothers. "He totally doesn't want to talk about it."

"Did you look at his file?" Jennifer asked with a wave of her arm setting her enormous stack of bangles jangling.

"Don't be crazy," Beth chided. "That would be illegal, even if I had access to the files. But I've dealt with lying patients before, I'll be able to tell if he's feeding us BS."

"Well, let's do this. Time to beard the lion in his den," Riley said with a wave toward the house.

"More like band the bull's balls. He's going to be pissed. This reeks of an intervention, and he hates it when we stick our noses into his business."

"It doesn't matter," Jennifer said tearfully. "We need to know exactly what's going on and how we can help."

"I know most of the blame lands square on my shoulders for ditching my ranch responsibilities to look for Hannah," Justice confessed. "I keep trying to step up to the plate but I can't, not with my daughter missing."

"Nothing is more important than finding Hannah," Riley injected. "I've always understood your agony, but I get it here, now." He tapped his chest. "More than ever, I appreciate what you're going through." He'd die if anything happened to Daisy. It would rip his heart out. How could Justice even survive not knowing where Hannah was?

"I'm no better," Ken said. "With two working ranches side by side, I should have been helping out instead of re-courting my wife. Besides, we can't let Mom carry the burden alone. We have to get a handle on this and pitch in."

The front screen door opened and they jumped guiltily apart when Sue addressed them from the step. "You know he's going to kick you out, right?"

"Yup," Carl agreed as they mounted the stairs to the house. "But he's just one man and we're a gang." Everyone chuckled. "It's time to put our heads together and figure out how to help Dad get through this."

"It's your funeral." A smile took the sting out of her words. "I wondered when this would happen. I figured a non-school night was most likely. So, I baked cookies and lemon meringue pies today." She turned to open the door. "I hope you know what you're doing," she called over her shoulder as she slipped back into the house.

"Me too," Riley and Justice said in unison.

"Who's taking the lead on this?" Beth asked.

Riley had pondered the question all day. Technically, Justice was first in line to run the ranch if anything happened to Robert, but Ken's spread was the next ranch over and the two were practically run as one. Jason, the family butcher had less stake; and Carl, as a mechanic, held only the responsibility of his garage and maintaining the ranch vehicles. Riley pitched in where he could while acting as vet for most of the town and the ranch.

As for the girls, Beth was a student nurse in training, home for the weekend. Candy spent most of her time on the road protesting questionable environmental practices and Jenn worked in the record store until she decided where to go to university and what to study.

Still, everyone had a stake in the ranch's welfare, and more importantly in Robert's health. They had to help out where they could before his problems put an even greater burden on Sue.

Riley took a seat on the arm of the couch across from Robert's cushiony leather recliner. Jenn hopped on Robert's lap and hugged him. "I love you, Daddy."

Riley noticed how much his stepsisters looked like his father. Their birth father had been built a lot like Robert and had similarly dark hair. He shrugged the thought off, they had bigger fish to fry tonight.

"You kids are too late, dinner's over," Robert teased, looking around the room. His expression darkened. "Did you ask them here?" He glared accusingly at Sue.

"I did not. They came on their own." She leaned against the doorjamb.

"You baked pies and cookies today, I should have known something was up. Dammit."

"For your information, I baked because Beth is home for the weekend. I had nothing to do with this—gathering."

"It was my idea," Riley spoke up. "You've been avoiding discussing your health for months now. Every time I walk into a room, you walk out. It's time to stop evading this conversation. You caught that bug and you've been under the weather ever since. I'm, no, we're worried about you. All eight of us."

"Nine," Sue interjected.

"There's not a damn thing wrong with me that being left alone won't cure." Robert crossed his arms over his chest and avoided looking directly at any of them.

"So why are you spending so much time alone in that tiny shed? Why are you practically grey?" Sue asked sadly. "You've got no color at all and we want to know why."

"The shed's the only place I get any privacy. It's my thinking spot. This is the tail end of a virus. You heard the doctor. I'm not an infant, I don't need the lot of you stirring up crap and worrying your mother."

Everyone looked at Beth for confirmation and advice. Riley mistrusted his father's words but had no idea how to force the truth out of him.

"Daddy," Beth said. "We are worried about you. You aren't healthy. I think you need to go back to the doctor. Maybe this *is* nothing. But it could be something serious. Better to get it checked out before something bad happens."

Robert grumbled and groused and they argued back and forth for nearly an hour before extracting an agreement from him to see the doctor. Sue promised to book the appointment and hogtie him if need be.

CHAPTER EIGHTEEN

After leaving the ranch, the Flints reconvened at Bar None for a drink. Riley and Ken pulled two tables together allowing them to sit as a group. Riley was barely sitting when his phone vibrated in his pocket and made a small chime. He pulled it out, glanced at the screen and frowned.

"What's up, bro?" Jason asked.

He typed a response before he answered. "Daisy's got a bit of a cough and she's sneezing a lot." The phone chimed again. "No fever though. Looks like she's coming down with a cold. I should go."

"Relax," Ken advised. "Kids get colds all the time. All three of mine had one last week. There's a bug going around. She'll be fine. I've hired those sitters dozens of times; they know what to do and they'll text if she gets worse. Take a load off and relax. You haven't been out for a drink since she arrived. One thing I can tell you about parenting, probably the only thing, is you have to snatch these chances when they appear."

"I don't know…"

"I think he's right," Beth placed her hand on his arm. "She'll be okay for a couple hours. Besides, how often do we get together as a family? Never! Stay, have a drink and we'll go home early."

He rolled the decision around in his head for a moment. The sitter had said Daisy was okay, just the odd cough and some sneezing. If Ken's kids had a cold last week, she likely caught it from them. Indecision taunted him. The veterinarian in him reminded him colds happen, even to animals. His new parent side said he needed to act on this now. "Maybe I should pack her up and take her to the hospital."

"Good grief no," Beth laughed. "It's not an emergency. You don't want to be cluttering up the hospital waiting room for a cold. I know it's tough, but she'll be fine. I can check on her tomorrow."

"Fine." He agreed reluctantly. "I'd appreciate it if you checked her over."

"Consider it done." She looked at him, her expression sincere. "You're going to be a good dad, I know it. Relax and take things as they come. Don't ignore problems, but don't go looking for them either."

"I'll try. I'm so lost most of the time. What am I saying?" He laughed dryly. "I'm lost all of the time. I feel like a fish out of water."

Ken joined in. "Having no idea what to do is parenting in

a nutshell. Kids don't come with manuals. Go with your gut and pick your battles."

"Meaning?" The last thing he needed was advice couched in riddles.

"Once she adapts to her new life, she'll start testing you. Stand your ground and stick by your rules. Even if you don't have many. Kids need boundaries."

His brain whirled. He wanted to run home and hug Daisy and protect her and he wanted to run and hide. The rest of him needed to sit and soak up all the advice he could get.

Out of the corner of his eye he saw Frank, the bartender, approach. Weirdly, he was pleased by the diversion in the conversation.

"Hey Flint family," Frank greeted them. "Jennifer Flint, I cannot believe you're old enough to drink,"

"Wanna see my ID? I'm almost nineteen."

"Trust me, I don't need to see your ID. I remember your eighteenth birthday party and the ruckus you caused." He chuckled.

"Hey, that wasn't my fault. I only had two drinks. Blame the idiots who crashed my party." She shrugged. "I'd never start a fight. The vibes are bad and Karma would kick my butt. You reap what you sow."

"Still the hippy then?" he teased.

"Ever and always, my dear friend." She smiled winningly at him. "But tonight, I need a drink. I'll have the usual. What about you guys?" She looked at her siblings.

"The usual," they chorused in unison.

"One bartender's root beer for Jennifer, and draft beer all

the way around, except Miss Beth who'll have a gin and tonic. Anything to eat?" Nobody requested anything. "Which one of you is designated driver?" Frank asked.

Ken raised his hand. "I've got the van. Carl, Jason and Justice will walk home. I'll deliver the rest safely. Switch my order to iced tea, please."

Frank nodded his approval. He tended to be a stickler about drinking and driving. On more than one occasion he'd taken away a customer's keys and called them a taxi. At least twice he'd called the police to intervene before someone drove under the influence. It wasn't about his bar or reputation; it was about community spirit and safety.

"He's so conscientious and adorable," Jenn declared when the bartender walked away.

"Gross, he's ten years older than you are," Beth said with a groan. "He's ancient. Besides, you're much too young to date."

"You're one to talk. You were sneaking around with boys behind Mom and Dad's backs when you were twelve. Besides, I'm sure not going to date any of the dweebs my age. They're all hormones and grabby hands." She followed Frank's movements until he was back behind the bar. "Mature men know how to treat women with respect."

Riley raised his hands. "Whoa. Stop. End of discussion. I am not being part of a dissertation on my sisters' romantic intentions. Leave me out of this."

"Hell yeah!" His brothers agreed.

"Speaking of love lives," Beth teased, "Riley, I see Tricia

Paxton over there with Houston and Jo. You should go say hi." She elbowed him in the ribs.

He couldn't help himself, he looked. They sat together at a table for four, Houston and Jo turned slightly away from him, facing Tricia. The shaking of their shoulders indicated they were laughing. Tricia's head was thrown back, and her mouth open. He could see her amusement, though he couldn't hear it over the rocking melody being pumped out by tonight's band. For the first time he could recall, he wished there wasn't the usual Friday night band to dance to. He'd seen her smile and laugh lightly, but he'd never heard full-on mirth.

He wanted to be there, beside his friends, beside her. He wanted to belong to her circle. He shook the thought away; tonight was about family. His family. He checked his phone in case he'd missed a message from the sitters.

"Relax, they'll text, or call, if they have any problems. By now, the kids'll be snuggled up with a movie if they aren't asleep already." Ken advised. "Trust me on this one. I don't get everything right, particularly when relationships are involved." His brow furrowed and his hands fisted on the table top. "But I do know babysitters."

"I'm still worried," Jennifer stated, her voice shaking. "Dad's not telling us the truth. I know it. There's something wrong besides a lingering virus." She looked from sibling to sibling, waiting for someone to answer.

"I think he's being honest," Beth said. "At least he's agreed to go for a physical. Until then, he's going to have to relax more, work less and eat better. If Mom can keep him walking on a regular basis, he'll do better. Working until he drops and then sitting and doing nothing isn't healthy. He needs to increase his moderate exercise. And you guys," she pinned each of her brothers with a hard stare, "you guys need to step up and do more of the heavy work."

Riley leaned back and sipped the beer Frank had delivered during the first part of Beth's diatribe. When she got on a roll, his sister had a knack for steamrolling over everyone and trying to run their lives. He had no doubt his turn was coming, but for now, he'd watch the others suffer.

"Justice Flint, you might want to consider moving into the cabin. Living in town puts you too far away," Beth shook her finger at him, the mannerism a perfect mimic of Sue.

"And my missing daughter?" He crossed his arms angrily over his chest.

"You might get more searching done living on the ranch. We've got high-speed satellite internet now. You could spend your daily commute time searching. Jason's still in town with his ear on the rumor grapevine. Living in the cabin you'd still have privacy."

Justice opened his mouth to reply and snapped it shut. "Holy crap. I never even thought of how much has changed out there in the past couple years. I might be able to make that work. Maybe I can get Dad to realize there are other ways to run things. Modern techniques and equipment could really ease the workload."

"Good luck," Ken jumped into the fray. "I've been harping on him for ages with no luck. He sees it working for me but won't consider upgrading for himself."

"And you, Candy could get a job and stop running around

the country protesting, or at least pay your own way. I'm working and going to school to keep the financial burden off Mom and Dad," Beth declared.

"If I work, I can't get to all the things I need to do. Do you know how much damage the oil companies and loggers are doing? They're devastating the environment. Somebody has to stand up for Mother Earth." Fire and enthusiasm rained from Candy's every word. She jerked to her feet, jostling the table and sloshing their drinks over the edges of the glasses. "You just don't care."

"You're wrong, Candy," Riley injected, grabbing the table with one hand and his glass with the other. "We all make our living off the earth in some fashion. We care about the world, and we advocate for it in our own ways. I think Beth is asking you to find a way to fund yourself. Dad would need less money if he wasn't helping you out. Less expenses could mean decreasing the size of the herd or being able to hire help." He held up a hand to stop her disagreement. "I get it, you're passionate about your cause, and I admire that, but this is Dad's life. He's treated you like his own daughter from the time he started dating Sue. You could repay his kindness by reducing your demands on him."

"And I could spend less time working at the record store or traveling. Of course, I pay my own travel bills. I could spend time on the ranch," Jennifer piped in. "I can't do the heavy lifting, but I can clean tack and wash vehicles and help Mom out so she has more time for Dad. I'll let the store know I'll need fewer hours for a while and I'll postpone the trip I was planning to the Grand Canyon."

Candy glared at Jenn and flopped back into her seat. "Fine. I'll find a part time job. And do more advocating from home. I'll try to stick closer to town. What about you two?" Candy pointed at Jason and Carl.

"They're already running full-time businesses. Plus, Carl does all the vehicle maintenance at no cost and Jason barely charges anything to butcher and deliver meat orders for Dad." Jenn grinned to take the sting out of her words.

"And Riley?" Candy asked petulantly.

"I do all the ranch's vet work for the cost of supplies, and in case you've forgotten, I've got a brand-new daughter," Riley injected. "But I'm more than willing to pitch in where I can. Frankly, I think if we all pull together, we can pick up a good chunk of the work and lighten Dad's load. I'm game if you are." He glanced around the siblings, impressed by how thoughtful they looked. Nobody was rejecting the ideas out of hand.

"I'm in," Ken declared. "I'll do what I can. Together, we can make this work. With eight of us each picking up a small portion of chores, it adds up to a much lighter load for Dad."

Riley raised his beer glass. "To working together and making the ranch and the family stronger." They touched glasses around the table and leaned back to drink.

"What are we celebrating?"

Riley looked up to see Jo, Houston and Tricia standing at the end of the table.

"Hi guys." he responded, trying his best not to stare at Tricia. "Not a celebration as such, more an agreement." He read the questions in their eyes and responded with a casual, "Family stuff. What's up with you three?"

"Just enjoying a night out. Mind if we join you? We could use some help planning the Harvest Festival."

After a shuffling of chairs, everyone was seated. Riley was thrilled to have Tricia pressed firmly against his side, almost sitting on his lap. He couldn't think of a place he'd rather be at that moment, even if having her near and smelling her sexy perfume was driving him crazy.

CHAPTER NINETEEN

Whimpering woke Riley from a sound sleep. He'd been up late after the impromptu Harvest Festival planning session in the bar. When he arrived home, he'd sketched up a plan for a petting zoo and an area for the local shelter to display rescue animals looking for homes. They'd need another tent, but he was certain the family's wall tent would do the job. Made of sturdy canvas, the floorless tent could handle a lot of traffic and the hazards of unpredictable fall weather. Next, he shot off an email to an old friend about adding fireworks to the festival.

He rose from bed and slipped into a bathrobe knowing Ken's kids were sleeping on the floor in Daisy's room. The boys slept soundly, but Jane was perched on the edge of Daisy's bed, her expression filled with concern.

"Uncle Riley? I think Daisy's sick," Jane informed him. "She's very hot. Put your hand on her forehead like this." She demonstrated the age-old technique of checking for a fever by placing a hand against the forehead. He humored her by doing as she said.

Holy crap. She was burning up.

"She is hot," he said, keeping the panic from his voice and smiled reassuringly at Jane. "I guess we better find some Tylenol. Hang tight, I'll be right back." Great, he'd barely become a father and now he was smack dab in the middle of a medical crisis.

"First you have to check her temperature. The doctor will ask," she added wisely. "Do you have a thermometer?" she asked doubtfully.

"I do. You sit here with Daisy and I'll get what we need." He strolled from the room even though every part of him wanted to break into a panicked run. Maybe he should call his mother. Nope, not yet. He was a veterinarian. He could handle a fever.

He fumbled with the lockbox in the cupboard over the fridge, the one Tricia had insisted he use for all his medications. He hadn't argued much at the time, he knew kids could, and would, get into everything. Now, the key was miniscule in his uncoordinated fingers and he wished he'd ignored her advice. He needed something to bring Daisy's fever down. Now. After several failed attempts, he got the box open, grabbed the drugs, clicked the box shut and shoved the unlocked box back into the high cabinet.

He quickly took Daisy's temperature. One hundred degrees. High, but not scary high. After reading the bottle and confirming the dosage he enticed Daisy to sip the over-sweet liquid and followed it with a few sips of cool water.

"You should take her 'jamas off. Mommy makes me be mostly naked when I'm sick and she puts a cool cloth on my head," she ordered, hands on her hips, clearly in full mother-mode.

"Good idea. Daisy, can you slip out of your pajamas? I'll help you and then get a cool cloth for your head."

"I want my mommy," she cried, her eyes glistening with tears.

His chest cramped like someone had driven a knife into his heart. He'd known this moment was coming and knew he'd never be ready for it. He could handle any animal crisis relatively unscathed, but a sick daughter who wanted her dead mother? Lord help him.

"Mommy's gone to heaven. She'd come if she could. I'll bet she's looking down on you right now. I'll only be a minute. Jane will hold your hand until I come back."

Jane eagerly pushed her way between them and clutched her cousin's hand. "Being sick sucks. I hate it. I'll keep you safe." Her voice trembled a bit on the last word. "Uncle Riley is the bestest. He's an animal doctor, he can be your doctor too. He knows lots." She gave him a squinted look warning him she expected him to hurry.

"Be right back." He hurried to the kitchen and filled an ice cream bucket with lukewarm water, grabbed a facecloth and hurried into the bedroom.

Tears dribbled down Daisy's face, she curled up in a ball and moaned. "Riley it hurts," she wailed.

"It takes a few minutes until the Tylenol kicks in," he advised her, placing the cool moist cloth on her forehead for a moment before wiping her face. He wiped down her arms and legs hoping, knowing, the evaporation would accelerate the cooling process and bring down her fever.

"Where does it hurt?"

"Everywhere. My arms, my legs."

"How about your tummy?"

She nodded.

"Oh oh, you better get the barf bucket," Jane declared.

"Can you get it?" Riley asked. "There's another empty bucket in the bottom of the pantry." He wasn't worried about her upset stomach. Yet. She showed no signs of nausea. He suspected it was a general ache from the fever. But best to keep Jane busy and distracted.

She returned in two minutes and set the bucket on the nightstand beside the framed picture of Mona he'd given Daisy for her birthday along with her first bike. The small, white bedside table was precariously laden with piles of books and dolls. Jane picked up a few books and returned them to the shelf, stepping carefully over her brothers as she went. In minutes the table was cleared of clutter, then she started fussing with the blankets, folding them down, one at a time, until she had a neat pile across the bottom of the bed and only the sheet remained.

"Thank you, Jane. That's a good idea. Daisy won't need many blankets until she cools off a bit." The mothering instinct in her was so much like Beth and Sue he had to smile and her bossy, take charge attitude was so much like her mother, Lindy, he almost laughed.

He glanced at the boys who slept undisturbed by the quiet

commotion. Ken had warned him boys slept through anything and girls were little homemakers at heart. He'd doubted it, but it sure was true in this case. Jane climbed up on the opposite side of the bed and settled down beside Daisy, close, but not touching her.

"It's okay," she whispered. "Uncle Riley will take care of you and I'll stay right here." She pulled the sheet over herself and lay facing Daisy. She looked up at Riley and said, "Have you got this?"

"I've got this. Thanks for the help." He ruffled her hair and turned his attention to looking after Daisy.

The sun was creeping over the horizon when her fever was finally down to almost normal and she settled into a more restful sleep, his hand clutched in hers. It was the longest three hours he'd ever spent. Ever. Bar none. How did parents survive this? Caring for a sick child, his child, was exactly like caring for a sick animal but at the same time, it was nothing like it. His compassion for animals knew no bounds but he was always certain he'd do his best. Yeah, sometimes he lost the battle, but that was rare.

But with Daisy, every moment was fear laden. Every agonizing groan and harsh breath stole his confidence and cut into him, heart and soul. He never wanted to do this again. How had Mona managed alone? How did parents survive this without going insane? He threw the brakes on that train of thought before it totally derailed him and drew in a few calming breaths.

He leaned against the side of the bed and closed his eyes, resting a moment before it was time to medicate Daisy again.

Her temperature had dropped but it wasn't gone, he'd have to stay on top of the medication until the fever was gone entirely.

Jane's indignant whispers woke him.

"I told you. Uncle Riley and I were up all night looking after Daisy. You have to shut up and be quiet."

Riley peeked his eyes open. Jane towered over her brothers who wrestled on the floor. He glanced at his watch. Six? Jeepers, less than two hours of sleep last night. Today was going to be a killer. With luck, there wouldn't be any emergencies at the clinic. He made a mental note to let Houston know what was going on in case he was needed. Thank heaven for business partners.

"Morning, guys. Why don't you head downstairs and watch TV? I'll be down in a few minutes to make breakfast. We need to keep quiet and let Daisy sleep."

They leaped up and scrambled out the door. He heard them pushing and shoving all the way to the family room.

"Boys," Jane proclaimed with disgust, making Riley laugh.

"Boys will be boys," he commented.

"Riley? Don't go," Daisy pleaded.

He settled on the bed beside her. "Hey, good morning. How are you feeling?" He stroked her forehead; her fever was rising. Again. Damn.

"I'm sick," she groaned. "I want Mommy."

Here we go again.

"I know, honey. I'm here and I'll look after you."

"Me too." Jane climbed carefully on the bed. "My

mommy is gone too. I'll stay with you. We should go watch TV; it helps when you're sick."

Daisy nodded but frowned.

Riley put the Tylenol and thermometer into the unused barf bucket. He dumped the water from the other bucket and rinsed it and the cloth he'd been using. He handed them to Jane. "Can you carry these downstairs for me? I'll bring Daisy and her stuff."

He helped her into an airy, bright yellow nightgown patterned with frolicking kittens. He pulled the sheet free, wrapped Daisy in it, grabbed her pillow and favorite stuffed animal and carried them all downstairs. He settled her in his recliner and gave her an additional dose of medication. He'd give this a few more hours and if she didn't seem on the mend, he'd take her to the clinic or get Beth to pop over.

"Dontcha have a couch?" Jane asked.

"You know I don't," Riley teased back, trying to keep things normal.

"You should get one. This place looks like a man cave. You have to step up to your 'sponsibilities. I heard Grandma say so."

Riley laughed. "You're right. But right now, getting Daisy better comes first. More furniture comes later. I've got enough chairs for now." He glanced over; Daisy had fallen asleep already. He shooed the kids into the kitchen, made some notes on Daisy's care on a notepad and started breakfast.

Daisy slept restlessly through breakfast and was still asleep when Ken came to pick the kids up. For a moment, Riley thought Jane was going to be a problem. She pleaded to stay and help, until Ken declared, "Jane, get your backside into the van this instant. If you listen, you can phone Uncle Riley later and check on Daisy. If not, it's straight to your room for a time out. The choice is yours."

Her face screwed up in anger and disappointment, she stomped to the front door and outside. Behind the boy's backs, Ken sighed and rolled his eyes. "Kids are a pain in the ass sometimes," he mouthed without making a sound.

Riley laughed. "Maybe so, but Jane was a big help last night and this morning. She's got a caring heart and great mothering instincts. Having her here kept me calm. If I'd been alone, I know we'd be at the hospital. Although frankly, I'm not sure going isn't still an option."

Ken gave him a stinging swat on the shoulder. "Buck up, bro. You've got this. It gets easier with time. I'd have been lost without Lindy." He shrugged. "I still am. Although after our meeting in Sangudo, I think she isn't finding city law as glamorous as she thought it would be. There's hope for us yet." He looked skyward. "From my mouth to God's ears. Call me if you need anything or just need to talk." He ushered the kids outside and closed the door behind them.

The silence was deafening.

Riley's gaze travelled around the front entry and the living room where Daisy slept in his recliner. Usually he was glad when everyone was gone. Today the solitude was crippling, the house felt empty. Who was he kidding? His house was empty. Barely enough furniture for one person, let alone two. He would remedy that as soon as possible. As for being lonely, Daisy would wake soon and he'd have company.

There wasn't anything missing in his life, he just missed his daughter. Yeah, that was it!

Waiting for Daisy to wake, he slid into the other recliner with his lap desk and laptop and started searching Watson's Furnishings' website for ideas. Quickly overwhelmed, he concluded he had no idea what he wanted, let alone barely fathom what he needed. This might call for in person shopping. He powered down the laptop and sat watching Daisy.

Her breathing was steady, though her sleep was still restless. Her face was flushed and pale. The longer he watched the more anxious he became. What if she was sicker than he thought? What if he should have taken her to the doctor? The thoughts circled inside his head until he leaped to his feet to pace.

"No," he said aloud. "I'm a doctor. Okay, a veterinarian. I can do this. I have to disregard my family ties to her. Right. Like that's going to happen." He raked his fingers through his hair and wandered to the window.

His reflection reminded him he was still in his pajamas and bathrobe. How had Ken let that go? He sprinted upstairs, cleaned up a bit and slipped into some jeans and a T-shirt. He was back downstairs in under three minutes. Record time.

After checking Daisy again, he made toast and coffee, wondering what to do while she was sleeping. Sue always went about her normal routine; confident she'd hear if the sick child needed her. He didn't even want to run out to the clinic to get magazines or paperwork for fear Daisy would wake up while he was gone. Waiting was making him crazy.

"Riley?" Daisy's voice warbled from the other room.

He rushed to her side and stopped her before she tumbled out of the chair. "Sit still, sweetie."

"I have to pee." She pushed against his restraining hand. "Oh!"

The next sound he heard was liquid splattering on the floor.

"I'm sorry," Daisy wailed. "I didn't mean to. I'll clean it up."

The panic in her voice chopped his legs right out from under him. "Hey. Relax. It's okay. Everyone has accidents. You're sick. Are you finished?"

She shook her head.

"Come on then, let's get you to the bathroom to finish up. We'll clean you right up and get clean pajamas." The deed was quickly finished, and he wiped down the chair with hot, soapy water and dried it off. Thank goodness it was leather and not some super-absorbent fabric. They had a brief struggle over pajamas.

"I want the kitty ones," Daisy declared, referring to the lightweight nightgown she'd been wearing.

"It's wet." He had to stop this before it turned into a tantrum. "Tell you what—I'll put the kitty pajamas straight into the washer and you can have them back as soon as they're clean and dry. Okay?"

"'Kay." She pouted, but she donned a T-shirt for pajamas and settled back into her chair.

"Do you need something to eat? Toast? Cereal?"

"No. I need Miss Tricia."

Wow. It didn't take long for her to turn from shy and agreeable to a pouty princess. He bit back a sigh. This wasn't her fault. She was like a dog torn from its home, injured and thrust into a new environment with strangers. She was way out of her element. He realized he'd mentally referred to his daughter as a dog. Again. Crap. He had to get a handle on the way his mind worked. She was a child. A sick, confused and lonely child. He knelt beside her.

"I know you don't feel well and I know I'm a new person in your world. But I'm your dad and I love you." God, did he love her. This little bundle of fear had climbed right into his heart and taken root there. "That means you need to listen to me. Miss Tricia is busy. She has things to do. She's your teacher and our friend, but she isn't our family. We can't call her every time we think we need her."

He was explaining this badly. He needed to think like a child. "Today is Saturday. Tomorrow is Sunday. Then Monday, which is a school day. You'll feel much better by then and you can spend the whole day in school with her. Okay?"

"I want her now." She broke into hiccuping sobs. "Or my first Grandma and Grampa."

Now what? He wracked his brain. He couldn't remember ever having a tantrum while he was sick. Even when her kids were ill, Sue had rules. Tricia's voice echoed in his head reminding him he needed to establish rules and a routine. Was now the time to start sticking to his guns? Good gravy. It didn't feel right to cause Daisy further anguish and upset, but calling Tricia felt too personal and wrong.

Daisy began to wail in earnest, hysterical crying and loud hiccuping sobs. If she kept this up, she was going to make herself throw up. He gagged thinking about it.

"Grandma Ruth had to look after Grampa Frank because he had an operation. How about if I call Auntie Beth or Grandma Sue?" he pleaded.

"Noo," she stretched the word out into three syllables before wailing again.

He might be a shitty father for caving, but he was going to anyway. "I'll be right back; I'm just going into the kitchen." He'd call first. No sense getting her hopes up if Tricia was unavailable. He left her sobbing in the chair and made the call.

CHAPTER TWENTY

Curled up in the corner of the couch in front of the open window with her tea in one hand and book in the other, Tricia debated ignoring her cell phone when it rang. Deep into a science fiction best-seller, she had no desire to talk to anyone. This was her reading day; she'd been planning it for weeks. Between having severed her ties with her family and her old life, and only begun building new friendships, she didn't get many calls. She sighed and picked up the phone.

Riley.

Her heart went pit-a-pat when she read his name on the screen. Why would he be calling her? She debated ignoring her over-eager reaction by not answering, but it might be about Daisy or the festival so she set aside her book and picked it up on the third ring.

"Hello?"

"Tricia, thank heaven you answered," Riley proclaimed over the wailing in the background.

"What's up? Daisy sounds upset." She tried to sound casual, but the outburst was so atypical it concerned her. Something must be wrong.

"Daisy's got a fever and wants her mother, or grandparents. The only person who will do is you. She's begging for you. I debated not calling, but our relationship is so new and fragile I didn't want to risk damaging it before it even forms. I mean, my relationship with Daisy." He sighed heavily. "I hate to put a strain on our friendship, but could you come over for a while and help me out? I can't get her to eat. She won't stop crying."

Tricia did a double take. Surely, he didn't believe she'd mistakenly think he meant his relationship with her. They had no relationship; they were barely more than acquaintances. The naked pleading in his voice made her smile. In the background, Daisy's wails increased in volume. Glory be, she couldn't let the wee one suffer. She'd already been through so much in her short life.

"I'll come. Once. This is the only time. After this, you're on your own." It felt like she was running to his rescue again. Three times in the few weeks they'd known each other she'd helped him out. This made four. She wasn't counting, exactly, but he was going to have to step up his game and become stronger. She sighed at her own callousness. Who was she kidding? He was a bachelor way out of his depth and she'd seen for herself that Sue, his first line of defense, was wrapped up in worries about the family patriarch's health issues.

"Tell her I'm on my way," she said into the receiver. "I

need to make a quick stop. Do you need anything? Do you have medication?"

"I've got meds. I can't think of anything. Thank you for this. You're a godsend."

Half an hour later she stood outside his door. Inside, Daisy was howling. The noise stopped instantly when she knocked. Oh yeah, full on tantrum. This was not good.

The door flew open as if he were waiting for her. "Come in! Please."

"Riley. Hi." She stepped inside and closed the door behind her. She leaned close to him and whispered, "Don't let her see you're upset. Let her think you're totally calm."

"Why?" he whispered back.

"You need to be in control. If she figures out you've lost it, she's in control. Kids need to know there's someone strong standing behind them to keep them safe. We'll talk about it later." She took a deep breath. Sweet heaven, he smelled delicious, like coffee, man and the barest hint of musky aftershave which must be leftover from yesterday, he had a serious five o'clock shadow she wanted to run her fingers over. She shook her head and slipped out of her shoes and walked inside.

"Hi, Daisy. Dad tells me you aren't feeling well. What's up?" Tricia sat on a kitchen chair beside the recliner. Riley must have put it there.

"I'm sick."

"That's what your Dad told me. I hear you're giving him a rough time."

Daisy hung her head and refused to meet Tricia's eyes.

"You have to cut him some slack. He's new to being a parent. He's still learning. Just like you're still learning to have a Daddy." She pressed her hand against Daisy's forehead, her fever was evident but not out of control.

"I miss my mommy."

Riley set another chair on the opposite side of the recliner and grasped Daisy's hand. "I'm sure you do."

"Tell us about her," Tricia suggested. "What did you like to do together?" She winked at Riley hoping to let him know this was a distraction technique as well as information mining.

"Mommy worked lots but we slept together every night after we moved to Grandma and Grampa's house. Mommy was sick." Tears brimmed again.

"I can't bring your mother back, but I'll look after you," Riley declared. "You're my daughter now. I'll protect you and love you."

Tricia nodded her approval. Getting Daisy to talk about her family was important. Kids needed to know what they valued was important to others. They talked a bit about Daisy's mom and she began to relax.

"Did you eat today?" Tricia asked. Daisy shook her head. "Sweetheart, you need to eat. How about some Jell-O or a popsicle?"

"Potsicle."

Out of the corner of her eye, Tricia saw Riley raise one eyebrow in question as she raised hers. Great minds think alike.

"Please," Daisy added, taking the hint.

They chatted while she slurped on the treat. How sad that

Daisy had lost her mother and her grandparents. At least her grandparents would be back when her grandfather recovered. Tricia helped Daisy focus her attention on the positives of sharing time and helping Daisy feel better. They watched television for an hour until she drifted off.

"Would you like a coffee?" Riley asked.

"Sure, coffee would be nice." She was desperate for a caffeine hit. Being part of this family was shaking her up and she needed the familiar stabilizing influence of coffee cradled between her hands. Tea was more calming, but coffee always helped her think and cleared her thoughts. Five minutes later, she had her coffee. "That was fast."

Riley smiled and patted the coffee maker. "Industrial pot. Brews in three minutes when it's new. But this gal is getting old, she's down to almost five."

"Very nice. I use a pod pot with a reusable pod. I dislike the waste of the throw away ones, but I don't often need a full pot. When I do, I use an old-school perk."

"Cowboy coffee. When we went camping as kids, Dad used a Coleman stove and a percolator. Best coffee I've ever had." A warm smile lit his face.

"You didn't camp with Sue?"

"We did, but things changed once Sue and the girls showed up on the scene. With dad and us five boys it was target shooting, fishing, hunting, horseback riding and quadding. You know, guy stuff. With the girls, it became nature walks and marshmallow roasts." His voice was soft with the memory. "Beth tried hunting, she's a wicked good shot, but Candy won't hurt or eat an animal. I can't imagine being a vegetarian, but it works for her."

"And you loved camping both ways."

He looked thoughtful. "You know, I did, but Sue changed everything. It kind of felt like they were stealing my family." He shrugged and sipped his coffee.

"That must have hurt you," she commiserated. How sad for a boy who'd lost his mother to feel like someone was stealing the rest of his family. They were close now, the Flint boys and the girls who'd joined the family, but for an insecure child, the transition must have been difficult.

"I'm okay. I survived." He stared out the window.

He was not okay. Anyone with half an ounce of empathy could see he still hurt despite his love for his extended family. What would it take for him to feel he belonged? What would it take for Daisy to feel she belonged? Perhaps their wounded pasts would bring them closer together and heal them both.

"You know, Daisy must feel similar, as if she doesn't belong," Tricia said. "She's lost her entire family and was taken in by a man with an enormous family. It must be mind boggling for her."

"I'm trying to help her see we all love her even though we're only getting to know her. I wish to hell I'd known she existed. I would have married her mother and supported them. I wouldn't have left them to make it alone."

There was no doubt Daisy's mother had loved her. Riley had told Tricia about the notes and videos Mona left behind for her daughter. It must be devastating to lose your mother's love and have your remaining family turn you over to a stranger.

"Take your feelings, your memories and use them to guide you in dealing with Daisy. They echo what she's feeling. Knowing you once felt like she does and have gotten beyond it will help her heal."

"That's what the shrink said," he said, his voice laden with disbelief.

"Oh. I didn't know you guys had seen a doctor." She knew he was thinking about it, but Daisy hadn't mentioned it even though she often told Tricia every detail of her life.

"I saw him. I thought it would be best to discuss things in advance so he'd know a bit of the history before Daisy saw him. We ended up talking about me a lot and how my life would color hers. Do you have any idea how difficult dealing with kids is?"

She laughed until her belly hurt. "Oh, Riley. Sorry. I'm not laughing at you. Well, I am but not the way you think. Did you forget I'm a teacher?" She chuckled when his smile turned to a frown. "I spend seventy-five percent of my waking hours with children. Okay, maybe not that much but it feels that way sometimes. One thing I do know is kids are all different with different needs and abilities. You've got to roll with the punches and deal with what life hands you. They'll surprise you more often than not. Kids are resilient and strong if they know they've got backup."

"She's got backup. Me. So why did she want you?"

"Easy. I spend more time with her than you do. I know you're her father, but you also split your time with her with your family. She doesn't have you to herself much." Part of him must feel like she was a traitor, stealing his child's love, she mused.

"She shares you with nearly two dozen other kids."

"And I'm always there for them. All of them as a unit. At least during school hours and I've pinch hit for you a couple times. To Daisy, I'm familiar, comfortable. You're a man, and therefore you're weird."

"I am not weird," he protested and dropped into the chair opposite to Tricia.

"You are to a six-year-old girl who spent most of her time around women."

Soft steps approached the kitchen and they dropped the subject as Daisy, sleep-rumpled and flushed entered the kitchen. She climbed into Tricia's lap and wrapped her arms around Tricia's neck.

"Hi, sweetie," Riley greeted her. "Feeling any better?"

She nodded but didn't speak.

"Would you like something to eat or drink?"

Another nod.

"Okay, first we check your temperature and then we'll feed you."

Riley checked her temperature and then his notes on when he'd last medicated Daisy, impressing Tricia with his thoroughness. "So, what's the verdict, Dad?" she asked.

"Still hot and climbing but it's too early for more drugs. I think maybe she should go to the hospital." He frowned when Daisy whimpered.

"What about the walk-in clinic?" Tricia suggested. "The

wait time is likely shorter and they'll send her to the hospital if she needs to be there." Coyote Creek had a dual-purpose medical clinic. Doctors booked appointments in the usual fashion for office hours, but they also remained open for unscheduled patients seven days a week, nine in the morning until nine at night. It was never difficult to get in to see the doctor on call.

"I'm hungry." After a miniscule serving of macaroni and cheese followed up by two tablespoons of Jell-O, Daisy's fever continued to climb.

"Do you think we should take her in?" Riley asked pacing back and forth in the kitchen.

"It's up to you. I'm no doctor, but I expect it's a virus. Lots of kids in the school were out with it last week."

"I am a doctor, well a vet, and I have no idea what to do." His fingers drummed on the countertop. "You know what? I'm taking her in. I need the peace of mind."

"Can Miss Tricia come?" Daisy's small voice piped in.

Riley and Tricia shared a look and Riley nodded. "This time, but next time you get sick, Miss Tricia won't be coming. I'm your daddy and it's my job to look after you. I *want* to look after you. We'll keep Miss Tricia as our special friend. Okay?"

Daisy looked like she might rebel but, in the end, she relented.

In his mid-sixties, the clinic doctor was quick and efficient. He pronounced the illness a virus and gave Riley a printout of follow-up care instructions. "She'll probably be on the mend by tomorrow, if this holds true of my other patients' experiences. She's quite thin and doesn't have much for reserves so it might take her a while to bounce back. I'd like you to book an appointment for a physical as soon as you can. Bring any records you have, vaccinations and family history."

He clapped Riley on the back. "You've got this. Parenting's tough but you've got a quick mind and strong family support. You'll make it through this. Some day you'll look back on this and wonder why you worried."

CHAPTER TWENTY-ONE

Riley sat on one side of Daisy's bed, Tricia on the other tucking Daisy in. The day had been interminable. Too sick to be awake, not sick enough to sleep all day, Daisy had been cranky and hard to deal with. She didn't want to read or watch television. She didn't want to play with her toys. She'd ask to be held and two minutes later she'd climb down and pout. Exhausted and overwrought, she struggled against sleep.

"I'll sing to you," Riley offered as he tucked her in bed for the tenth time.

Daisy stopped struggling and looked at him expectantly.

"I'm not very good, but here goes." He started singing ABCs. Then Twinkle Twinkle and every other kid song he could think of. Her eyes were growing heavy but she wasn't asleep and he was out of material. He glanced helplessly at Tricia.

She opened her mouth and softly began singing an old country song about angels. Riley stared slack-jawed at her. Her voice was strong and true. She'd never make a career singing, but she had a lovely voice. He joined in at the chorus and by the time the song was finished Daisy had drifted off.

They eased off the bed and tidied up the room without speaking.

"The photograph's a nice touch." Tricia pointed to the picture of Daisy's mother. "So is that." She indicated the three-picture frame hanging over Daisy's bed. The pictures were from their shopping trip the day after Daisy arrived. Daisy's photo was on the left and Riley's on the right. Between them was a picture of all three of them hamming it up for the camera.

Riley grinned and his cheeks flushed. "I wanted her to remember her first day with me. You were a big part of the day. I developed all the pictures I took. They're in an album on the bookcase. There are a few of us shopping and in the park. Half a dozen candid shots from Mom's birthday and a couple taken after her room was set up."

"Fabulous. They'll mean a lot when she's older."

"I hope so. I also made an album of the few pictures in the box from the Ables. There weren't many. I expect Mona, Daisy's mom, couldn't afford to print many. Later I'll get to the hundreds of pictures on CD." He sighed heavily. "I wish I'd followed up in person rather than just calling after I stopped seeing Mona. One of life's hard lessons. Everybody lies."

"Not everybody," Tricia countered.

"Everybody. Some only tell little white lies, others tell whoppers. Keeping Daisy from me was more than a whopper. Although I'm glad she named me on the birth certificate. I'm glad the Ables found me and brought me into Daisy's life. Though I wonder if they would have if they were stronger and healthier."

Tricia crossed the room and gripped his arm. "She's lucky to have you. And me. She has your entire family. Plus, I'm sure half the town, or more, is rooting for her. Although I've heard a complaint or two because you aren't in the bar much lately."

He groaned. "My reputation as a lady's man is highly overstated."

"Is it undeserved? I heard a lot of stories about you taking women home. A different one every night." Her hand flew from his arm to her mouth. "Sorry."

"Relax. I know all about the rumors. I drive them home. I rarely have more than one beer, two max. I'm a big boy. I can have two drinks and not be drunk, especially when they're spread over several hours. I drive drunk women home and drop them off. If I don't go back to the bar it's because I came home." He dropped to the floor against the wall. He bent his legs and rested his head on his knees.

"I let the rumors go unchecked. They keep the serious long-timers, the happily ever afters, away. I'm not ready to date seriously, now more than ever. The trouble is, I have to figure out how to keep my reputation from hurting Daisy. I mean look at Kyle Broderbund. The kid's never done anything wrong. His dad's a drunk and his mother works like a dog to support him. The kids are mean to him because of his father. It isn't right."

"Kids can be cruel. They're fighting to find their place in the world. It'll work out. Especially now that Daisy and Jane have taken him under their wing. He's got friends now and the other kids are more accepting. Your daughter has a big heart, like her father." Tricia slid down the wall to sit beside him, her shoulder brushing his. She nudged against him as if reinforcing her words.

"Is that how you see me? Just like that, you believe in me?" he asked.

"I believe in you."

Something loosened in his chest at the firm statement. "And you trust me?"

She was quiet for so long he thought she might not answer. Eventually, she spoke. "I trust you with children. I know you're great with animals and are trying to do the best you can for your family and friends." At his questioning look she added, "The rumors don't match with what you're saying. But they don't not match either."

"I explained that. Don't you believe my innocence?" He couldn't stop himself from poking at it like sticking his tongue on a sore tooth.

"Honestly? I'm undecided."

Her shoulder shifted against his arm, warm and soft and welcoming. Despite her words, tension flowed out of him.

Talking to her was easy. She seemed to pull thoughts and feelings out of him with little effort, almost as if she could see inside to who he really was. "I appreciate your honesty."

"Honesty is important to me," she replied. "Which doesn't mean I go blurting out my life story to everyone. My past is over and done. It doesn't reflect who I am now."

"I disagree. Our past shapes who we are, who we become. We change because of our life experiences, and they definitely influence our decisions." He jumped to his feet, uncomfortable with the sudden depth of their conversation. "Want some dinner? Wine?"

She looked up at him, questions in her eyes, leaving him with no doubt she'd revisit this conversation if she got the chance. She held out her hand and he pulled her to her feet. She stumbled a bit and slipped into his arms. Before he could react, she'd slipped her arm around his waist and guided him toward the door. "Feed me, cowboy."

"I'm a vet, not a cowboy."

She laughed. "Right, you've got the boots, the jeans, the Stetson and the button-down western shirts. You've got horses, you're from a ranching family. You, Riley Flint, are a cowboy through and through. Your past made you who you are."

"And you, Tricia Paxton, what are you?"

"Hungry." She skipped down the stairs to the kitchen leaving him staring at her back and wondering what she was avoiding talking about. He suspected now wasn't the time to push it. She was fast becoming a good friend and he didn't want to risk chasing her away. She wasn't close to many people in town, he felt privileged to be one of them.

Three hours of light conversation, a steak dinner and two bottles of wine later, Tricia started to yawn. "I really should be going."

"Are you serious? After all that wine? There's no way I'll let you drive anywhere." He'd already hidden the car keys she'd left on the table by the front door.

She reached across the table and patted his cheek. "Aw, Riley, my hero. Every woman's hero. I'll call Jo for a ride."

Her palm was warm and soft against his cheek, for a moment, he wanted to turn his head a fraction of an inch and kiss her palm, which would result in a sound smack unless he missed his guess.

"Leave Jo alone. It's late. You can sleep in my bed and I'll sleep with Daisy. I was planning on sleeping with her anyway. You won't be putting me out."

"I have no pajamas."

"I'll lend you a shirt."

"I have no toothbrush."

"I've got spares. Any other objections?" He grinned knowing he was winning this argument come hell or high water.

"I suppose not. Lead the way, cowboy. I'm ready to hit the hay."

Upstairs, he gathered what he needed to sleep in Daisy's room and showed Tricia to his room. He gave her a toothbrush and they said goodnight and stood for a moment looking at each other until he stepped out of the room and closed the door behind him. Leaning against the wall, he listened to the soft sounds of her moving around in the bedroom and bathroom. Only when he heard the bedside lamp click off did he head into Daisy's room and stretch out on the floor.

CHAPTER TWENTY-TWO

Tricia was surprised to see Riley outside her classroom when the dismissal bell rang the next Friday. He usually met Daisy outside the school or had one of his siblings pick her up. After the first week of school, Tricia realized it was standard practice for a random member of the Flint family to pick up the kids. Sometimes it was Sue and Robert or one of their girls. Once, Jason had picked them up and walked them to the butcher shop. Rarely did anyone enter the school after Tricia became aware of the family's casual, yet flawless, pickup system.

"Mr. Flint, what can I do for you?"

"Hi, Riley," Daisy greeted him.

"Why don't you run outside and play with your cousins in the playground? I'll be right out. I need to talk to your teacher for a minute," he said.

"Okay. Bye, Miss Tricia," Daisy called and raced into the

hallway. They listened to her steps until they faded around the corner.

"What can I do for you?" Tricia asked. "Is everything okay?"

"Everything is great. She's bounced back from the virus and is gaining some weight. Doc gave her a clean bill of health and her immunizations are up to date. I'm not here about Daisy." He paused and studied the polished toes of his boots.

"What is it Riley?" She touched his shoulder.

"I was wondering…"

"Yes?"

"Well, I was wondering if you'd-like-to-have-dinner-with-us, tonight?" He rushed the last words together into one breathless word. She didn't reply, so he looked up from his boots. She was smiling. He floundered, waiting for an answer. Was she laughing at him?

"We can go to my place if you don't want to be seen in public with me?"

"So, this is to be a dirty little secret then?" The corners of her mouth twitched.

Was she kidding? Talking to women had never felt like a minefield before. "Um. No. I didn't mean it like that. I just meant… I know you don't date much and I don't think you'd feel comfortable dating a parent. I thought—" his flood of disjointed words ground to a halt.

"Relax, Riley. I'm teasing. Dinner at your place will be fine. Unless you'd prefer to go out." She quirked an eyebrow in question.

"We can go out if you want to."

"What do you prefer?" she asked.

"To spend some time with you. No pressure. No games. No interruptions. You and I eating and talking. I enjoyed your company last weekend while we looked after Daisy. I'd like to spend time with you without worry intruding. I can get Sue to babysit so we can go out, I'm sure she wouldn't mind. Or we can eat early with Daisy or you could come over later after she goes to bed; which would be my choice. Quiet, adult time. Daisy goes to bed around seven-thirty. Any time after that would be great. I thought we could do either grilled chicken or steak. Baked potatoes and salad." Good grief, he couldn't stop the words from spewing out.

"I'd love another of those delicious steaks. I'll bring dessert."

"Can I pick you up? Oh, crap. Daisy will be asleep." He groaned. It was incredibly frustrating to be suddenly tied down and unable to drive off whenever he chose to.

"I'll drive myself. The drive is beautiful this time of year with the leaves starting to turn color." She laughed. "Listen to us. We sound like two strangers. I thought we were friends."

He ran the conversation over in his head. "Wow, awkward. I apologize. I haven't asked anyone out in a long time. Too long."

"Is this a date or friends meeting for dinner?"

What did she want it to be? He couldn't tell. He just wanted to spend time with her; nothing more, nothing less. Yet. "Can we decide later? Start as friends and see what happens?"

"I think I'd like that. I'll see you around seven-thirty, Riley."

They stared at each other awkwardly for a moment. Tricia blushed and Riley grinned. "Catch you later," he said with a wink and turned to walk away.

TRICIA HURRIED home from school and took a long relaxing bath. She styled her hair and put on her minimal makeup. Discrete jewelry, her favorite linen skirt which ended, perfectly demurely, above her knee. Silk blouse and low heels. She looked personable, slightly professional, approachable and dare she say it? Dateable. One last check in the mirror and she was ready for her non-date date. She glanced at her watch. Wow. She'd spent two hours in the tub.

Thank goodness the bakery was open late. She didn't have anything even remotely resembling dessert in her apartment. She snatched her purse and keys off the counter when her phone rang. She glanced at the display.

Jo. Darn.

She didn't have time to talk to her bestie but if she didn't answer Jo would keep calling. She clicked the icon to accept the call.

"Hi, Jo."

"Hey. Houston and I are going to the Bar None tonight for a couple beers. Want to join us? He's going to ask Riley."

Tricia performed some mental gymnastics to find an

answer and settled on a half-truth. "Gee, I'd love to, but I've already made other plans for the evening."

"Like what? Washing your hair? Pedicure?" Coming from her best friend, the teasing didn't hurt. They were her usual excuses.

"I'm having dinner out. With a friend." Silence followed her answer.

"You never go out," Jo blurted.

"I know." Tricia sighed. "It's the first time since I came to Coyote Creek. It's not a date, exactly, it's dinner with a man. We can talk about it later. I'm running late already. Bye." She disconnected the call and ignored the subsequent ringing and the questions that would follow if she answered.

"Hi, Elsie," Tricia greeted the peppy senior citizen and owner of Cakes and More, the ever-popular bakery which shared a building with Jason Flint's butcher shop and two other stores. She'd always adored the two-story red brick building with its white shutters and delicate trim work. The smell of fresh baking enticed her to stop in, more often than her waistline needed. Tonight, chocolate, cinnamon and vanilla tickled her nose and fired up her taste buds. The entire bakery smelled of comfort and love.

"Tricia, so good to see you. You haven't been in since— probably since the start of summer vacation. What can I get you?"

"I'm not sure. I'm joining a friend for dinner and I said I'd buy dessert." She studied the well-stocked displays of cookies, cakes, donuts and tarts. Every sort of baked good was displayed deliciously.

"Well, Jo's partial to the mint chocolate cheesecake."

"It's not for Jo." She looked away to hide the color staining her cheeks.

"Ah, you'll want the black forest cake then. It's the last one. Made fresh this morning." She winked. "It's Riley's favorite, aside from the delicious things Sue makes."

There was no sense denying it. To pretend she wasn't seeing Riley would add to the rumor and speculation. She might as well meet it head-on. "Perfect. How did you know?"

"Basic math. You've been helping Riley with wee Daisy. Tragic story. I'm glad she's finally with her father. You've got your car and you usually walk. You don't go out much and it isn't with your bestie, Jo. Who else could it be? Riley's a keeper, you mark my words and ignore the rumors about him." She hustled around boxing the cake and tying it with a bright blue ribbon. "All those boys are well worth any trouble they might cause. Once, I thought my own granddaughter, Nicole, might end up with Jason, but she ran off to the city. She'll be back though; Coyote Creek has a way of calling her people home and when it calls her, Jason'll be right where she left him."

Tricia's cell phone rang in her purse. She let it go to voicemail. It rang again.

"Aren't you going to get that dear?" Elsie quirked one eyebrow.

"No, I'm ignoring her."

"Jo? No doubt she'll have a thousand questions." Elsie laughed, a wide, knowing grin lit her face. "She's persistent.

Ignoring her might be a smart move. Anything else for you today?"

"Not tonight. Thanks."

Tricia, head spinning from the one-sided conversation, paid for the cake and hot footed it to her car. How could she have forgotten the ever-efficient rumor mill. If she'd gone to the grocery store, she could have had a dessert without the fifth-degree. She knew better for next time. If there was a next time. But then, as good as grocery store baking was, it didn't compare to Cakes and More.

Tricia knocked and waited for Riley to answer. After a moment, she knocked again, avoiding the doorbell; she didn't want to wake Daisy. Muffled cussing came from inside and the door flew open.

Riley stood there, his jeans unbuckled, dipping wet and shirtless. Holy cow. She tried not to stare but her eyes wouldn't abandon the curves of his muscles or the flat planes of his abdomen.

"Come in. I'll go get dressed." He turned and walked away.

"What happened?"

"Small accident with a bottle of salad dressing. Stay out of the kitchen until I clean it up. Please. Give me two minutes." He raced up the stairs.

An accident with salad dressing that ended up with him soaking wet and half naked? "This I've got to see." She set her purse on the table by the door, slipped out of her shoes and wandered to the kitchen. Thick, creamy, fuchsia liquid dripped off every surface. Fridge, counter, table, doors, walls, even the ceiling had something dripping off it. What kind of dressing was fuchsia?

Laughter threatening to seep out, she minced to the sink and started filling it with hot soapy water. Rummaging through the drawers, she found two dishcloths and clean tea towels. There was no way they could eat until the mess was gone. There wasn't much she could do about the stains on the ceiling but she could wipe down the cupboard doors and walls. She started close to the sink, the epicenter of the explosion and worked her way outward.

"Tricia? Where are you?"

"In the kitchen," she called back. "Getting a head start on the explosion."

"You didn't have to clean up. I would have gotten it." He paused. "Holy crap, it's worse than I thought. But then, I was half blinded by Sue's creamy raspberry ranch dressing. And she said it was easy."

"Apparently not," Tricia chuckled. "Is the taste as explosive as the dressing was?"

"Hardy har har. Not funny."

"No, it's funnier. Look at this place." She waved around the kitchen and tossed him a damp cloth. "Get cleaning, Chef Riley. How'd you manage this anyway?" she asked as he deftly snagged the rag out of the air.

"It doesn't matter. We'll have to eat store dressing tonight."

"Oh no." She mock glared at him. "You're not getting off so easily. 'Fess up, cowboy." There was a good story behind this, she could feel it.

"I'll finish cleaning up the mess." He dodged answering her.

"'Fess up or I'll pitch the Cakes and More black forest cake I brought into the trash."

He opened his mouth, closed it and opened it again. He swallowed hard. "You play dirty, Tricia Paxton. Really dirty. I chopped up the berries, added all the ingredients to the jar." He waved at the mason jar in the sink. "I shook it up and opened it to taste it. It wasn't sweet enough. I added a bit of sugar and screwed the lid back on and all hell broke loose."

Laughter bubbled inside Tricia as she imagined his surprise. "You didn't screw the lid on all the way, did you?" She laughed until her stomach hurt. "How hard did you shake it to make it explode?"

"Yeah, yeah. Laugh it up. You're not the one wearing raspberry cologne." A smile curved up the corner of his mouth.

"Raspberry cologne? Let me see." She stepped up to him and inhaled deeply. "Oh yeah, you do smell berry good." She snickered. "Wait, what's that behind your ear?" She reached out and grabbed something pink from behind his ear. "A raspberry?"

"It is not," he declared.

"Is too. Didn't you shower?" she teased, trying to hide her laughter.

"I did but I was in a hurry. I didn't want to be showering when you got here. As it was, I was getting out when you knocked. Have you ever tried putting jeans on wet legs?"

Tricia laughed harder. She clamped a hand over her mouth. "Sorry," she mumbled through her fingers.

He squinted at her. "Watch yourself, there's still dressing everywhere. It's not too late to dress you up."

She groaned at the bad word play and raised her hands. "I promise not to tease you too much." She backed away from him and picked up her cloth. After rinsing it in the sink, she resumed cleaning. "You going to stand there or are you going to help out? I'm starving." She gave him a quick glance over her shoulder. He looked torn between laughter and chagrin and completely undecided about what came next.

"Suck it up, cowboy. Accidents happen but I won't be responsible for what happens to you if I don't get fed. I'll get hangry…very hangry." She winked over her shoulder and whipped back around to face the sink, hiding her amused reaction to the stunned look on his face.

Twenty minutes later, the steaks were on the grill, Tricia had rescued the potatoes from the oven and the threat of over-baking. The table was set and a salad with oil and vinegar dressing sat waiting. Tricia's eyes widened when Riley slid a platter with two enormous rib-eye steaks on the table.

"Holy cow, those are huge, and they smell incredible," she exclaimed. "I think barbecued beef just became my favorite smell. I'm hungry, but I don't know if I can eat that much meat with potato and salad." She looked at the food spread before her. Everything looked delicious and smelled even better. The steak had perfect grill lines and the fatty edges were curled up and crispy without the center appearing overdone.

"Take the small one, I'll eat the bigger one. The meat scraps and bones will go to Dad's dogs. They like a treat now and then. You said medium-rare, I cooked them as close as I could. My barbecue is getting finicky. I think it needs a new regulator. It's on my ever-growing to-do list." He joined her at the table, he closed his eyes, inhaled deeply and after a moment he opened his eyes and started eating.

He waved his fork at her. "Go ahead, dig in, before it gets cold."

"I will and thank you for supper."

Conversation was light and easy while they ate. She was impressed by his devotion to his family and the animals he cared for. A secret part of her heart whispered if she was looking for a man, for someone to share her life with, Riley had serious potential to be that man. She brushed the thought away. She wasn't looking for romance. She was getting by, day-by-day, and hoping to build a life here and keep her reputation intact.

They delayed dessert for a while and settled into the family room's mismatched recliners. Riley insisted she take the new, more comfortable one. Out of the blue, Riley hit her with a bomb of a question. "What brought you to Coyote Creek? Jo said she knew you in the city."

"We went to school together. She used to spend summers here with her grandmother and loved it so much she applied for a teaching position straight out of university." Maybe the non-answer would satisfy his curiosity. She didn't want to get into her history and why she ended up in this tiny town in north central Alberta and far away from the city she grew up in. Were there rumors? Did everyone know? Panic flashed through her veins as she fought to stay seated and sip her wine when every instinct told her to cut and run.

"That explains how Jo ended up here, but not you. You lived in Edmonton. What prompted you to leave?" His glance was casual. Interested but not prying.

"I was desperate for a job. Jo told me there was a temp position here and I applied. I guess small towns aren't the most popular places to get a job. I know I hadn't considered it until it got tough to find work in the city."

"I didn't realize teachers found it hard to get jobs."

She stared into her wine glass. She came to Coyote Creek to escape her past, not relive it. Her stomach clenched and the delicious dinner she'd consumed threatened to make a return appearance. Maybe if she ignored the question, he'd let it drop.

"You don't have to talk about it if you don't want to. I'm not one to gossip, but last week I bumped into Jo and she warned me you had things in your past which weren't what they seemed."

Tricia gasped. How could Jo betray her?

He held up his hands reassuringly. "All she said was if I heard anything about your past to take it with a grain of salt. I've known her for a couple years, I trust her. Does your past have anything to do with having trouble finding a job?" His tone was gentle and he seemed genuinely interested.

Why was he pushing this? More importantly, what had possessed her best friend to gossip about her? Her chest tightened. She felt like she was whirling out of control. It was the old days all over again. Friends abandoning her. Her fiancé dumping her for her best friend and acting as if Tricia had never been in his life. It was a knife stab to her guts all over again.

Her hands formed into fists. Her shoulders bunched and rose to her ears. She battled the urge to roll into the fetal position and hide. Tears loomed and her vision blurred. Time to go home.

She collapsed the footrest of the recliner with a thump. "Listen, thanks for dinner. It was great." She swallowed hard. "I have to go."

He was beside her, a gently restraining hand on her forearm before she got to the door. "Hey, I didn't mean to upset you. We don't have to talk about this. I'm sorry I upset you. Please stay."

She eased her arm from his grasp. He released her without complaint and she sucked in a shuddering breath. Shoot. She closed her eyes and counted to ten. This was going to follow her forever. She might as well get it out in the open now. It wouldn't hurt her job, the school board was aware of her history, they always had been and she had a glowing performance review from parents and Principal Keller at the end of last year. She'd be okay. Professionally. Personally, not so much.

She looked up at Riley. He smiled reassuringly. Would an honest, hard working man like him be able to understand her twisted past? Could she make him understand she was nothing more than an innocent pawn? Did it even matter what he thought?

Yeah. It did. He was happy and fun to be with. He was working hard to become a good father. And she liked him. A lot. More than she should from a professional standpoint. Suddenly, she wanted him to know. Could he understand her past and how it crushed her and made her wary of friendships? Aside from Jo and Houston, he was her only real friend. The people she worked with were acquaintances. Fear kept her from opening up to them.

Her gaze flitted around the nearly empty room, lighting for a moment on the jumbo television and the two recliners. The room held precious little else. A few discarded books and toys lay in one corner, a sure sign Daisy was branching out and becoming comfortable enough to abandon her precious possessions and know they'd be there for her later. If Daisy could put her trust in this man, maybe Tricia could too.

"Please don't go," Riley repeated.

She pivoted and returned to her chair. Electric jolts of tension sputtered through her creating a feeling of chaos, like a flickering light bulb. She perched on the edge of her chair; hands clenched together.

"What do you want to know?" she blurted.

"Only what you're comfortable talking about." He sat on the front of his chair, leaning toward her, elbows on his knees, hands dangling between them. At a glance, he seemed relaxed; but his jaw clenched and his eyes squinted a fraction of an inch as if he were the one with everything on the line.

"I worked for a private school in Edmonton," she began. "I taught grade one. Since I was a kid, maybe seven, I wanted to be a grade one teacher. Not grade two or three. Grade one. I think, maybe, I was in love with my teacher, Miss Marple. She was perfect. Kind, loving, generous. She never lost her temper. She was amazing. I wanted to be exactly like her. All through school, through teachers, good, bad and worse, the vision never faded. I hurried through university, taking summer school every year to finish early." She felt her lips curl up at the memories. She shook her head.

"I scored a temp job at a private school; I was filling in for maternity leave. The teacher never returned and I kept the job. I think private schools and small-town schools have a little more leeway in their hiring practices than fully public schools." She waved the idea off. "Doesn't matter, I got the job and I kept it.

"It was great. My parents worked for the school. I met my fiancé there." And boy howdy, didn't she wish she'd never met him.

"You have a fiancé?" He sounded incredulous.

"You don't have to sound shocked. I'm not totally un-dateable. And it's ex-fiancé now."

"Thank heaven. I wouldn't want to hone in on another man's territory."

There were so many issues with his statement she didn't know where to begin. She ignored the idea of a woman being a man's property, certain he didn't mean it the way it sounded. But honing in? Weren't they just friends? She raised her eyebrows at him.

"Can I finish? This isn't easy for me to talk about." She didn't wait for permission. If she stopped talking, she'd never finish. The memories were knives to her soul, hacking off slices and slashing her heart to shreds. But he asked and he'd get the full, unedited version and she'd walk away.

"A few years later, an audit revealed there was money missing from the school's accounts. A lot of money. An investigation was started. When the culprits were found, the fallout was brutal." The hand wrapped around her wine glass ached and she worried she'd snap the fragile stem. Her other hand fisted on her knee. Her neck and back ached with tension from holding herself in place when she every instinct said to flee.

"My parents, the school's accountants, embezzled nearly three million dollars." She dashed away the tears rolling down her cheeks. "I was fired along with them. After all, I was family, I must have known," she drawled sarcastically. "I didn't know. I had no idea. But I was tarred and feathered along with them. Nobody would hire me. It took every penny I had, and then some to prove my innocence. When it was all cleared up, I went camping in the mountains for a week to think and settle myself. To calm down and regroup. When I came home, I found my fiancé in our bed with my best friend. I kicked them out and got rid of the bed."

"Shit." His low, muttered curse touched something inside her.

"Our wedding was six weeks away." Her voice shook. "She was supposed to be my maid of honor. Not only did I lose my family, my fiancé, my closest friend and my job, I lost thousands of dollars in wedding deposits. My credit cards were maxed out. I was on the verge of being homeless and living in my car when Jo called me and told me about the position here.

"Nobody in the city would hire me. Not the public schools or the private ones. Certainly not the Catholic ones. Although I was exonerated, they wouldn't take the chance. When the Coyote Creek School Board agreed to hire me, I jumped on it, even though it was temporary. I'd already sold everything I had of value. I packed up my clothing and sleeping bag and moved here. Jo let me sleep on her couch or I couldn't have come." With trembling fingers, she set her glass on the side table and rose to her feet. Pacing slow circles around the room she avoided his gaze.

This was where he'd back off, where he gave her the 'you're a criminal' look or the pity face. Then, she'd never hear from him again. She'd been on more than one date where she should have kept her past a secret. She was tired of being abandoned. Why had she opened herself up to it again? Yeah, he was a great guy but he was nothing to her. Sure, she liked him… she cut off the thought before it could even develop.

"Fricken bastard," Riley snapped. "How could he do that to you? How could she?" He jumped to his feet and stomped across the room. He slammed his fist into his hand a couple times. "I should beat the crap out of him."

"What?" She stared at the usually quiet man in front of her. He was defending her honor? His reaction stunned her.

"Oh, I wouldn't really." He held up his hands in a placating gesture. "But it pisses me off. Why didn't he stand by you and help you fight it? A real man doesn't let a woman be treated so poorly. Hell, he doesn't let his friends, male or female, be treated like that. He fights for them. Your ex must have been a lowdown, good for nothing jerk. No offense."

Tricia laughed; her heart suddenly lighter. "None taken." She walked up to him and brushed a kiss across his cheek. "Thank you. Nobody, besides Jo, has ever taken my side. It means a lot."

She whirled away and stared out the window, her back to him. Shoot. What was she thinking? Her fingers flew to her lips. She'd kissed him and she wanted to kiss him again. She was in serious trouble here. Big trouble. Time to leave. She turned to face him.

"Well, thanks for dinner. I'll go now."

"What? Why? You bare everything to me and then run. Don't you want to talk about it, get it off your chest? Sue always says things get better when you share them. Stay, have another glass of wine. Please."

She gave him a long, hard look. There was no pity in his expression, no revulsion either. Only compassion. "I don't want to talk about it anymore."

"Stay, we'll watch a bad movie or something. It can't have been easy to talk about this. I'm sorry you were hurt, but I'm not sorry we talked about it." He paused. "I don't know you well, but this explains some of the questions I had about you."

"Like what?" She couldn't help herself, the words whipped out. Two glasses of wine with dinner had turned her into a blabber-mouth.

"Like why you don't socialize much. Why you just stick close to Jo and don't attend many of the teachers' informal gatherings. You're keeping yourself apart from everyone, hoping to protect yourself from being hurt. I get that. Everyone gets hurt; hiding away isn't going to help. I also understand why you don't drink when you go out and why you seem to triple-think everything you say. Your hurt shows in the extra compassion you have for the kids, in how you have a gift for making them feel loved and wanted. You're giving them what you lost and you're protecting yourself from being hurt again."

She stared at him speechless. His words were thoughtful and dead-on accurate. This Riley didn't seem much like the different-woman-every-night Riley. He'd always seemed so light and carefree. Was this side of him a result of his new father status or was it who he'd always been?

"How about if we watch a movie?" she blurted. "Or I could go and get some sleep? You should be sleeping while you have the chance. You won't get many nights alone now."

He chuckled. "I have a million more questions, but I'll let it go. For now. But I warn you, I want to know everything about you. Come on, pull up a chair and we'll watch something mindless."

Tricia slid into a chair at Jo's kitchen table the next day. She straightened the blue rose patterned placemat and set her coffee carefully on the center of the mat and glanced around the apartment's small kitchen. It had a homey welcoming feel with it's sunny yellow walls, blue and white accents and mismatched wooden furniture blending harmoniously. The enormous bouquet of roses and daisies on the table was a nice touch.

"More flowers from Houston?" she asked, already knowing the answer.

Jo laughed, but a frown marred her joy. "How'd you guess? The man won't stop sending them to me. You know, sometimes I think they're a distraction technique to keep me off balance. He's a great guy. Fun to be with. Dependable. Honest—I think. But every now and then, it feels like he's avoiding certain subjects. I can't put my finger on which ones exactly, but if we've talked about something and he skips topics, I get flowers the next day. Last night I asked him about his sister and he changed topics. Her picture is on his mantle, but he never talks about her or his family." She waved her hand at the flowers. "And today, voilà, more flowers."

"Have you asked him about it?" She hesitated to suggest it, deep questions could be off putting when you had secrets you didn't want to share. She'd brought a few dates to an end with her refusal to talk about her past.

"I haven't pushed him yet but I really like him." She sighed and flopped into the maple chair kitty-corner to Tricia's pine one. "I think I could fall for him, but it worries me he keeps secrets. My life's an open book. His seems to have secrets and shadows."

"Everybody has secrets. He seems like a great guy; Riley likes him. He must trust him, they're partners. Maybe he needs time to open up. Having secrets is scary. You live in constant fear that people finding out will ruin your life. Despite Riley taking it in stride, I'm still nervous that if the lovely residents of town knew about my parents, I'd lose my job."

"No worries. You've helped so many kids and you're an amazing teacher, your job is safe. Besides, you were fired but you're innocent. If you'd interact more, you'd have more friends and people to back you up if shit hit the fan."

Tricia sighed. It sucked when the truth was right in front of her but she didn't have the guts to accept it. She made a mental vow to accept the next social invitation which came her way. "I'm trying to open up. It's not easy."

"Neither is broaching a touchy subject. Like…how was dinner with Riley?"

Tricia ran the evening through her head recalling the fun and camaraderie of cleaning up the exploded dressing, the good food and light conversation and the surprising results of her revelation. It had been a nice evening. One she'd like to repeat. "Dinner was good. The steak was delicious. And boy, can Riley pack away cake."

"All those Flint boys love their desserts. Sue keeps busy baking for them all. Well, except Jason, he's always in the back room of the bakery letting Elsie feed him sweets. Of course, he repays her with simple repairs and snow shoveling. I think it's his way of helping out without leaving her feeling obligated. I know she's hoping her granddaughter comes home and takes up the business. But that's all irrelevant. How *was* Riley?" Her emphasis on was left Tricia no doubt this was an innuendo.

"Nothing happened. But I did tell him about my parents and my ex. He didn't run screaming from the room which is a good thing." She kept her tone level despite wanting to jump up and fist pump the air.

"So, you're dating him?"

"No. That would be inappropriate. I'm not saying I wouldn't like to, he's nice. He's got a quiet strength and kindness I find appealing. Daisy is wonderful, but she's my student, putting Riley into the no-go camp." For a moment, Tricia's mind wandered into the fantasy of her, Riley and Daisy as a family. Nope. She wasn't going to go into that no-fly zone.

"Two years ago, one of the grade six teachers dated a student's father. They got married. Nobody cared. They've moved away because he was transferred, but it wasn't a big deal. Be discrete, don't favor Daisy over the other kids and it'll all be fine. I should say don't favor her more than you already do."

"I don't favor her." Tricia couldn't help but laugh at her lie. It wasn't even a little white lie; it was a whopper. "Okay, I try not to favor her, but she's adorable and she's been through so much. It's only been weeks but she's already coming out of her shell and she learns so quickly." She wished her bias and her caring wasn't so evident in her voice but Jo was her best friend, she had been since university, and she'd understand. She'd stood by Tricia in the fiery aftermath of her destroyed career and broken engagement.

"We've all got favorites, every teacher does. Hell, every parent does. It's the way it is. We just try and keep it under control. I say, if you want Riley, go for it."

Jo's words echoed in Tricia's head all the way into Edmonton and back that afternoon. She wanted some extra curriculum aids and didn't want to wait for them to ship, so she made a hurried trip to the city and the teacher's supply store for supplies. Her fall harvest display was going to be epic this year. She'd driven past her old apartment and school and several of the places she'd hung out with Troy, her ex. Seeing her old haunts didn't hurt as badly as it had before she left. Maybe she was healing, which opened up moving on and put dating Riley into consideration. Could she risk it? Was the chance of building a new relationship worth the chance of getting hurt again? He had taken her confession well. He seemed okay with the shadows clouding her reputation.

On impulse, she pulled into his yard instead of passing right by on her way back to town. The house was nearly dark, but a light glowed brightly in the clinic behind it. She eased to a stop outside the clinic and jumped out of the car.

In the few moments she waited for Riley to answer the door, she debated leaving half a dozen times. A secret hope he'd want to see her was the only thing helping her stand her ground and wait.

"Tricia!" His face was wreathed in a huge welcoming smile. "Come in. I was just finishing some paperwork. What brings you out this late in the evening?"

"I was going by and thought, maybe, you'd have time for coffee." Her hands twisted together and she jammed them into her jeans pockets to hide her nervousness.

"Come in." He bowed low and flung the door open all the way. "I'll give you the five-buck tour. This," he waved expansively around the room, "is our reception area."

Decorated in shades of green, the waiting room boasted a dozen chairs. A television hung high on the north wall. Posters of kittens, puppies and horses decorated the walls. The desk was wide and clean. The floors and windows gleaming. Overall, it had a warm, comforting appeal.

Riley showed her his office where he shut down the computer he'd been using and quickly stowed a few files in their proper place. He clipped a baby monitor to his belt. Down a short hallway from the office he shared with Houston, there were three examination rooms, a small surgery, and an enormous room of cages divided in half by a glass wall. One side held pens and crates for cats and birds. The other was set up for dogs and small animals. Large animals such as horses, cows and the occasional goat were treated in the barn out back. He told her about the wild animal cages further out on his property where they rehabilitated injured wildlife.

"It's beautiful," Tricia praised. "So clean and tidy. You could do people surgery here. I've been in medical clinics that weren't this pristine. Plus, it feels comforting and calming. You've got a great place. No wonder your practice is booming."

"Thanks, Houston and I designed it together and had an architect turn our concept into reality. But this is my favorite part." He led her through a short hallway with hanging hooks for lab coats and messy gear and a small sink for washing up. They went from the clinic to his back entry and through into his kitchen. Riley laughed when Tricia gasped at the changes he'd made.

"What the heck?" She stared at the colorful plastic children's picnic table, complete with umbrella sitting beside his kitchen table.

"It's for the deck. I ordered it for Daisy, but she wants it inside for crafts, she informed me. Come check this out." He led her into the living room.

A large leather sectional sofa filled one corner of the room. It was flanked on either end by tables and his recliners. A sturdy wooden table occupied the center of the room. A dollhouse and two bookcases filled one wall and there was a basket of toys in the corner.

"Whoa, what happened?"

"We spent a day in Edmonton visiting the Ables. I want Daisy to know they'll always be part of her life. Mrs. Able, Daisy and I hit a furniture store and chose it together. It just came yesterday. Daisy's thrilled."

"I love the distressed look of the table and the sofa looks super comfy," Tricia praised.

"It is. Trust me, we napped on it this afternoon. And the distressed look? A deliberate choice. Sue warned me kids are murder on furniture. I was thinking glass and chrome. She nearly split a side laughing. But she was right. Daisy dropped my coffee mug on the table today. It smashed to bits, but the table is barely marked. I'd hate to think what would have happened if I'd gone with glass."

They chuckled together.

Tricia settled in the corner of the sofa, wine in hand. Riley sat to her left, close enough to touch, his body twisted to face her. "What do you think?" he asked, wondering why it mattered.

"I like it. It's big and comfortable. The leather's plush and durable. It's the perfect family couch. Lots of room for cuddling."

Her blush was adorable.

"I meant for you and Daisy to curl up and read, not…" She paused and took a gulp of wine. "I didn't mean to imply."

"Relax, Tricia. I get it.' He was not going to admit her words had sparked an image and longing inside him. The couch was easily deep enough for two people to lay together and cuddle. His jeans grew tight. Time to change the subject.

"I confirmed all the parade participants today. The band is booked. I can't wait to dance." He shimmied in place on the couch.

"Ew." She groaned.

"Right, you don't like to dance." Heaviness weighed him down. He'd forgotten that little fact. He'd been looking forward to taking a turn on the floor with her at the Harvest Dance. He'd been hoping for a sexy, slow waltz.

"It's not because I don't like to. It's…I can't dance." Her voice was so low he barely heard her confession.

"Anybody can dance. You did fine in the short time we danced at the Bar None. You just feel the rhythm and move your feet and arms to match. I can show you." Suddenly eager, he set his glass on the table and jumped to his feet to turn on the sound system.

After a long, drawn out and lackluster discussion, she joined him and they pushed the heavy wooden table aside. "If I'd known I'd be moving this thing, I would have gotten a smaller one." He danced in place, gesturing for her to join him.

CHAPTER TWENTY-FOUR

Tricia stared at Riley as he danced about the room. He was as graceful at home, alone, as he had been dancing in the bar. She didn't want to do this but if she was going to dance at the Harvest Dance as expected, she'd have to learn how or risk looking like an idiot which would interfere with her goal of staying relatively anonymous. But learning to be a half decent dancer was better than making a total fool of herself.

"Come on, Tricia," he beseeched. "Don't be afraid. There's nobody here but us and your secret is safe with me." He danced around her, snagging her hand on the way by.

Lightning shot up her arm. The man packed a punch. Static electricity. Nothing more, she told herself. She shifted with his motions to keep her balance.

"That's it, move your feet, listen to the music, feel the rhythm." He kept a light grip on her fingers as he moved. She followed his motions, trying to match her steps to his. "Close your eyes, don't look at me, *feel* the music."

Her eyes drifted closed as she shuffled about, trusting his grip on her hand to keep her from bumping into anything.

"You're doing great," his voice whispered in her ear.

When had he gotten so close? She sucked in a breath. Sweet heaven, he smelled divine. Like wine with undertones of man, cedar and antiseptic.

"You smell like antiseptic." She laughed.

"Occupational hazard. I usually shower before I go on a date. I've got this citrus scented soap I use on my hands to minimize the antiseptic. Sorry about the smell." He tugged her gently toward him.

Suddenly, she was in his arms, her chest pressed against his. Their bodies aligned. She stiffened and pulled back.

"You lied to me," he whispered, easing her back against him. "You can dance. You're a pretty decent dancer and you feel lovely in my arms."

His words knocked her off kilter, she stumbled and stepped on his foot. His booming laugh rang out, startling her. "Guess I spoke too soon."

She stopped moving and looked up at him. Those beautiful, Flint-green eyes stared back at her, stealing her breath. His five o'clock shadow caught her gaze, her hands fisted against his shoulders to keep from touching. Would his whiskers be deliciously soft or delightfully scratchy? Her gaze flicked away and came to rest on his lips. Plump, full and deliciously kissable. She rose on her toes and brushed a kiss against his lips without thinking.

Whirling away, she separated herself from his endlessly tempting attributes. Her body urged her to go back. She shook her head. Being in his arms, in his life felt too right, too comfortable.

"What?" he asked kindly. "Come back. Dance with me. It won't hurt and I enjoy dancing with you."

"I can't. We shouldn't. It's not right." She floundered to express the conflicting emotions rioting within her. She doubted he'd ever understand. He'd been bred and born in Coyote Creek, his family was a beloved institution in town, which gave him an edge and the acceptance she didn't have as an outsider. Jo had said Tricia would be an insider before she knew it. Her promise hadn't come true, perhaps because she refused to take the risk of friendship.

Years ago, Tricia had believed risk was part of life but she'd been burned without taking a risk and now she feared incineration if she stepped out of her comfortably safe box.

"We can. We should. It *is* right. And we will," he countered, stepping forward and pulling her into his arms. "Dance with me. Call it practice for the dance. We're alone and nobody will be the wiser and you'll be prepared. You're better than you think you are."

Maybe he had a point. This was private, there were no prying eyes and he danced like a god. She melted into his arms as the music slowed to an intimate waltz. The lyrics, something about broken hearts, mending fences and new love burned into her. Heart and soul. She was falling for him. He filled a need deep within her. She wanted companionship. She needed Riley. In a moment of weakness, she knew if she let him, he'd take over her heart.

They shared a few glasses of wine and danced, song after song. Some fast, some slow. Some delightfully, utterly romantic and sexy. A crack formed in the barrier around her heart with an almost audible snap. She was doomed. Gloriously, deliciously, perfectly doomed to fall for this man.

"What made you think you can't dance?" He whispered against her ear.

For a moment, she was lost in the sultry heat of his breath, the feel of his hard body against hers. Then the question penetrated and her heart shattered.

"It doesn't matter." She stepped out of his arms and turned away. "I think I'll go now."

"First, you've had too much wine to drive. I know, you're not drunk, neither am I, but there's no sense taking a risk. You're staying until we sober up. Second, it does matter. Who put the ridiculous idea that you can't dance into your head?"

His softly spoken words bounced off her back like bullets off a steel plate. They ricocheted and jumped, inflicting damage she was helpless to block. Had she been wrong to give up her love of dance because one man claimed she couldn't? Had she been so wrapped up in public opinion, his opinion, she'd blocked her own pleasure, her identity. Worse, with her ex, Troy, long since out of the picture, why was she still doing it?

"Tricia?" His voice was low and questioning. "He did this to you, didn't he? Your ex. He made you think you had to be something you're not. What kind of asshole does that?"

She whirled around to face him, a reprimand for interfering on her lips.

"You're a beautiful woman with a huge heart. You're kind, loving and generous. You're great with kids and their parents. Your dancing is more than acceptable. In fact, I haven't been this turned on for years." His eyes widened as if he were shocked by his words. He dragged his fingers through his hair and sighed. "I've done enough damage for one night. Come on, I'll get you a shirt to sleep in."

He was right, she shouldn't drive. Nor should she spend another night in his house. It was go to bed, or be tempted by his nearness. Giving in to the inevitable, she followed him upstairs, refusing to stare at his delectable backside in his Wranglers. Nope, she would not look. She sighed softly. She was looking and enjoying every second of it. Was it only weeks ago, in the bar, when all she wanted was a dance and to go home? Now they'd danced, she'd loved it and she felt irrevocably tied up in his life and dang it all, she liked it. Now she had to figure out how to back out gracefully. Maybe she should call Jo for a ride home. A glance at her watch showed it was nearly two in the morning. Nope, not going to call Jo and have to explain why she was here. Besides, Jo was probably curled up in Houston's arms and she didn't want to bring him into this.

"Hang on a minute and I'll get you something to sleep in. I'll sleep on the couch."

"Riley, it's two a.m. Give me a blanket for the couch and you take your bed."

He looked at her like she'd grown two heads. "Do you

really think I'd let you sleep on the couch while I was comfy and cozy in bed? You've lost your marbles." He rummaged in a drawer and tossed her a T-shirt emblazoned with the University of Alberta logo. She caught it midair. "I'd let my brothers sleep on the floor, or the lawn, but until my guest room furniture arrives, you get my bed. No complaints." He eased the door shut behind him. "Good night, Tricia," he called through the door. "Your toothbrush is still in the bathroom. See you tomorrow."

CHAPTER TWENTY-FIVE

Tricia wasn't sure when it happened, but Riley had started calling her every week night to check up on Daisy's progress at school. Initially, it had been compensation for Daisy's lost notes and the missing phone message. Somehow their conversations had wandered all over the map. They discussed the Harvest Festival, his clinic, his patients, Daisy, his family. They talked books and movies. Each call was longer than the night before.

Last night she went to bed without a call. She lay there, disappointed. He didn't call his patient's families every night and she had no right to expect him to give her special treatment but she'd come to enjoy their conversations. To look forward to them. She debated calling him but discarded the idea as smacking of desperation. She wouldn't be that woman.

Her cell phone jangled and she looked over at the display. Riley. It was past midnight. Panic raced through her. Was Daisy sick? Injured? Was Riley okay?

"Hi, Riley. Kind of late. Is everything okay?"

He sighed. "It is. Just got home from a call. Remember the horse I had to look after on Daisy's birthday? I was called back tonight. She'd been attacked again. I don't think it's wolves or coyotes like the owner claims. I think it's his dogs."

"Oh no!" Her hand flew to her chest. "Are you okay? Did they hurt you?" Who would let their dogs attack a horse? What was wrong with people?

"I'm fine. It was an excruciatingly long night. I had to call in the police. Amy Baxter came out to investigate. She confiscated the dogs and they're impounded in my clinic for now. I had to haul the horse back to the clinic for treatment. I'm not sure she's going to make it."

"That's terrible. Dealing with mistreatment must kill you inside."

He agreed and vented for a few minutes. She didn't know who the owner was, or where he lived, nor did she want to. She let Riley talk until he wound down to silence. The best part of a friendship was knowing your friend would listen without judgment and she was wordlessly offering comfort to Riley.

Conversation rolled from work to Daisy who was testing her limits against Riley's authority and becoming increasingly difficult when she chose to dig her heels in over something she didn't want to do. Tricia suggested staying strong and consistent would help, as would the stability and routine of the nanny he was planning to hire.

Tricia knew all three women and agreed they'd all make

great caregivers for a young, active girl. She asked Riley if he'd narrowed down the initial three applicants.

"I ruled out one, she didn't drive in winter and Daisy will need rides to and from school. Plus, I want her cared for at home, not at someone else's house."

"Logical, the stability of home will be good for her. What about the other two?"

"We interviewed them. Daisy and I. Both seemed like an excellent fit for our needs. Daisy preferred Mrs. Quarry, so that's who we went with. She started today. I meant to tell you, but it slipped my mind."

"Daisy will love Mrs. Quarry; she volunteers at the school. All the kids adore her. I think you and Daisy chose well." It wasn't any of her business, but she sensed Riley was still uncertain about his decision.

Every night, Tricia and Riley traded the details of their days, almost as if they were in a serious relationship. Part of her yearned to be closer to him, part of her was scared of getting in too deep.

RILEY CLIMBED the stairs to Tricia's apartment after she buzzed him in. It was the second Sunday in October and he'd caved to Sue's requests and had invited Tricia to join the family for Thanksgiving dinner, even though Sue could have done it herself.

Tricia stood in the hallway, one shoulder leaning against

the doorjamb of her apartment, a big grin on her face. "You look like a man on his way to the gallows."

"I feel like it."

"Come on, family dinners can't be so bad. Besides, I adore your family. I've gotten to know them quite well."

"It's not my family, it's the blatant matchmaking. Sue was great for a while, but since Daisy entered our lives, she's become hell bent on setting me up. She believes every child needs two parents. Funny, she'd been alone for over a year with three daughters before she married Dad. But now, she thinks you're perfect for me. Doesn't she understand I'm my own man? I'll find a woman if and when I'm ready?" He paused mid-step, one foot on the floor, the other poised mid-air. He lowered it to the floor. "Wait, what do you mean you've gotten to know my family?" He scratched his nose and stood there, feet spread, hands fisted with tension.

"I was your nephew's teacher last year. I'm Jane's teacher this year. I see Ken a lot. I see Jason at the butcher shop now that you've gotten me hooked on Flint ranch beef. Sue's been to see me a time or two to drop off desserts." Tricia laughed. "They're sweet in their determination to see you happy."

"Maybe we should just skip dinner." He growled.

She chuckled. "Buck up. Look at it this way, if they're trying to hook you up with me, a woman who isn't looking for a relationship, you're safer than if they wanted you with someone eager to marry and bear your children."

"What?" He gaped at her.

"Come on, we're friends. Friends protect each other. At

least, I thought we were friends. Who else, besides, friends, talk for hours virtually every night?"

"I guess. You're just easy to talk to. You let me vent and bounce ideas off you. You shoot me down when I've gone way off the rails but otherwise, you let me figure this parenting thing out. I appreciate the help and support."

"Glad to assist, it's what friends do. Now come, grab this box. It's awkward to carry. I've made a couple pies to bring and I don't want to risk dropping it on the way downstairs." He grabbed the box, she locked up and they headed to the ranch.

"I love this drive," Tricia exclaimed as the last buildings on their way out of town gave way to fields of ripe grain interspersed with sections of golden leaved trees where cattle have eaten away the undergrowth. It's pretty in the summer, but the oranges mixed with greens is so soothing to me. I never had views like this in the city."

"Small town charm, I guess." They fell into a comfortable silence. Tricia stared out the window, watching the scenery go by.

Riley studied her profile. She was lovely. Smooth perfect skin, glistening black hair and long lush lashes. He couldn't see her eyes, which was probably a good thing because those knowing, flashing blue eyes could see right through him.

He could get used to looking at her. He was no stranger to dating, usually fun-loving short-term women. He'd never felt comfortable sharing his doubts with any of them. With Tricia, his concerns came out unbidden and she never made him feel inadequate when he felt lost or terrified by being a father. She gave him encouragement and strength to figure things out. Whether it was the teacher in her or her inherent nature, he had no idea, though he suspected they were one and the same. If he were looking for someone to share his life with, she'd fit the bill nicely.

They hadn't seriously kissed. He'd been tempted more than a time or two but didn't want to risk jeopardizing their friendship. He couldn't, wouldn't, risk what he had in the vain hope of something more. He'd likely lose. His dad had lost his mother. Sure, he'd found Sue years later but if Riley built something with Tricia and it ended, Daisy's world would crumble again. It wasn't worth the risk, no matter how tempting she was. He wasn't just risking his heart; he was risking his daughter's too.

"You're quiet this afternoon," she said, turning to look at him.

"Resting up for the chaos to come. Most of the family was already there when I dropped Daisy off earlier. She wanted to play with her cousins as long as she could and I could use the break." He smiled when he said it so she'd understand he was just talking, not actually complaining.

"I have days at school when nothing's wrong, but it seems like everything is too much. I think it's why we have professional days. They're as much about resting as updating our skills."

"I heard there was a kerfuffle at the school on Thursday. Mr. Broderbund?" He already knew the details; Jane had expounded on it all the way home.

"He came in drunk. He drove to town after drinking. He

wanted Kyle to come home and help him fix the tractor. He stormed into the classroom; I thought he'd hit me. I've never been so scared in my life."

"You never told me! I tell you all my problems and you keep a near assault a secret?" Didn't she trust him?

"Confidentiality. I wanted to talk about it, more than you know. I just couldn't. Sometimes being a teacher involves keeping my mouth shut. Although, if I feel a need to call the authorities, I will and I did."

"Well, you can talk about it now. Jane and Daisy filled me in." He pestered her for details, asking questions based on Jane's enthusiastic report and Daisy's less excited comments. She didn't offer any information, just corrected him where he was mistaken. Despite his knowledge of the event, it wasn't her place to tell the story. As they pulled into his parents' driveway, the conversation ground to a halt. "The police gave him a choice, rehab or jail. He took rehab, he won't be bothering you for a while."

"Who looks after Kyle when his mother's at work?"

"Mrs. Quarry goes straight from our place to theirs. Sometimes, Kyle comes over to play until I'm finished at the office. Houston and I have tweaked the schedule, he does the early mornings and I start once I've dropped Kyle and Daisy at school."

Tricia leaned over and kissed him on the cheek, her hand resting warmly on his shoulder. "You, Riley Flint, are a good man and a great father. You do such wonderful things and never tell a soul. I'm impressed."

He grasped her hand and stared into her eyes. Beautiful

blue eyes he could get lost in. He felt like he was falling into something deep and eternal. Something he'd never get out of. He smiled and kissed her hand. "And you, Tricia Paxton, do the same for your students and my family. You're here to appease my stepmother and to protect me."

"No, I'm here because I want to spend time with you." She extracted her hand and with the box of pies held tight against her chest, she slipped out of the truck and climbed the stairs to the front door. He raced to catch up and take the box from her hand.

"Trying to take credit for my pies?" She teased, opening the door for him.

"Yup. I can use all the brownie points I can get. Anything to help me fit in." He bolted inside before she could pressure him on his spur of the moment response.

"It's about time you got here," Sue chided, hurrying to embrace Riley.

He shifted the box of pies to protect it. Sue looked into the box. "What's this? You brought food? You know better," she chided her son.

"He might, but I didn't. I don't like to show up for dinner without bringing anything. I baked a couple of mince pies. I hope you like them."

"I love mince. It's the one pie I never mastered but then, I don't make my own filling and the jarred stuff is a touch on the sweet side."

"There's a trick to it. A few extra ingredients. I'll show you my grandmother's recipe sometime, if you show me how to make pastry. Mine's always a little on the tough side."

The two of them wandered into the kitchen chattering about baking, leaving him standing alone at the front door. Tricia turned back just before she was out of sight and gave him a broad wink. His heart did something funny and a smile quirked his lips.

"Dude, you're smitten," Jason teased as he opened the screen door behind Riley. "She's got you eating out of her hand."

"Don't be an idiot." He cuffed his brother on the shoulder. Jason pushed back.

"You're totally done for. Wedding bells are next."

Riley gave him another shove. Jason balled up a fist.

"Take that crap outside," Robert demanded as he came around the corner from the living room. "Your mother hates when you boys wrestle. Something always gets broken."

"How are you feeling, Dad?" Riley asked, dropping the near fight as if it never started.

"Okay. A little run down. I'm taking it easy. Thinking of hiring a manager until Justice gets his life together."

"He should be here helping out until you get over the bug plaguing you. You been to the doctor again?" Jason asked. "I haven't seen your truck in town."

"Got an appointment coming up. Expect he'll order a bunch of useless tests that'll say it's nothing but old age creeping up on me."

Riley squinted at his father. Beneath his tan, Robert was pale, his skin had an almost grayish hue, but he looked better than the last time they'd visited. Maybe it was a nasty virus. A nagging in his stomach told him otherwise. He'd like to push the issue but it would cause an argument and ruin the family dinner. "Could be time to slow down a bit," he advised Robert lightly. "Running a ranch isn't easy. I became a vet because it was easier than ranching."

"You became a vet because you're got a squishy, girly, marshmallow heart. You're practically a chick," Jason quipped.

Robert laughed. Riley squinted and shrugged. "I'll admit it, I've got a soft spot for animals. I always have."

Robert clapped him on the shoulder. "You do good work, son. I'm proud of you." He looked at Jason. "And I know all about how you help Elsie at the bakery. People like you make the world a better place. I'm proud of all my children."

"You raised us right." Riley hugged Robert.

"Come inside, visit with everyone before we eat. There's probably a game on TV somewhere." Riley and Jason shared a glance, Robert never was one to accept a compliment gracefully, instead he pretended it never happened.

"I'm not much for football, are the kids playing video games?" Riley asked. "I'm up for some Mario Kart."

"You and those darned video games." Robert laughed.

"He's just too weak for real sports," Ken added joining the group at the front door. "We should be outside throwing around a baseball. We could teach the kids to catch."

"I'm in," Riley proclaimed. "I haven't thrown a ball around in months."

"Boys, come help haul the food to the table," Sue called from the kitchen. "It's ready to eat. Jason, you go haul those kids up from the basement. Robert, the turkey is on the table, can you carve please?"

So much for a ball game. They dispersed to do as bidden.

The familiar dining room table seated twelve and was covered with a white linen table cloth, at least Riley thought it was linen. There was a smaller table set up nearby where the children would eat. He wondered what would happen when his brothers found wives and had more kids and the small table wouldn't hold them all. He had a sudden vision of an older Daisy sitting beside a toddler with Flint-green eyes and Tricia's dark hair.

Crap. He pushed the thought away. He wasn't going there. Hanging around his family was giving him ideas he wasn't ready for.

The table virtually groaned with the spread of food on it. The air was redolent with the smell of roasted turkey, mashed potatoes and candied yams. Riley's gaze roamed the feast as he decided what to offer Daisy. Peas from the garden, fresh beans, the last of the year's corn on the cob. Turkey, two types of stuffing, gravy, potatoes, salad, cheese, pickles and so much more. And sweet heaven, Sue's homemade dinner rolls. He was going to weigh a thousand pounds before he left today.

The children sat at their table, the adults stood behind their chairs, Robert at one end, Sue at the other. "Before we begin, let's just take a moment to close our eyes and be thankful for the bounty before us," Sue suggested.

Riley peeked at Daisy who glanced at Jane and copied her closed eye expression. He banked a smile and closed his eyes.

This was a bountiful day. Good food, family and friends and his new daughter. A silly grin stole across his face.

Robert began carving and Sue offered a choice of red wine, white wine, water or milk to the adults. She served watered down ginger ale to the kids.

"Daisy, darling. Pop over here and help your daddy pick your food. He's not sure what you like," Sue called.

"Can I pick too?" Jane asked.

"You'll get what I give you," Ken responded. "You know the rules. This is a special meal for Daisy. It's her first family Thanksgiving. Next year, she'll eat what she's given just like you."

"Oh." Jane frowned. "Try the green beans, Grandma puts bacon and parmesan cheese on them."

Daisy climbed up in Riley's chair and pointed to a few things, including the beans. He added corn, stuffing and sweet potatoes as well. "Two bites of each, just to try them," he advised. "It's important to try new things and eat a big meal. Besides, if you don't eat enough, Grandma won't let you have dessert." He winked so she'd know he was teasing.

She nodded solemnly, climbed down and took her plate to the table.

Tricia was seated across the table, beside Jason who kept whispering in her ear and making her laugh. Riley frowned at his brother and kicked his ankle under the table, warning him off.

"Dude, what the heck?" Jason glared at him then smirked and leaned in to whisper something else.

Riley's blood pressure skyrocketed. His brother was

honing in on his girl. Whoa! His girl? Oh man, he was losing it. Tricia wasn't his. They were friends. Just friends. He'd ignore them. The idea was simple, the reality not so much. He focused as much as he could on the conversation and kept half an eye on Daisy who reluctantly, but obediently cleared her plate.

"Riley, why don't you help me clear the table for dessert?" Sue asked, rising from the table.

He popped to his feet. Anything to get away from his brother putting the moves on Tricia. What had happened to Jason's fixation on Elsie's granddaughter, Nicole? He'd had a thing for her in high school though he'd never acted on it because she was younger. She was all grown up now and had been back to visit a time or two. Was he tired of waiting? Or was he using Tricia to fill Nicole's spot until she returned to town and he could court her?

He gathered a stack of plates and carried them to the kitchen.

"Stop gritting your teeth," Sue whispered. "He's egging you on. He has no interest in Tricia and he knows full well she's yours and off limits."

"She isn't mine," Riley responded, flipping the dishwasher open. He started rinsing plates and dropping them in.

"Be careful. Those are my good dishes. And she is yours, you just haven't figured it out yet. Neither has she. I can see it in your eyes when you watch her. She watches you when she thinks nobody is looking. When the universe sends you love, you don't get a choice." She reached down and closed the dishwasher. "We'll get those later. Time for coffee and dessert." She patted his cheek. "Son, I don't know why you fret so much. But something has you scared of love. If you ever want to talk, I'm here. I may not have given birth to you, but I love you like my own." She smiled sadly, grasped his shoulders and turned him back toward the dining room. "Go, get those dishes so there's room for dessert."

He stumbled forward until he caught his balance. He paused and looked back at her. "Thanks." He wanted to say he loved her. He did love her. Somehow, he'd never been able to form the words. He wondered if she knew how he felt. She probably did, Sue didn't miss much. Guilt swamped him, he wanted to say the words, fear held his tongue in check. If he said the words, she might vanish like his own moth had.

They toted a few loads of dishes and leftovers back into the kitchen. He ignored Jason's blatant attempts to rile him. After a few minutes, the table was cleared and loaded down with desserts, tea and coffee. Sue stood behind her chair and cleared her throat.

"I'd like to try something new this year. We're going to go around the table and express what we're thankful for. I'll go first. I'm thankful for my enormous, boisterous family and the love we share." She sat down and nodded at Beth, seated to her right.

"I'm thankful for my family and my nearly perfect exam scores on my midterms." Everyone congratulated her.

One after another, they expressed their gratitude. When it was her turn, Tricia cleared her throat. "I'm thankful for my job and my new community. I'm especially thankful for you guys." She waved her arm to encompass them all. "You've welcomed me into your home and treated me like family. It means a lot to me. My parents broke some laws and implicated me and they're no longer part of my world. I'm glad to have you guys. The love you so easily share is beautiful."

Mouths dropped open and the room fell silent. No one moved, not even the children. Everyone stared at her. Riley's heart ached when she dropped her head and stared into her coffee.

"I'm thankful for all of you," he blurted. "To Tricia for helping me with my beautiful new daughter. To Daisy for coming to me and making my life better. And to my family who supports me in everything. Dad, Mom, crazy siblings, I love you all."

The uncomfortable silence after Tricia's revelation was nothing compared to the one which followed his. He hadn't planned to speak; the words, the sentiment just exploded from his heart. Part of the impulse was to turn the attention from Tricia but more of it was the truth he'd never been able to express. He couldn't recall a single time when he'd told his family he loved them. He'd always held the feelings, the words, in check.

"Why is Grandma crying?" Daisy's small voice broke the silence.

Sue rose and knelt beside the kid's table. She grasped Daisy's hand. "I'm happy crying. Sometimes when your heart is so full of love, you cry. Your daddy gave me, gave us, the biggest gift by saying he loves us."

Daisy patted their joined hands. "I love you, Grandma."

Sue swept her up in a big hug and carried her over to Riley. "I love you both." She hugged them together until Daisy wiggled and complained she was being squished. Sue released her and Daisy hurried back to the kids' table.

"Thank you, Riley. I always knew, but the words mean so much." He embraced his stepmother. No, his mother, he corrected himself, the only mother he'd ever known. She may have arrived late, but from the first time she'd stepped foot in the house, she'd been there for him through everything, good and bad.

Her gratitude surprised him, as did the sudden lightness in his heart. He looked up at Tricia, her eyes brimmed with tears and her face was wreathed in an enormous smile.

Women. Crying when they were happy. He'd never understand them.

"This really is the perfect Thanksgiving," Robert proclaimed. "Let's celebrate with dessert!"

Riley and Tricia laughed along with everyone at Robert's declaration.

CHAPTER TWENTY-SIX

After dinner the evening progressed to games, puzzles and good-natured teasing. Tricia and Riley helped with the dishes, and the family went outside for an impromptu game of catch. Before long, the kids were back in the basement playing video games.

Tricia polished the last crystal wine glass and slid it into the china cabinet in the dining room while Riley rinsed the sink. She draped her dish towel over the stove handle to dry and joined Sue at the small kitchen table.

"Dinner was delicious, thank you for inviting me. I've eaten so much I'm stuffed to the gills. I may never eat again." She laughed.

Riley settled at the end of the table with a piece of blueberry cheesecake. He offered Tricia a forkful and laughed when she accepted. "I thought you were full," he teased.

"I was, but who can resist cheesecake? Especially this one. You outdid yourself on this one, Sue." Her praise was heartfelt. The entire day was picture perfect. She felt blessed to be invited into the family, even if there was a poorly hidden agenda to hook her up with Riley.

"We should go soon," Riley suggested around a mouthful of cake.

"Don't talk with your mouth full," Sue and Tricia chorused in unison. They looked at each other and laughed.

Tricia's eyes were captivated by the bobbing of his Adam's apple as he swallowed the bite before speaking. He kept captivating her with simple, everyday gestures. A wave would draw her gaze to the length of his fingers or the strength of his hand. Or she'd catch a glimpse of a muscle flexing under his shirt or a bulging bicep. His tender gestures toward Daisy twisted her heart into jealous knots. It wasn't that she didn't want him to love Daisy, it was more she wanted a share.

She didn't want to want him, but her heart kept defying her wishes. Every time she had the chance to be with him, she took it. She needed to stop, she was getting in too deep and depending on having him to talk to. If she didn't watch herself, she'd fall for him. He didn't seem the type to hurt her like her parents and her ex, but she hadn't expected to be burned by them either. Life had no guarantees and she wasn't sure she was up for the risk.

"Are you ready to head out?" Riley's question jerked her from her musings. "If you are, I'll grab Daisy." Moments later, they were in his truck, headed back to his place, Daisy nearly asleep in the back seat. "Want to stop in for coffee?"

"Yeah, I'd like that." She'd enjoy more time with him.

Alone, away from his family. She'd probably regret it later; she was becoming entirely too attached to him.

Riley slipped off his cowboy boots, flipped his Stetson, wallet and keys onto the table beside the front door and invited her in. She dropped her purse beside his things and hung her sweater in the closet.

With Daisy tucked snug in her bed, they settled on the couch. She'd expected him to sit close, but not this close. She got up, adjusted the drapes and sat cross-legged on the end of the couch, facing him. "So how is it going with Daisy?" she asked, trying to fill the awkward silence.

"Really well. Didn't we have this discussion on the way to the ranch?" He paused and looked at her, questions in his eyes. "Are you nervous?"

"No. I'm fine," she blurted the words out all at once.

He reached out and tugged on a lock of her hair which had fallen over her shoulder. "You are nervous! Why now? We've gotten together a few times."

"I'm fine." She sipped her coffee nearly scalding her mouth on the hot liquid. "Damn."

"You are nervous. Hell, I'm nervous." He blew into his coffee before taking a cautious sip. "I'm never nervous around women."

They looked at each other for a long moment. "Something's shifted," she offered at last. "I thought we were friends, but after you put yourself on the spot at dinner to protect me from questions about my family, something is…weird."

"You're right. Seeing you put yourself out there gave me

the courage to share my feelings. I've never told them I love them."

She reached out and touched his arm. His skin was warm and pliant, his downy arm hairs tickled her palm. "They knew how you felt."

"I should have told them long before now. I just couldn't find the courage. Or the words. You gave me that strength. I owe you. You're helping me express myself. Half the time I'd be lost without your help with Daisy. You're becoming important to me. Very important."

He reached out and cupped her cheek. His thumb brushed over her lips. Her body tilted forward of its own volition; her face pressed against his palm. He was going to kiss her. She blinked slowly and he grinned.

"I'm going to kiss you," he warned. "I've waited way too long already. If you don't want this, you better tell me now." He paused, waiting for her response.

She needed it as badly as he seemed to. Tender need glowed in his eyes, stoking her own desire. Was she ready for this? Her life had been a whirlwind since the night in the bar when she'd refused his first offer of a dance. Everyday their lives had become increasingly entangled until they felt inseparable. Sometimes she didn't know where her life ended and his began. They'd merged into one.

When she didn't say anything, his hand dropped to his lap. "You're not ready."

"What? Oh. I am. Kiss me, Riley Flint." She leaned toward him, barely resisting the urge to crawl into his lap, to become part of him.

He was quick to obey. His fingers threaded through her hair, cupping the back of her neck, drawing her closer. Their lips brushed, softly, tentatively and then with breath-stealing intent. His kiss was magical, touching her heart, caressing her soul. This was where she needed to be. In his arms. For all time. Briefly, it flitted through her mind that fate was funny, ruining her life and then sending her here to find the man of her dreams.

A whisper of sound distracted her from the divine taste of him.

She pulled back. He came back for more.

"No. I mean, yes. But I think Daisy is awake. You better go check on her." She pushed the words out past the lump of emotion clogging her throat. Her tone was husky, hardly audible over the pounding of her pulse in her ears.

Riley kissed her forehead. "Don't go anywhere. I'll only be a moment."

But he wasn't. twenty minutes later, she could hear him talking to Daisy, trying his hardest to get her to go back to bed.

"No. I want you to sleep here. I want *her* to go home." She spat out the pronoun.

"Miss Tricia is my friend, and your teacher. She came here to visit."

"I want you. She should go to school." The harshly whispered argument floated downstairs. The pain and fear in her voice was heartbreaking.

Wow. This was a no-win situation if ever she'd heard one. Time for her to go. She'd talk to Riley again. Soon. After

Daisy had calmed down and realized sharing her father wasn't all bad. She rose and put her glass in the kitchen sink. She paused at the base of the stairs.

"Riley, I think I'll go now. Good night Daisy. Sweet dreams. I'll talk to you guys later."

She grabbed her purse, slipped into her sweater and headed for home, suddenly overcome by weariness. Just when she thought her life was turning the corner.

Bam!

Sleep would be a long time coming tonight. She never should have taken the risk. Daisy was too fragile. She didn't need to feel like she was competing for her father's attention.

CHAPTER TWENTY-SEVEN

"Good morning, Daisy," Tricia greeted her young charge a week later. "Did you have a good weekend?"

"Yeah." The response was decidedly lackluster at best.

Disappointing. Tricia had held out a vain hope that once she stepped away from Riley, Daisy would warm back up to her and they could be friends.

"I had a good weekend. I did some shopping, visited some friends. What did you do?"

"Nothing." She squinted her eyes and frowned at Tricia. For a moment, a mean smile flashed over her face but it was gone in an instant and Tricia disregarded it.

After school, Riley came into the classroom and sent Daisy outside to play with her cousins and her Uncle Ken.

"Riley, hi." She smiled warmly. "Is Daisy going to be okay with us seeing each other?" Might as well broach the subject head on. There was no sense denying the girl's jealousy.

"I hardly think it matters." He frowned and crossed his arms over his chest.

"You don't think it matters if she's jealous of me?" She couldn't keep the confusion from her tone. Why was he being so cold?

"I want it back." He held out his hand, palm up, as if he was expecting her to put something into it.

"Want what back?" unease stirred in her chest.

"Don't play dumb. I want my wallet back."

She shook her head, confused. "Why would I have your wallet?" A sinking feeling came over her. Oh no. He couldn't think she took his wallet, could he? Why would he think that?

"Don't play dumb. My wallet is gone. I left it on the table by the front door the other night. It's gone and you were the last one near it. I'd like it back so I can go get gas."

"I didn't take your wallet. The last time I saw it, you put it on the table."

"My point exactly. I'd like it back."

"Riley, I didn't touch your wallet." His accusation stung. Being accused of something this heinous was worse when the accusation came from a friend, from the man she'd fallen in love with. How could she have been so wrong about him?

Riley glared at her. God, she must think he was an imbecile. Stealing his wallet. He never should have trusted her. Maybe she wasn't as innocent as she claimed. "Give it back and I won't call the police. We'll just go our separate ways and pretend we never met." Riley watched the blood drain from her face as his words rained down on her like physical blows.

"I don't have your damned wallet." She stomped over to the desk, pulled out her purse and slammed it on the desk. "Check for yourself."

Suddenly doubting his earlier conviction, he hesitated before opening it. He unzipped it and spread it wide. There, right on top, was his wallet. He snapped his head up to stare at her. She looked as shocked as he was. Deep inside, he'd harbored the hope he was wrong, that she hadn't taken his wallet. He'd held out an insane hope and looking into her purse, had destroyed it.

"I don't know how your wallet got into my purse. I swear on my life, I didn't take it. Maybe Daisy…" she trailed off.

"Don't start blaming my daughter for your light fingers." He flipped through the wallet ensuring everything was in place, and nothing was missing. "I'll thank you to stay away from my home, my family and my possessions. I'll leave Daisy in your class. For now." He pivoted on his heel and stomped from the room, anger and disappointment clenched the muscles in his neck and shoulders.

Funny, walking away hurt. Badly. As if he were making a mistake. Could she be right? Could Daisy have put his wallet into her purse? She'd been at the base of the stairs last night when she'd interrupted their kiss. Angry at his own doubts, he shoved the thought away and strode out of the school.

CHAPTER TWENTY-EIGHT

Hours later, Tricia paced laps around her apartment. Into the bedroom, back out, through the kitchen. Step after step, trying to get a handle on his accusation. Bile rose in her throat. She paused in the bathroom and downed several antacids hoping to quell the burning in her gut. How could he believe she'd steal from him?

From the bedroom she heard the muted ringing of her cell phone. She stomped to the front door and rummaged through her purse to extract the offending instrument. It better not be him blaming her for something else she hadn't done. She stared at the display for a moment before Jo's name registered.

She flicked the phone open with a sigh. "Hi."

"Wow, what an unenthusiastic response. What's up?"

"I don't want to talk about it." She flopped on the couch

knowing Jo, in typical best friend fashion, wouldn't let it go until she'd heard what needed to be said.

"Didn't you have Thanksgiving dinner at the Flint's? Did it go badly? Houston says their dinners are a blast."

Tricia couldn't muster a response besides tears.

"Shoot. Are you crying? What did Riley do? Hang tight, I'm on my way over."

The phone went dead in Tricia's hand. She was still sitting there, staring at the blank screen fifteen minutes later when Jo used her key to let herself in. "I brought ice cream and wine. Spill it, girl. Did he dump you?"

A hiccuping laugh escaped Tricia. "How could he dump me? We weren't dating."

"Aha," Jo pounced on her slip of the tongue. "Weren't dating? But you wanted to. I knew it all along. What can I do to help? Want me to get Houston to beat him up for you? I could run him over with my car. Maybe we can have him thrown in jail overnight on some made up charge."

Tricia laughed weakly at the outrageous suggestions. "Hook me up," she waved toward the kitchen. Jo laughed, grabbed the grocery bag she'd brought with her and headed to the kitchen. Dishes clanked, silverware rattled, a cork popped and the fridge door slammed. A bowl of ice cream and a flute of champagne appeared in front of Tricia.

"Champagne? This isn't the time for celebrating."

"Liquor store closed twenty minutes ago. This is all I had at home. Shut up and drink. What happened? You blew out of the school like your butt was on fire."

Her candor and friendly bossiness were just what Tricia needed. She accepted the offerings, leaned back and raised her glass. "To the Flint men, may they rot in hell!"

"To the Flint men," Jo echoed. The modification of the toast didn't go unnoticed. They clinked glasses and sipped.

"It's gonna be hard to get drunk on this."

"Well, I brought tequila, but I'm not sure you're ready for the hard stuff, you're not much of a drinker. Eat." She waved a spoon of ice cream in a hurry up gesture.

"I'm getting myself six cats and declaring spinsterhood," Tricia vowed.

"I thought you'd already declared that." Jo laughed around a mouthful of ice cream.

Tricia scooped up some ice cream and shoved it into her mouth. "Maple walnut? With champagne? What about strawberry or chocolate? Maybe even vanilla?" She shoveled in more.

"In an emergency, flavor doesn't matter. Booze and ice cream are always the solution."

"And pizza. I need pizza. Triple pepperoni, ham, spiced beef, mushrooms and pineapple. And fresh tomatoes." She looked up to meet Jo's incredulous stare.

"You don't eat triple meat! You sure you don't want anchovies too?"

"Ew. I'm pissed off, not crazy."

They were on their second glass of champagne and their bowls sat empty on the table when the doorbell rang. "Check the peephole," Tricia ordered. "Don't let *him* in."

"Do I look stupid?" Jo laughed, opened the door and paid for the pizza.

Tricia slid to the floor and grabbed a slice as soon as the box hit the coffee table. "I probably shouldn't eat this."

"So how *did* supper go? I haven't talked to you since then."

Delightful. Amazing. Friendly. Loving. Teasing. So many adjectives fit. She'd never experienced anything like it. Thanksgiving was fun, but to be included as part of the family, it had been beyond her wildest dreams. She'd always wanted a large brood of kids. "Supper was great. The aftermath sucked. I mean really, epically, sucked."

"Do tell."

The champagne bubbles must have gone to her head because before Tricia knew she was going to speak, she blurted out the entire story of how she suspected Daisy had slipped Riley's wallet into her purse. Daisy had seemed pretty upset that Tricia was with Riley the other night. She ended with a blistering diatribe of how Riley had jumped to conclusions and accused her without question and how he wouldn't believe she had no idea how his wallet got into her purse.

Her past continued to haunt her and she was beyond mad. She was disappointed. She clamped a hand over her mouth to stop the endless flow of words and recriminations

"I'll lose my job if he mentions this to anyone. He refused to believe I didn't steal from him."

"You won't lose your job. First, I doubt he'll say anything. Second, he isn't that kind of man. Third, you didn't do anything. Do I need to go on?" She towered over Tricia like an avenging goddess.

"Except for parent-teacher conferences, I won't be seeing him again. I hope people forget I was ever attached to him."

"What's to forget? You never went out with him in public. You had your secret dates at his place and a bunch of secret, late-night phone calls. You never had a relationship. You never took a risk. You squirreled him away like you were ashamed of him, and his family welcomed you anyway. You know I'm your best friend. But the way you kept him in the closet has bothered me. You're so scared of being burned you kept Riley like a shameful secret; which doesn't lead to much trust coming back." She peeked out the window into the evening.

The darkness outside matched the feeling in Tricia's heart.

"How ever this goes, I've got your back. I always will, but you need to expand your vision and figure out who you are and what you want. You're human and us mortals open ourselves up to love and hurt. We make mistakes and suffer for them. If we're strong, we pick ourselves up and get on with our lives. With or without Riley."

As if she'd finished her speech and had nothing left to say, she dropped into her chair and sucked back the last of her champagne and glared at the empty bottle.

Tricia thumped into the kitchen and brought back a bottle of wine. She twisted off the screw cap and refilled their glasses.

"I didn't take his wallet."

"You think I don't know that? I'm your best friend. We'll

figure out a way to convince him and you guys can repair your relationship."

"Nope. I'm done with him." She slugged back the rest of her wine and poured another. There was nothing like alcohol to deaden the pain of a broken heart.

$\mathcal{M}$orning came way too early, bringing with it a colossal headache and pouring rain. The temperature plunged from a weekly average of seventeen to a frigid three. Snow couldn't be far behind.

"You cooking your hangover cure?" she said by way of greeting Jo who stood in the open fridge door.

"Yup." She didn't move from the fridge or look at Tricia.

"Anything else to say?"

"Nope. Not until I kill this abominable headache. I hold you responsible for it, by the way."

A laugh bubbled out of Tricia. "Friends don't blame friends for their hangovers. Or their past mistakes." She sobered. All traces of alcohol evaporated like her moment of levity at the reality of her words.

"God, I really screwed up. I never should have started seeing him. I thought he liked me. How could he believe I'd steal from him?" She wrapped her arms around herself. Damn, she was freezing inside and out.

"You have to admit, to someone who hasn't known you all your life, the evidence was pretty damning."

"He should have trusted me." The world was so unfair. She thought they'd had something together. Apparently, she was mistaken.

Hip checking Jo aside, Tricia grabbed eggs, bacon, a red onion, peppers and cheese out of the fridge and whipped up omelets. Protein and grease were the best cure for a hangover.

They were drying the last of the dishes when the doorbell buzzed. Tricia froze on the spot, her heart racing.

"Relax. It's Houston. I texted him for a ride. We've got a date with a flea market today."

Tricia flipped open the lock without looking and opened the door. Riley stood there, hat in hand. "I'd like to talk, if you don't mind."

Jo pushed past them. "That'll be my cue to exit. I assume Houston is downstairs?"

Riley nodded without taking his gaze off Tricia. She felt like he saw every dirty secret in her soul. She stepped back and he followed her inside, gently closing the door behind him.

"So," she began.

"I'd like to talk," he said over her single word.

His smile was awkward and a bit touching.

"Go ahead, talk to me. Yell at me. Tell me how you feel," he suggested. "Can I come in or do you want me to stay at the door?" He shifted back and forth on his feet. His glance darted around the room.

"Come in. We might as well be comfortable while we're being awkward." It wasn't a gracious invitation, but it was more than she wanted to give.

He toed his boots off and set them neatly by the wall and set his hat on the table. It seemed like they'd argued days ago rather than hours.

"Where's Daisy?"

"Ken's got her for a few hours. He owed me one."

She settled into a wing chair and looked at him. He looked exhausted. And handsome. He'd changed his clothes and shaved since last night. How did men do that? She probably looked like she'd been awake and crying for a week. She hadn't combed her hair, brushed her teeth or changed. She had pizza sauce on the white cotton sweater she hadn't changed out of after school yesterday. Well, no sense worrying, he'd already seen her. Finding a place to start the conversation wasn't just hard. It was impossible. She sat in silence waiting. He came to her; he must have something to say.

"I've been thinking," he began. "I was completely out of line yesterday."

"You were," she started but he halted her words with a stop motion of his hand.

"No talking. Please. Let me finish. Good grief, now I sound like the teacher instead of you. I jumped to the wrong conclusion. I know you well enough to realize you aren't a thief. And with Daisy's acting up, the missing notes, I realized she was up to something. I talked to her this morning. After losing her mom and being separated from her grandparents, she's afraid you'll take me away from her. She heard someone talking about your past. She thought if I caught you stealing, I'd send you away. She was right. I panicked."

The strength and conviction of his words rang out, ricocheting off her heart. There was no doubt, Riley Flint was a good man who regretted jumping to conclusions. The problem echoing in her head was whether or not he made a habit of it. She hadn't seen him do it before, but she still had her doubts. Her twisted past, her dishonest parents, her cheating ex, they made it hard to trust people. Everything in her life added up to an inability to trust her own judgment and that wasn't easy to get past.

"I've never had a seriously close relationship with a woman. Sure, I've had short term ones, but this one, this relationship between you and I, this one is different. It's… important. For the brief time, I thought you weren't who I thought you were. I freaked out. He cracked his thumb knuckles. "The moment I opened my mouth I knew I'd screwed up; I was wrong. It was your stunned reaction that really blew me out of the water. I'm so sorry."

There was a sad honesty in his words which touched her heart. Moved or not, she wasn't sure she could forgive him.

"Thanks for the apology." She stood and walked toward the door. He didn't follow.

"I want to start over." He stared at his feet, his gaze darting up for a second to clash with hers before returning to his intense study of the hardwood floor.

"What?" She stared. Could she take a chance on him?

He'd been pretty quick to think the worst of her. But at the same time, he'd been forthright and honest about everything so far. Would he continue on that way? Should she risk her heart?

"Now, I beg for forgiveness and grovel at your feet. I'm sorry. Daisy is sorry and promises she'll apologize. We talked about her misdeeds for a long time. She understands what she did is wrong. I'm sorry. I might have, I did, overreact without getting all the facts. I don't have this relationship thing figured out yet. Or fatherhood, but I'm working on it. I'm in it for the long haul, the paternity test came back and I'm definitely her father, though I never had any doubts."

"I'm glad you've taken her in and are doing your best to be a good father." Despite priding herself on her honesty, the truth of her words shocked her to the core. His stand-up nature was one of his best features, it even outweighed his mesmerizing eyes and delicious physique.

"Thank you. She'll always have my love. But I see now she'll need more time and more discipline. I know how badly I screwed up with you. There's no going back on that mistake. I can't change what I did, what I said. But I'd like to try and move past it. Can we be friends? I'll understand if you don't want to be seen with me anymore but I would like to continue our friendship. Your support means a lot to me."

"Why didn't we ever go out?" she blurted, with Jo's earlier observations flashing through her mind.

His mouth fell open and he stared. "I don't know. We never planned anything, except Thanksgiving dinner. We always ended up at my place, with Daisy snug and soundly asleep in her bed. Does our not going out bother you?"

"I didn't realize it before last night. You and I had a friendship nobody knew about. We kept it hidden. My fault, I think," she said. "I worry about my reputation because of my past. I hide from life. I dragged you into the dark with me."

"I didn't mind. I was so wrapped up in my own problems I didn't see your fear. I'd like to try again. Begin with friendship, in public, and see what happens."

"What if we don't work out? What if we can't maintain a friendship? What if Daisy gets hurt?" She watched him mull over her words and knew he was giving them serious consideration.

"This is a small town. She'll see you around. We can be civil, we're adults. In the event things go awry, we'll get beyond it and help her through it. But I want you to know I intend to see you without her as well as with her. No hiding, no sneaking around. If you agree." The last words were as much a question as a statement.

It was her turn to ponder the situation. The solution sounded reasonable but life was seldom as simple as it seemed. Fear shook her and she clasped her hands together to hide her tremors. She was scared. Truthfully, she was terrified. She could blow her reputation and lose her job. She could lose everything and be right back where she'd started. Jobless, homeless and alone. Memories of Riley's kindness marched through her mind. She'd seen it firsthand with his treatment of his daughter and his animal patients. He was awkward but caring with his family and his reputation was sterling.

Realization dawned, if she passed up the chance to deepen their friendship, she might come to regret it. She had enough regrets. She wanted to live. Jo, and others, had assured her dating Riley wouldn't put her job in jeopardy and she was going to take them at their word.

"I think," she said, "I'd like to go out with you, Riley Flint. One date. You buy. Wining and dining. And if it goes well, I'd like to repeat it. My treat."

His nervous frown morphed into an ecstatic grin. "I accept your terms, Tricia Paxton. Pick a day and say the word. I'll find a sitter. Tonight?"

"Wow, you move fast. I was thinking maybe the Harvest Dance."

"But we'll be working," he complained.

"Is this how it's going to be?" She grinned. "You're already shooting down my ideas. Besides, our shifts are day shifts, the dance is in the evening. We just have to help clean up after. Besides, a gentleman I know taught me how to dance and I'd like to try it out in public."

"We haven't known each other long," he said with a frown. "I don't want to wait two weeks to go out with you. If I can find a sitter for tonight, would you consider going to dinner and a movie with me?"

"If you can find a sitter, I'll agree to an early dinner, no movie. Nothing fancy, maybe Allie's or Tammy's. I'd meet you there."

"I prefer to pick up my dates," he countered running his fingers through his hat flattened hair.

He was adorable when he did that. He looked as nervous

as she felt. "I prefer to meet my dates at the restaurant. Safety first. I'll let you pick the place and I'll meet you there. A woman can't be too careful on the first date."

"The first date?" he blurted incredulously. "We've spent a hundred hours together. Or more!"

"Yes, we have. As friends. If we're going to walk this friendship into something deeper, we're going to do it properly." She winced. "I mean, the entire town will see us, it needs to be fully above board. I'm learning Coyote Creek has different standards, but I want this on the up and up. I want everything in the open. No questions, no rumors, no chance of people misunderstanding. I want everyone to know we're dating, but I don't want them to believe we're sleeping together."

His frustrated sigh tickled her heart, but she needed to know he was willing to do this the right way. Her way.

"Lady, you drive a hard bargain." He ambled over to her and pressed a kiss against her cheek. "I'll find a sitter and call you with details." At the door he grabbed his hat and slipped into his boots. "Lock the door behind me, I need my second-best girl to be safe."

"Second best?" She sputtered then laughed. Knowing she fell behind his daughter in the importance chain didn't bother her a bit. "Get out of my apartment." She tossed a throw cushion which bounced harmlessly off the closing door to land on the floor.

Nine hours later, at seven, she stood outside Sammy's Steakhouse, straightened her slim fitting, navy, knee length skirt, and ensured her shoes were shiny and dust free after her walk. She smoothed her silk blouse and relaxed her grip on her handbag. They'd argued briefly on the phone over the relatively formal atmosphere of Sammy's and she'd caved gracefully. She pulled the door open and stepped inside.

The enticing aroma of grilled meat and seafood tickled her nose and she inhaled deeply. Mm. Garlic toast, avocado all overlaid with fresh chocolate cake. Yummy.

"Miss Paxton, nice to see you," the teenaged hostess greeted her. "Mr. Flint is in the corner, follow me."

Riley stood as she approached. She stumbled a bit as she took him in. Perfectly groomed hair, Stetson nowhere in sight. An elegant black suit and burgundy tie had replaced his typical semi-formal cowboy attire of pressed jeans and button-down shirt.

"Close your mouth," the hostess giggled. "You're drooling."

She snapped her mouth shut. "Riley. Hi. You look—nice."

"You look incredible." He reached out, took her hand and pressed a light kiss against her knuckles. He pulled out her chair and slid it in as she seated herself.

Her knees wobbled. Jeepers, the man sure knew how to impress a lady. She could get used to being treated like this. Who knew cowboy Riley had this in him? No wonder half the women in town were chasing him. She sobered and pushed the idea away, prepared to take him at his word he wasn't a Lothario, just a good friend to many.

He slid gracefully into the seat across from her. "I hope it's okay, I've taken the liberty of ordering wine?"

"Um, yes. I walked so a glass or two won't hurt," she

replied as the owner stepped forward to set a bucket of ice with the wine beside them. He showed Riley the bottle, opened it and offered them each a small taste. The Chablis was cool, smooth and delicious.

"Thanks, Kiefer. This is perfect." Riley smiled and slipped the tall tawny-skinned man a tip. He nodded and walked away.

"How was your day?" Riley asked politely.

"Quiet. I had a nap." She chuckled at the awkward conversation. "Is this how it's going to be? Formal and stuffy? We're beyond that, aren't we?" she asked. They'd shared exploding salad dressing, many meals, hours at Daisy's sickbed. It seemed silly to return to the stiff formality of a first date, but their disagreement still hung awkwardly between them.

Riley slid a small flat package wrapped in silver paper with a blue metallic ribbon wrapped around it across the table.

She squinted her eyes at him.

She eyed the package like it might burst into flames. "Do you always bring gifts on a first date?" Did he have a system down pat, a series of moves he used to charm the ladies? Or was she just being extra suspicious? He held up his hands defensively. "It's nothing. I saw it in the drugstore and thought you'd get a charge out of it. I'd have bought it anyway."

"Thank you." She picked up the package and opened it. A flat, curved metal hook slid out into her hands. Attached to one end was a string of colorful beads interspersed with numbered beads. The hook was engraved with the phrase,

Teachers Do It With Class. She read it and laughed. "I don't know if this is funny or inappropriate," she confessed.

"A little of both I think. I thought you could use it in one of those steamy romance novels I noticed on your coffee table. You know, to make you think of me." His face flushed and he grabbed his wine and choked down a large swallow.

"I'll do that." She smirked at his discomfort. Maybe Mr. Smooth wasn't as good with the ladies as the town seemed to think. The idea was reassuring.

Dinner was a quiet affair virtually without interruptions. Riley nodded to people he knew and Tricia greeted a few teachers who happened by. Strangely, nobody questioned them being together or lingered long after saying hi.

After dinner, he left his truck at the restaurant and walked her to her door. Tempted though she was to invite him in, she left him standing on the front porch of the building as she slipped inside.

They shared three dinners that week and two the next. Sometimes, they were alone, others Daisy came with them. She seemed to have accepted Tricia and Riley's relationship and had, reluctantly, apologized for her behavior. It wasn't much, but it was a start. Daisy loved the hotdog cart in the park where they spent Saturday afternoon. On Sunday, they went to a children's flick at the cinema in the city and stopped by Daisy's grandparents' house for a short visit. Initially, there were some awkward pauses, but eventually, they bonded over their love for Daisy. The Ables planned to come to Coyote Creek and share Christmas with Riley and Daisy. Bruce was recovering from his surgery and Ruth's new medications were starting to control her pain.

The next Wednesday, after a childless dinner and movie, he walked her home. "Do I get to come inside for a drink tonight?"

"You can walk me to my door."

"And a drink?"

"No drink."

She was a bit disappointed at his easy acquiescence to her insistence he not come in. Standing in the open doorway of her apartment, he reached out and stroked her cheek. "Thank you for coming out with me, Tricia." His hand dropped to his side. His mouth opened and closed like he might say something else.

"Would you like a beverage?" Her words startled them both.

"I don't think so."

"Oh, for Pete's sake," Mrs. Adelson called from her doorway down the hall. They pivoted in unison to gape at her. "Go inside. Nobody cares. Watching you two dance around each other is driving us all half nuts. Get it together. This ain't the turn of the century. Girl, if he don't try and cop a feel tonight, dump him. He's not man enough for you." She stepped back into her suite, thunking the door shut behind her in emphasis.

Riley looked at Tricia and she giggled. He laughed along with her as she pulled him into her apartment.

"I guess you better stay awhile and prove your manhood," she teased.

"Guess so," he agreed and toed off his boots.

"Wine? Tea? Coffee?"

"I'll have ice water, if you've got it. I have a surgery at six a.m. tomorrow. I have to be at my best."

They settled, side by side on the couch with their glasses and she flipped on the television to a cooking show. They chatted over the show, only paying a smidgeon of attention to the on-screen antics.

Riley set their glasses on the table and turned toward Tricia. He bent low, his mouth just inches from hers. "I can't leave my masculinity in doubt," he teased and brushed his lips across hers.

She grabbed the back of his head and pulled him close, deepening their kiss. Her eyes fluttered closed as sensation rocketed through her. The kind, gentle touch of his lips; his hand buried in her hair holding her close; the minty taste of his mouth; and the heady scent of his light cologne made her head swim. But the rightness of his kiss, his embrace left her no doubt, she'd fallen for him without even knowing it.

Endless breathless minutes later he pulled back and stroked his thumb over her lips. "I should go."

"But…" her mind ground to a halt. She wanted him to stay. She sighed. He was right. They were growing closer, but they both had reputations to protect.

She walked him to the door. After several long, intense kisses, she was tempted once again to ask him to stay. Instead, she opened the door.

"Daisy and I will meet you at the parade. We're watching

from the roof of Jason's shop." He brushed another kiss across her lips and kissed the top of her head. "Goodnight, Tricia."

"Goodnight, Riley." She leaned against the doorframe and watched him amble away. He paused outside Mrs. Addison's suite and knocked.

"Goodnight, Mrs. Addison."

"Goodnight, Mr. Flint," she replied.

Riley turned and winked at Tricia. He waggled his fingers and jogged the short distance to the stairs and disappeared.

CHAPTER THIRTY

"Look at the people," Jo crowed and shoulder bumped Tricia and Houston who stood on either side of her. The crowd lining Main Street was enormous, the noise deafening. "We've got a dozen more floats than last year. I talked to the desk clerk at the hotel this morning, they're booked solid for the weekend. This is huge."

"We've hit it out of the park for sure," Houston agreed.

Tricia watched the duo celebrating their victory. Last year had been her first Harvest Festival. She'd taken in the merchant mall and the bake sale but skipped the parade and dance. They'd planned so much more for this year she was worried they'd never pull it off. They stood on the roof of Jason's butcher shop behind a waist high protective fence. Their vantage point allowed them a clear view of the goings on up and down the street.

Vendors sold cold drinks, cocoa, roasted nuts and hotdogs. Clowns circulated through the crowd handing out balloon animals or creating them on demand. It was chaos, beautiful happy chaos.

Riley jogged across the roof to join them, side stepping Daisy and her cousins who waited excitedly for the parade to begin. "We're all set. Mayor Chowdry is going to set off the inaugural firecrackers any minute." Right on cue, tiny explosions rent the air and the gathered crowd started cheering.

A fire truck rolled down the street. The assembled firemen tossed candy to the children and waved to the crowd. The high school marching band followed, playing a jaunty, if somewhat out of sync jazz number. As they rolled out of hearing the tune morphed into *When the Saints Go Marching In*. Dozens of businesses had floats. The rescue society paraded dogs down the street. Ranchers and farmers rode their horses. The Lions and Kinsmen Clubs drove clown cars and gleefully tossed candy to the excited kids.

"Aw, we can't get candy," Jane complained.

"Ah, but you can." Jason raised a bag of candy and waved it in the air. "I like having you guys up here where I can keep an eye on you but I didn't want you to miss out."

"Thanks, bro," Riley praised. "You think of everything."

Tricia laughed at the gratitude in his voice. After the parade, Riley and Tricia strolled through the vendor's market, with Daisy dancing happily ahead of them, hand in hand with Jane. His hand brushed against hers a few times and she was tempted to grasp it and hold on. Her heart and her body were getting ahead of her mind. Anticipation flowed through her as she thought ahead to the dance.

They rode carnival rides and got lost in the corn maze. They even took a few turns in the super popular bouncy castle. They feasted on corn dogs, fries and sugary lemonade before Riley took Daisy home to change for the dance. Tonight, just this once, she was allowed to stay up past her bedtime and attend the dance.

Riley arrived, Daisy in tow, to pick Tricia up precisely at seven. Daisy danced excitedly in front of him, her sunflower print, layered netting dress bouncing and fluttering with her motions. Her curly blonde hair was clean and freshly combed. "You look lovely. I adore your dress."

Tricia looked from Daisy to Riley. His hair was neat and still a bit damp; his jaw was shaven smooth. He'd exchanged his standard Wranglers for a casual suit and blinding white, button-down shirt. He was devastatingly handsome; his warm smile stole her breath and sent her heart racing like kids abandoning the classroom on the last day of school.

"These are for you," Daisy thrust a bouquet of fall mums into her hands, drawing her attention away from Riley. "You have to put them in water."

"Thank you, they're beautiful. Come inside and give me a hand, I don't want these to wilt while I'm at the dance." She took one last glance at her date and turned toward the kitchen, her knees weak and legs trembling. Glory, he was too pretty for words.

"Riley has something for you too. Don't you Riley?"

He ruffled her hair. "I sure do, princess." He held out a small package covered in Sweet Heaven's familiar pink and white striped paper.

"It's chocolates," Daisy piped in excitedly. "I helped pick them."

"Thank you. That's very sweet." She winked at Riley knowing he'd let Daisy choose to keep her involved.

Together they settled the flowers in a water filled vase and set it on the kitchen table.

"They're lovely, thank you."

Nervous energy fluttered through her stomach making her regret eating two corn dogs. She rested her hand against her stomach and breathed slow and deep until she felt calm enough to face Riley. "I guess I'm ready then. Shall we go?"

Daisy hopped between them, holding their hands as they descended to the street and climbed into Riley's truck. As they drove toward the fairgrounds outside town, Tricia glanced around. His truck was always clean, today it was spotless. Not a lick of dust, no gravel on the floor mats and not a single wrapper or coffee cup to be seen. The windows and chrome shone brightly in the descending sun. He'd cleaned his truck for this. What a sweet gesture.

"Daddy cleaned the truck so we didn't ruin our pretty dresses," Daisy exclaimed.

Riley slammed on the brakes and pulled over to the curb. Tricia's heart threatened to jump out of her throat at the abrupt action. Daisy's words penetrated and elation washed over her.

Safely stopped, he turned to stare at Daisy. Tricia watched them both.

"What did you say?" he asked quietly. He didn't quite hide the small tremor of emotion in his voice.

"You cleaned the truck." Daisy replied, squinting at him.

"Before that, sweetie. What did you say before that?"

Her brows pinched together as she pondered the question. Tricia held her breath in anticipation, Riley reached across the seat and clutched Tricia's hand nearly crushing it.

"I said, Daddy cleaned the truck to keep our pretty dresses clean."

Riley swallowed hard, the sound loud in the breathless silence following her declaration. Tricia fought for air and tried to hold her tears back.

"You called me Daddy," he whispered.

"You are my Daddy. You told me so. Mommy told me one day we'd find my Daddy and he'd love me as much as she did." The progression of her thoughts was logical and emotional. "She wanted you to have me because she was sick." Her lip quivered and she unbuckled her seatbelt and launched herself over the seat into his arms.

Her hard-soled shoe connected soundly with Tricia's eye leaving a stinging welt she was barely aware of.

"I love you, Daisy. I always have and I always will." He hugged her tightly. "And I love your mommy for giving me to you." She pushed back against him and scowled.

"No. You're supposed to love Miss Tricia. Jane and I decided. Miss Tricia is gonna be my new mommy and you're my daddy and we'll be a family with Grandma Ruth and Grampa Bruce. And Grampa Robert and Grandma Sue. And everybody else."

Tricia stifled a groan. This wasn't going to be an easy situation to extract herself from, no matter how badly she wanted to be part of their lives.

"I'm so glad you called me Daddy. You're my best girl. Maybe someday, Miss Tricia can be my other girl. But that's not for you to decide." He tickled her chin and hugged her close. "It's a special thing for us adults to talk about, but I'm glad you love her as much as I do."

Tricia stared at him. He winked at her over Daisy's head and her heart sputtered into overdrive. Maybe Daisy wasn't so far off the mark. They'd resolved their differences and revealed their pasts and moved beyond them; perhaps, now they could think about the future. She gave him a small smile. He returned an enormous grin.

"Come on, Daisy. Back into your seat and we'll go to the dance and have our first father-daughter dance."

She climbed back and buckled up. "And then you can dance with Jane and Miss Tricia." Her wide grin melted Tricia's heart. "Okay, Daddy, I'm buckled up. Let's go."

Riley turned toward the road and placed both hands on the wheel. His eyes shone with moisture and his smile stretched ear to ear. He was the happiest person she'd ever seen. She gripped his thigh and squeezed. He flashed her a wink and put the truck into gear.

They heard the music as they rounded the corner into a wall of parked vehicles. It looked like the entire town had come out to take part in the dance. After locking the truck, they wandered down the rows of parked cars and trucks and through the wide-open barn doors. Jerry O'Reilly, whose ranch adjoined the fair grounds and was for sale, had opened his vacant barn for the town's use. Laughter and country music spilled out into the early evening.

A bonfire roared a safe distance from the makeshift pallet bar erected outside the barn. A bold sign hanging over the door declared free rides home were available for everyone. All you needed to do was turn in your keys and order your drink. Tricia waved toward the sign. "Great idea," she declared.

"They do it every year. Carl and his employees and a couple others donate their personal vehicles and act as designated drivers for the event. Different people pitch in for the Christmas dance."

"Incredible. This town is fabulous. I can't believe I spent so much time hiding away from everyone." Regrets nagged at her. Well, everyone had regrets and it wasn't too late to let herself shine and get to know the people in her new hometown. She'd start tonight. Filled with hope and resolve, she grabbed Daisy's hand and leaving Riley behind, they raced into the dance.

Laughing, he ran up behind them, scooped Daisy into his arms and whirled her around. Wrapping his warm, strong arm around Tricia's waist he pulled her to the floor, stealing her breath. It was easy to see why so many women were attracted to him and continually vied for his attention. As they waltzed around the floor Tricia noticed two single mothers standing by the indoor bar, talking and pointing at them. They frowned and shook their heads. Her resolve to ignore rumors and live her life wavered under their scrutiny until one of them gave her a big smile and thumbs up. Maybe this wouldn't be so bad after all.

Two songs later, Daisy rushed off to play with Jane and

some classmates. Tricia whirled around in Riley's arms, her cheeks aching from her unstoppable grin.

"Mind if I cut in?" Jason stood beside them, a challenging look on his face.

"Not at all," Tricia declared. "I'd love to dance with you."

"I mind. Back away, bro." Riley's voice was laced with warning.

"I can't let you hog the most beautiful woman in the room. She's the catch of a lifetime. There are plenty of others for you. Besides, it's just one dance. Unless you're worried she'll fall for me and dump you in the five minutes a dance lasts."

"Not a chance." He stepped back and winked at Tricia. "Do your best, Jas. My manly charms outweigh yours a thousand percent. You don't scare me; this filly is mine."

Catch of a lifetime? Filly? Rural men sure had a way of putting things. In her old world, the words would have been rude and insulting. Here, they were a compliment of the highest order and she graciously accepted them as such.

"If you *boys* are finished bickering like *schoolgirls*, I'd like to dance with someone. Is Ken here? I could easily dance with him."

Jason bowed low and held out his hand. "Care to dance?"

Riley swooped in and dropped a fast kiss on her lips before they could dance away from him. Unable to contain her joy, she laughed lightly as they swung into a two-step.

"So, you and my baby brother, eh?"

"I've helped him with his parenting. He's got a lot to learn."

"From what I've heard, you've been seen around town

together. Dating," he whispered dramatically, pretending to be scandalized.

"We've dated. There's no law against it." His teasing didn't bother her. They'd become friends during their shared Thanksgiving dinner.

"He likes you."

"I know. Is this going somewhere or are you trying to distract me from your sub-par dancing?" His dancing was divine. Better than Riley's but somehow, she wasn't enjoying it as much. She preferred to be in his brother's arms.

"I didn't think he'd ever realize, or maybe admit, he loved his family. He's been elusive since he was a kid. You gave us that and we're grateful. Thank you."

His words humbled her, but he was mistaken. "I think you should thank Daisy."

"Daisy *and* you. Welcome to the Flint family." He twirled her around and around until they reached the ladies by the bar. He bought Tricia a soda, grasped one of them by the arm and led her to the dance floor.

"Hi," the other woman said. "I'm Francine Schmidt." She offered her hand, her spiky blonde hair glittered with flecks of color, her smile was broad and engaging. "I see you've taken Riley off the market. Today, all the women of Coyote Creek weep. Of course, since you're one of our own, we celebrate your success." She raised her glass and clinked it against Tricia's.

"Um. Thanks?"

"You're welcome. I work at Marcy's. Stop by and we'll get to know each other and do some crafts. Maybe you can teach me to knit. Jo tells me you know how. I've never mastered it."

"Hey, Franny, want to dance?" Carl injected. "I've got time to cut the rug a bit before I start giving rides home." He didn't wait for a response, he tugged on her hand and laughing, she followed him on the floor.

"Don't call me Franny." She looked back over her shoulder. "Stop by and see me."

"Hey, beautiful, are you alone?" Riley's voice whispered in her ear. "If you are, I'd be honored if you'd dance with me."

She nodded and his arm slid around her waist. Warm and comforting it echoed the welcome she was receiving from everyone tonight. Contentment flowed in, replacing the last of her reservations about opening herself up to the residents of Coyote Creek.

They waltzed again and again, moving in perfect unison. Only once did she stumble and step on his foot. He laughed it off and spun her around in a dizzying move. "I have a proposition for you."

"A proposition?" She had no idea where the conversation was headed.

"More like a proposal." He dropped down on one knee and took her hand as the song ended. The room gasped. Light twitters of conversation flickered through the crowd. "Tricia Paxton. I'm not perfect. I've got flaws and a history and a daughter. You'll love her. She's adorable. We've fallen in love with you. Would you do the honor of marrying us? Will you be my wife? Her mother? We're broken without you; you make us whole. You're everything I ever wanted in a woman, in a wife. Please. Say yes."

Her hands flew to her mouth, covering the enormous smile she couldn't contain. Her body tightened with thrilled anticipation. Love for this man, for his child, flowed through her. Suddenly, she realized this was her dream. A dream she'd waited an eternity for. To be happy, accepted and loved.

Daisy tugged on her hand. "Please say yes, Miss Tricia. Please be my new Mommy. Marry us! Say yes!"

Someone in the crowd whispered, "yes."

"Do it!" Jo called.

The crowd chanted. "Yes, yes, yes." The volume grew as more voices joined the chorus.

Her stomach trembled and her knees locked. A bubble of fear trickled up her throat and popped. Calm descended over her as the crowd fell silent.

"Yes. Yes, I'll marry you!" She threw her arms around him. Their lips locked and he spun her around the room until they were both breathless and dizzy. Daisy danced behind them. Riley snatched his daughter up and the trio tumbled to the floor in a glorious, laughing heap. Blissfully happy, she kissed them. "I love you Riley, more than I ever thought I could." She dropped a kiss on Daisy's cheek. "And I love you too, Daisy."

"Thank God," he declared. "You hesitated. I thought you were going to say no."

"I say yes. Again, and again." She winked. "Although I don't see a ring."

He paled. "I knew I forgot something. So much for the perfect proposal."

"Here, Daddy. Use mine." Daisy handed him her enormous pink plastic 'diamond' ring and he slid it on Tricia's finger.

"It's beautiful," she told Daisy. "This is the perfect proposal. You two made it perfect."

The crowd erupted in congratulatory cheers and swamped them right there, in the middle of a barn during the Harvest Festival dance. Tricia was offered best wishes, hugs and kisses from people she knew only by sight. The crowd swelled and separated them.

"Stop!" Riley's voice rang out. "Let me have my fiancée back." The crowd parted and pushed them together. She fell into his arms, laughter bubbling from her lips. "You are the most beautiful woman I've ever known. Inside and out."

The band struck up a waltz. Giddy with excitement, she stepped fully into his arms and twirled around the room. Daisy's grandparents had accepted Riley's invitation to come to the festival with them, they stood beside his parents on the sidelines. Daisy stood on a chair, between the couples, clapping her hands excitedly as Riley and Tricia danced across the floor and into their new life together.

Love the novel you just read?
Your opinion matters.

Review this book on your favorite book site, review site, blog, or your own social media properties, and share your opinion with other readers.
Thanks in advance, Katie.

I hope you enjoyed Riley and Tricia's story.
Stay tuned for Justice and Amy's story.
Coming soon to a retailer near you.

CONTACT KATIE O'CONNOR

Katie loves to hear from her readers.
Feel free to contact her anytime.

Website: https://katieohwrites.com
Email: katieoconnorwrites@gmail.com

Reviews are an author's lifeblood.
To thank readers generous enough to leave a review, Katie
holds a monthly draw for a free e-book.
To enter, simply email your review link to:
(katieoconnorwrites@gmail.com)
Each month's winner will receive the e-book of their choice
from Katie's publications.

Thank you in advance, Katie.

Katie O'Connor lives in Calgary, Alberta, Canada. She married her high school sweetheart and is living her happily ever after. She is the mother of two grown daughters and is extremely proud of her five grandchildren. She has two wonderful sons-in-law and a large support network of friends, family and fellow authors.

Katie's career path has been long and twisted, with most of her life devoted to her family. She's been a waitress, chambermaid, cashier, store manager, as well as a lab and x-ray technician. She is an avid quilter and crafter.

She's dabbled in writing since high school because something drives her to create stories. She swears that it's impossible for her NOT to write. Unsatisfied with one genre, Katie writes contemporary romance, erotic romance and erotica. Recently, she's crafted her first cozy mystery with the intention of publishing a cozy mystery series.

She believes in all things magical; including dragons,

fairies, UFOs, ghosts, and house pixies. But most of all she believes in love, romance and hope.

Katie likes to make it up as she goes along and dreams of publishing a mixed genre novel. It is going to be an erotic, shape shifter, vampire, steampunk, sci-fi, murder mystery, adventure, romantic, western, historical, thriller. It will be her biography.